HIDDEN IN THE SAND

ELENA AITKEN

Also by Elena Aitken

Destination Paradise

Shelter by the Sea

Escape to the Sun

Hidden in the Sand

Ever After

Choosing Happily Ever After

Needing Happily Ever After

Wanting Happily Ever After

Fighting Happily Ever After

We Wish You A Happily Ever After

Keeping Happily Ever After

Finding Happily Ever After

Seeking Happily Ever After

Cherishing Happily Ever After

Ever After: Volume One (Books 1-4)

The Springs Series

Summer of Change

Falling Into Forever

Second Glances

Winter's Burn

Midnight Springs

She's Making A List

Summit of Desire

Summit of Seduction

Summit of Passion

Fighting For Forever

The Springs Collection: Volume 1

The Springs Collection: Volume 2

The Springs Collection: Volume 3

The Springs Complete Collection - Books 1-10

The McCormicks

Love in the Moment

Only for a Moment

One more Moment

In this Moment

From this Moment

Our Perfect Moment

Stand Alone Stories

All We Never Knew

Drawing Free

Sugar Crash

Composing Myself

Betty & Veronica

The Escape Collection

Vegas

Nothing Stays in Vegas

Return to Vegas

His to Tame

His to Seek

Hers for the Season

Bears of Grizzly Ridge: Books 1-4

Bears of Grizzly Ridge: Books 5-8

Halfway Series

Halfway to Nowhere

Halfway in Between

Halfway to Christmas

Hidden in the Sand

Chapter One

HIS PULSE THUNDERED in his ears and he worked hard to control his breathing.

In. Out. In. Out.

Dean Harrison knew he had less than thirty seconds before he would be discovered behind the tarp-covered barrels. Thirty seconds before the bullets would start to fly and he would start running.

Fast.

He forced himself to focus on the count in his head.

Ten…nine…eight…

A blast from somewhere farther off in the boatyard shook the barrels he was hiding behind.

"Shit." It was early. Or his count was off. *Dammit.* He hated it when he was off.

Not that there was anything he could do about it now. With another curse under his breath, Dean squeezed the revolver in his hand a little bit tighter, and took off running through the boatyard. Just as he expected, the yelling started and the deafening sounds of guns firing rang all around him. Adrenaline fueled him and narrowed his vision, blocking out everything but the obstacles in front of him. He jumped and dodged just the way he'd planned and visualized in his head for the last few days.

An explosion sounded directly in front of him, and he jumped to the right, just barely avoiding the blast. He landed hard on his shoulder; a hot, sharp pain shot up his neck as he rolled in the dirt.

Shit.

But still Dean didn't stop. He jumped to his feet and once again started to run through the boats that were propped up on blocks and stands. The cargo net, and the crane it hung from, was only ten yards away. Dean knew if he could get there, jump on, and swing over the dump truck that, once he was on the other side, they couldn't stop him.

He pushed himself harder. He was almost there. *Just a few more—*

"Cut!"

The word ripped through him, and reflexively, Dean's body slowed right as he reached the cargo net, his fingers wrapped through the netting.

"Cut!" the director yelled again. "Everyone, cut!"

Reluctantly, Dean let his hand slip down. His head dropped and he silently cursed the situation before he turned around. "Come on, Wes. I was almost there."

Wes Reacher jumped down from the platform where he'd been watching the progress of the scene and joined Dean on the ground. "You know you're not doing that scene, Dean." The director patted him on the back, sending a fresh shot of pain from his shoulder into his neck. Wes didn't miss the flinch. "My point exactly. You landed hard back there."

Dean handed the prop gun still in his hand to an intern who'd run over to collect it, and used his free hand to massage his shoulder as he rotated it. "It's nothing. I'm fine."

Wes gave him a sidelong glance, but didn't push it. He knew better. They'd worked together before. In fact, *Run From the Sun* was the fourth Max Silver movie they'd shot together. Wes knew exactly how far he could push Dean. And vice versa. As big of a movie star that Dean Harrison was, Wes Reacher was just as big of a director. The fact that they'd worked together for so many projects had been mutually beneficial.

"Go to medical and get it checked out. I can't afford the downtime if you screwed your arm up."

Dean swallowed a growl. He was fine. He just landed funny, that was all. And if Wes would just give in and let him do his own stunts, he'd have even more training in how to fall properly and things like this wouldn't happen. It was an argument they'd had more times than he could count. Still, Dean wasn't going to give up. He hated not doing his own stunts. And he hated even more being told he couldn't do something.

Dean stopped walking and turned to his director and friend. "Wes, seriously, man. I think it's time that I did at least—"

"I can't talk about this now. We have exactly ten minutes to set up for the next scene and you know just as well as I do that time is money." Wes started walking again.

Dean swallowed hard, bit back a reply and caught up with the director. He wasn't a demanding star. Never had been. But he was starting to get tired of being treated as if he were going to break if he did the slightest thing. The Max Silver movies were the hottest thriller franchise in decades. And sure, they revolved completely around his character, which meant if something did happen to him, shooting would come to a halt. But they were also action-packed thrill rides and dammit, Dean wanted to be part of that ride. And, as the star, was he not entitled to make a few demands?

"Okay," Wes conceded, as if he knew exactly what argument Dean was going to try next. "We'll get you involved in some of the stunts."

Dean grabbed his friend by the arm so he stopped and finally turned to look at him. He needed the director to look him in the eye and say that. "Seriously?"

Wes nodded, although somewhat reluctantly. "Yes. There's the boat chase scene that could work. You swim, right?"

Dean nodded.

"Okay. We'll work with your double, Eric, on it and I'll have him show you a few things so you don't kill yourself."

Dean worked hard to control the smile that was blooming across his face.

"I mean it, Dean. Do *not* kill yourself."

He lost the battle and let his grin take over as he slapped Wes on the back. "I promise," he said as he turned to head to his trailer. "No dying."

"No dying!" Wes called after him. "And for God's sake, go get that arm looked at before your next scene."

Phoebe Flynn stood off to the side, in what she hoped was an inconspicuous spot. She knew she probably shouldn't be on set when it wasn't time for her call, but *Run From the Sun* was her first major film. Hell, it was her first film at all. She wasn't a movie star. She wasn't an actress. And she definitely wasn't Silver Starlet material. She was completely out of her depth, and if she didn't figure it out soon, everyone was going to see what a fraud she was.

She watched the scene in front of her play out. Dean was a pro. He moved quickly and without hesitation through the set. Phoebe could see the way he controlled his face, perfectly in character as he ran through the boatyard, occasionally looking over his shoulder just the way Max Silver would. He made it look effortless, the way he turned into his character. She'd heard stories about Dean Harrison on set, and the others who she'd been hanging out with since arriving in Panama had filled her in on what it was like to work with him.

A total pro.

Intimidating.

Humbling.

And her new friends were largely all the stunt doubles, so they didn't actually exchange lines with Dean. *What would it be like playing his leading lady? What would it be like to—*

No.

Phoebe would only work herself up further if she let herself think about shooting the sexy scenes that were coming up. Sure, Dean Harrison's movies were famous for being fast paced, intense action movies, but that wasn't their only defining feature. For as much action as they contained, they also were chock-full of steamy scenes. Like everyone else in the world, Phoebe had watched them all. She'd known exactly what she was getting herself in to when she'd accepted the role of Misty Falls, the female lead.

It was a decision that had made enough sense in the moment. But now that she was actually here, on set in Panama, it was starting to feel different. Very different.

The director yelled cut and just like that, the boatyard filled with people, all with a job to strike the set and prepare for the next shot. With all the chaos, controlled as it was, Phoebe took her chance to slip away and go for a walk.

Since arriving, her time had mostly been occupied with wardrobe fittings, running lines, and a multitude of other things to prepare for the actual shooting of the film. She'd been lucky when some of the stunt doubles had invited her to join them for a quick getaway in Bocas del Toro, a few hours away at a jungle-themed bed-and-breakfast type of hotel. It was a perfect little holiday to help her break the ice with some of her castmates, who all tended to think she was really stand-offish, or stuck up. She wasn't either of those things, just shy and completely terrified that she was about to make an epic mess of things the next day when she shot her very first scene with Dean Harrison.

She wasn't a complete newbie, though. Phoebe had already shot a few scenes back in LA in the studio, a fact she was grateful for because at least she was able to warm up a little bit before being thrown to the sharks.

Leaving the boatyard and the movie chaos behind her, she made her way toward the breakwater that kept the rough ocean seas from the harbor and the boats moored in the bay. The ocean breeze whipped all around her and pulled her long, dark hair from the loose ponytail she'd tied it back in. It had been almost two weeks since she'd arrived, and still Phoebe was having trouble getting used to the muggy heat of Panama. It sat on her like a weighted blanket when she was inland. But the moment she got near the water, where the breeze washed over her, she felt lighter.

The breakwater was one of her favorite places because from that vantage point, she could look out to sea and see the massive container ships anchored out in the deep water, waiting for their turn to go through the Panama Canal system. Despite the waves that crashed up on the rocks below her, the anchored ships hardly seemed to move. Occasionally, a sailing yacht or power yacht would go by, and they'd look like a toy boat next to the container ships. She'd never seen anything like it.

Of course, she hadn't traveled far from her small town in Montana, either. Except for a few trips when she was a kid, Phoebe hadn't really been anywhere before she was *discovered* at the mall serving frozen yogurt. She laughed every time she thought about that day when Lorilee, her now agent, had ordered a scoop of the strawberry before demanding to know who represented her. As if that were a thing in the middle of nowhere, Montana.

It wasn't.

When Lorilee finally accepted that Phoebe was not in fact *represented* by anyone, whatever that meant, she had insisted on having a meeting with her when she was done with her shift. Preferably before she was done. Finally, Phoebe had to agree so she could serve the other customers in line. Of course, she didn't expect anything to come of the meeting, and no one was more surprised than Phoebe when Lorilee had insisted that she sign her to the agency because she had the *perfect role* for her.

That had been a little over three months ago. Everything had happened so fast, she'd barely had a chance to catch her breath. Let alone think about what any of it meant.

Her cell phone chirped in her pocket. It was Kristen, the assistant who'd been assigned to her for the duration of the film.

"Where are you? Mr. Harrison wants to meet you."

Mr. Harrison. Dean Harrison.

Phoebe's stomach flipped.

She'd have to do it sooner or later. After all, Dean Harrison *was* the star of the movie. And her character's love interest.

She exhaled slowly.

The fact that he had a reputation for seducing his leading ladies didn't mean anything.

No.

Just because he'd been romantically involved with every single one of his costars didn't mean the same thing was going to happen to her.

Phoebe squared her shoulders and tipped her head back, letting the breeze wash over her.

No. None of those things meant anything. Nor did it mean anything that Dean Harrison was drop-dead gorgeous with sexy, dark eyes and a smile that made it hard to breathe.

Nope. Didn't matter.

Maybe those other actresses fell for his smooth operator act. But that didn't mean she would. If anything, it only made her more determined not to.

She took a deep breath before typing in her response to Kristen. She was on her way.

Chapter Two

HE WATCHED her walk out on the breakwater. Her hair blew behind her in the wind. She wore a simple tank top and cut-off jean shorts. But even from a distance, Dean could tell she was beautiful.

Of course she was beautiful.

She'd been cast as his leading lady.

An unknown who would become a star.

The way they all did.

Every single one of his leading ladies had been plucked from obscurity and literally catapulted into stardom. It had become part of the Max Silver franchise. Just as much part of things as the heart-pounding action scenes and the steamy sexy scenes, the world also waited anxiously to see who the next Silver Starlet would be. Revealing her was almost as important as the movie premiere.

Almost.

Dean was still the star who pulled in the viewers. It was just an added bonus that he always ended up dating his leading lady by the time filming wrapped. A bonus that was almost always carefully executed by Bruce Warner, his manager.

It was also the part Dean was starting to hate the most, and he'd resolved not to date this female lead. No matter what.

He watched as Phoebe held her arms out into the wind, completely unaware that her life was about to change. She looked so innocent, so free. And so real. Like a real person, not the fake, over-plucked and over-polished women who tended to dominate his social circles.

His phone rang in his back pocket. Without even glancing at the caller ID, he knew who it was. Bruce had a sixth sense.

"What's up?"

"Give me good news, Harrison."

Dean shook his head and lifted his arm to run a hand through his hair before the pain in his shoulder reminded him he was supposed to report to medical. "Dammit," he muttered under his breath and shook out his arm.

"What's that?" Bruce never missed a thing. "Are you referring to a certain star you're supposed to be getting to know, or the accident you had on set today?"

Dean swallowed back a sigh. The man truly knew everything. It was beyond annoying. "It wasn't an accident," he said, ignoring the comment about Phoebe. "I just landed a little strange in a roll. No big deal. Probably just a bruise. It'll be fine by tomorrow. Wes finally agreed to—"

"A stunt," Bruce interrupted him. "I heard."

"Shit. How do you hear everything? I swear, you know things before I do."

"I do." Dean could picture the man on the other end with his trademark shit-eating grin. "That's why you pay me the big bucks, Deano. It's my job to know things before you even *think* them."

Dean laughed. "Oh yeah?" He turned and once again locked his eyes on Phoebe in the distance. "What am I thinking now?"

"Easy one. You're thinking of a way to tell me that you're

not going to make a move on that sexy beast of a woman who is your newest costar, which is absolutely crazy since she's very likely the hottest one you've ever had. I mean, Jess Jenkins was pretty cute, but no tits to speak of, am I right? But Phoebe? Damn. I saw her casting photos. That girl has curves in *all* the right places. You should be sending cookie bouquets or some shit to the casting directors for finding her for you. Am I right?"

"Yes," Dean answered before he realized what he was agreeing to. "No," he added quickly. "You're not right. I mean, yes. She's gorgeous. Of course. But no, I'm not sending a thank you-gram or whatever to anyone because you were also right about the other thing. I'm not dating her, Bruce. I'm done with that crap. It's not—"

"It *is* friggin' brilliant, is what it is. You know as well as I do that the public eats it up and they expect it, Deano. And hey, don't forget whose idea it was in the first place."

Dean sighed. Bruce used it as an argument every time. But it wasn't as if Dean had meant to start something when he'd dated his first costar, Emma Dennis. That had happened naturally. And no matter what anyone thought, it hadn't been constructed. It was real. Even if it wasn't meant to be.

And then his next costar, Ashlyn Bay. He'd genuinely liked her. It wasn't until after the premiere when she broke it off that Dean had realized he'd been played. Ashlyn wasn't dumb; she'd seen what dating him had done for Emma's career. And by the third movie, when Bruce suggested he play nice with Jess Jenkins, he'd gone along with it. Because why not? He just hadn't expected to feel so dirty afterward. It wasn't who he was. He wasn't that type of guy. He wasn't interested in playing with people's feelings or using them. Even if they didn't think twice about doing it to him.

"No, Bruce." He was putting his foot down. He wasn't going to play that game anymore. It was why he'd waited so long to even meet Phoebe Flynn. Normally he liked to meet everyone early on and have a cast meeting. Filming was always more fun if the cast felt like a family. But he was more than aware of the expectation on him to hook up with Phoebe. It seemed easier to keep a distance from everyone this time around.

"Don't make me get on a plane," Bruce said. "You know I don't like the humidity. Besides, I've already reached out. Her assistant is going to set something up for…right now."

"Bruce, I—"

His objections fell on deaf ears. Bruce had already hung up.

Kristen was waiting for Phoebe at the Dockside Inn, the main building of Shelter Bay Marina. It was still a working marina during the filming, with boat crews and yachters coming and going. The movie crew had more or less taken over the premises and the combination was an interesting mix of people mingling together all the time. It actually relaxed Phoebe having *non-movie* people around, too. Made things more normal somehow. If that was a thing.

"I didn't think I had a call until tomorrow," Phoebe said when she got close enough to her assistant, who she'd very quickly come to depend on. Not only was Kristen the most capable and organized person Phoebe had ever met, who knew the movie industry in and out, she was also a genuinely nice person. It hadn't taken long for Phoebe to think of her as a friend. "I assumed I'd meet him then."

She actually hadn't assumed anything. But she had hoped that there wouldn't be any awkward meeting with Dean Harrison.

"You don't," Kristen said as they walked up to the deck of

the Dockside. "But I got a message from his assistant that he'd like to meet you before then. And you know——"

"I know." Phoebe cut her off. "You can't say no to Dean Harrison." She tried not to roll her eyes, but judging by Kristen's smile, she wasn't very successful. She didn't know whether she'd ever get used to the *game* of everything.

"You got it." Kristen squeezed her arm. "But it won't be so bad. I promise. He's actually a really nice guy and——"

"Phoebe! Over here!"

Both women spun to see Mason Wells, one of the stunt doubles Phoebe had become friendly with, standing on the other side of the open-air deck restaurant with a bucket in his hand. Phoebe raised her arm in a wave and started to walk toward him.

"Don't do it, Pheebs. He's it!" Layla, her stunt double, appeared next to her with a cup of water in her hand. Her hair hung wet and dripping down her back.

"What the——"

"Water fight!" Layla turned and, before Phoebe could react, threw the glass of water at her.

Phoebe shrieked. A sound that immediately turned to laughter as—pending meeting forgotten—she ran after Layla, grabbing a jug of water off a nearby empty table as she went. It didn't take long to catch up to the other woman, and she dumped the water over her head with a splash and a laugh.

"You are so dead," Layla playfully threatened before dissolving into giggles.

"You're both in trouble!" They turned together to see Mason approaching. His bulging arms lifted the huge bucket with ease.

Phoebe and Layla exchanged a look, eyes wide. It was a massive bucket.

"Fend for yourself," Layla called and took off down the deck.

"Where are you…" Phoebe started to call after her, but Mason was approaching quickly. Sitting around waiting to accept her fate didn't seem like a solid plan, and with only one other direction to run in, she scanned the deck. There were only a few tables with actual customers. There was one table, just behind the pillar, with only one person sitting at it. If she was quick, she could get to the empty chair next to the man who had his back to her and use him as a shield. No way would Mason throw water on a *civilian*. It was her only chance.

"No way, Mason!" Phoebe laughed as she darted through the tables toward her target. "Not today." She landed with a thud in the empty chair and, out of breath and giggling, dropped her head to her chest in an effort to pull herself together.

"Excuse me?" Her table mate cleared his throat.

"Sorry." She glanced behind her, but could no longer see Mason and his bucket of water. "I'm just hiding from my friend." She turned to introduce herself. "I hope it's—"

Dean Harrison.

His sexy, dark eyes sparkled with humor and instantly, it was hard to breathe.

"Dean? I mean…Mr. Harrison." What *was* she supposed to call him? *Shit.* "I'm sorry. I thought—"

Her words were lost in a tidal wave of water that flooded over her, plastering her hair to her face and soaking her to the skin.

Above her, she could hear Mason celebrate his victory with a shout. "Got ya! I—oh shit. Dean?"

———

He sputtered and coughed as an incredible amount of water rushed over him. One second, he'd been looking into the most

14

dazzling blue eyes and the next, he was trying not to drown on dry land.

What. The. Actual. Fuck?

"Got ya! I—oh shit. Dean?"

Dean managed to wipe away enough water from his eyes to look in the direction of the voice above him. "Mason?" He could see the other man trying hard not to laugh. It was a battle he was mostly losing.

"Dean," Mason sputtered. "I'm so sorry, man. I was trying to get Phoebe and when she sat down here, I just assumed you were Eric. I mean…"

"We look alike," Dean finished for him. They did look alike. Eric was Dean's stunt double and from the back…well, he could see how Mason could have made the mistake.

"Exactly! And man, you got caught up in an epic water fight." Mason looked over Dean's head and covered his mouth with one of his big meaty hands as he burst into laughter. "Phoebe, oh shit. You are—"

"Drenched." Next to him, his costar stood up and pulled her long, dark hair from her face and wrung it out.

Dean tried and failed to notice the way her tank top stuck to her curves. Dammit, Bruce was right. The girl had curves in all the right places.

No.

He chastised himself. No matter what Bruce—or the public —wanted, he was not getting involved with Phoebe Flynn. No matter what.

"Nice one, Mason." Phoebe shook her head, but she didn't look mad. In fact, her smile lit up her face and she was positively gorgeous. "I thought I was home free," she continued. "I completely underestimated your desire to soak innocent people." She laughed and looked down at Dean. "Sorry, Mr. …"

"Dean." He extended his hand. "Call me Dean. Please. It's

nice to meet you, Phoebe. Even under the rather wet conditions."

"Damn." Mason looked between them. "You two hadn't even met yet?" He wiggled his eyebrows and Dean resisted the urge to glare at him.

He knew exactly what Mason was thinking. It was the same thing as virtually everyone else on set. But no. He wasn't going to hook up with his costar. Not this time.

"We haven't." He flashed Phoebe a grin. "But we were just about to."

"It's nice to meet you, Dean. I'm—" The smile on Phoebe's face dipped a little as she took his hand. She froze for a moment before continuing. "I'm sorry I got you caught up in this." Her smile returned as she pulled her hand away from his.

Dean instantly felt the loss of her touch.

"I'm sure you weren't expecting this when you sat down."

"I wasn't." He laughed in an effort to keep things light. Mostly so he didn't focus on the way his body had reacted to the simple touch of her skin on his. "Thanks for that, Mason."

The big man saluted comically and backed away. "I think maybe I'm needed on set or maybe…well, anywhere but here. I'm out, guys. Have fun." He took his bucket and with a few huge strides, he was gone, leaving Dean and Phoebe, both completely soaked, alone.

"Maybe we should reschedule our meeting?" Phoebe picked at her clothes.

He watched as she glanced over her shoulder at a blonde woman in a ponytail, standing at the edge of a restaurant. She held a clipboard and a cell phone. Phoebe's assistant.

"Later? After we've dried off, maybe?" Phoebe added as she turned around again.

Dean knew there would be no later. His schedule was almost always accounted for, down to the minute. If Bruce had cleared a few minutes for him to meet with her now, it was likely the only chance he'd have for a while. And more importantly, he didn't want to reschedule. Now that he was in her presence, he didn't want to be away from her. She had a strange magnetic pull about her. It was innocent, as though she had no idea that she had that power. Likely she didn't. Whatever it was, Dean liked it.

"Nonsense," he said. "If your schedule looks anything like mine, we won't get another chance until we meet on set. And I always think it's a good idea to get to know someone before I kiss them, don't you?" Her face morphed, and at once she looked mortified. Dean instantly regretted his words. "Not that we're going to kiss…I just meant…"

"I know what you meant." Phoebe had recovered, the playful smile back in place on her face. "And I agree. But I don't think that's our scene tomorrow." She winked at him, and his entire body reacted at the simple action.

"Okay." Dean cleared his throat. "I'll tell you what. I'm going to grab us each a drink and then maybe we can go sit in the sun and dry off. Sound good?"

She nodded.

"Beer okay?"

She nodded again, and before she could change her mind, Dean went to grab the drinks.

Chapter Three

IT DIDN'T TAKE the intense Panamanian sun long to dry them out completely. And it took even less time for Phoebe to relax into the conversation with Dean Harrison. They'd found a grassy area, off to the side of the marina. It was away from the action of the movie set, as well as the busyness of the boats coming and going at the docks. Most importantly, it was far enough away from the rest of the cast and crew that they wouldn't inadvertently get caught up in another water fight.

"So what do you think so far?"

Dean drew her from her moment of daydreaming. "Think about what?"

He smiled and it was dangerous. Never mind his acting ability; there was a reason he was one of the most popular movie stars in the world right now. He was deadly gorgeous. If she found it hard to breathe when she saw a photo of him, she was going to need some sort of inhaler if she spent too much time with him. She glanced down at the grass and started to pick at the blades. Phoebe had never been shy around men. And she'd definitely not been the type to get star struck. Not that there had been a lot of celebrities in her hometown. Or any at all.

"The movie." He waved his arm around to encompass the marina on one side, and the rain forest just behind them. "Panama. All of it." He shrugged casually, as if it were all no big deal. Which, to him, it probably wasn't.

"I think it's amazing," she answered honestly. "I've never seen anything like this."

"The movie set? Or Panama?"

"Both." Phoebe laughed. "But definitely the movie set. I watched a commercial for a local car dealership being filmed once. But I'm sure I don't have to tell you it was nothing like this. Not even close."

He grinned and leaned back on his arms.

Phoebe tried not to look at the way his tanned muscles bulged under his T-shirt. The man really was something else.

"And were you the star of the commercial?"

She laughed again. "No way. I was only twelve."

"So you weren't a child star then?"

He was flirting, but she didn't mind. To her surprise, Phoebe actually kind of liked it. It was easy and fun. "You don't know my story? I assumed everyone had read the article in *Star* magazine."

He shook his head and although it would have been easy for him to lie, she got the distinct impression that he was telling the truth. It was a surprise, but a nice one. "I try not to read those things. Even the magazines that claim they aren't tabloids. It's hard to know what to believe, ya know?"

She nodded despite the fact that she hadn't considered that. Obviously, she knew that a lot of the magazines and websites were nothing but gossip mills, but the journalist who'd come to her hotel room in LA and interviewed her had seemed very professional and the article was entirely factual. There was no way Lorilee would have let her do the interview if it was going to be trashy. Still, she wasn't nearly the star that Dean was, so it probably wasn't a fair comparison.

"Why don't you tell me the story?" Dean suggested. "Pretend you're reading me the article. Don't leave anything out." He tipped his beer to his lips and drank deeply.

Phoebe swallowed hard. "Nah, it's stupid."

"Clearly not, if you got an entire article in *Star*. I'm sure it's a great story." He sat up and leaned forward, resting his arms on his bent knees. His beer bottle dangled casually from one hand.

Everything about the man was easy and authentic. He had a way of making her feel as if she'd known him forever in only a few minutes of conversation. She almost felt stupid for a moment that she'd been so stressed out about meeting him. Obviously there'd been nothing to worry about.

"I already know you weren't a child star," he prodded. "But I don't know how you got here, in Panama, with me. Fill me in."

He genuinely looked interested in what she had to say, and there was no reason not to, so Phoebe sighed and told him the story about how she was working a crappy part-time job in the mall scooping frozen yogurt, when her agent Lorilee had discovered her. She'd been in town visiting her brother.

"It was fate," Dean said when she was done recounting the story. "If Lorilee hadn't been in that mall that day and you hadn't been serving her, you wouldn't be here right now."

She shrugged. "I guess not."

"So why was a beautiful, and based on first impressions, intelligent, woman like yourself working at the mall anyway? Were you between jobs or…"

A parrot squawked somewhere in the rain forest, and Phoebe turned toward the trees, but of course she couldn't see anything. When she turned back, Dean was still watching her, waiting for the answer. "You could say that. The truth is…well, the truth is that it's kind of embarrassing."

"Working an honest job is never embarrassing."

"It is when you'd just spent the last four years racking up so much student debt that it was hard to breathe under the weight of it all to finish your business degree, only to decide that you would rather sleep in a bed of spiders—which I don't, by the way—than spend one more day behind a desk, crunching numbers for the local car dealership."

He raised an eyebrow and she laughed. "Yes," she answered his unasked question. "*That* car dealership." He nodded, the explanation making perfect sense. "At any rate, it turns out I'm not really cut out for a desk job. It was making me crazy."

"So you went to scoop fro-yo?"

She nodded and laughed. "I know it sounds crazy."

"It does. But hey, if you weren't happy…then it doesn't seem all that crazy."

Phoebe had heard her share of opinions when she'd quit the dealership. Her friends from school thought she was insane. Her uncle had been disappointed and her sister… Kate had been livid. A single mom with two young kids, neither of which she'd planned on, Kate had always pinned all of her hopes and dreams on Phoebe, which was exactly how she'd ended up taking the role of Misty Falls in the first place, and had ended up in Panama sitting with Dean Harrison on a grassy hill. It was Kate's dream to be a star and shine in the spotlight, not Phoebe's.

If she was honest, it was the last thing she'd wanted. But then again, she didn't really know *what* she wanted, just what she didn't want. And you couldn't spend your life that way. Not really. And especially not when there were bills to pay. So, with no other options, she'd taken the job. Even if Phoebe hadn't been excited about it, Kate had been over-the-moon thrilled, and for a girl who'd always had her big sister take care of her, Phoebe couldn't deny that it felt good to do something that made Kate smile. She more than deserved it.

It didn't really matter why she'd taken the role, just that she had.

"I appreciate that," Phoebe said after a moment. "I don't usually hear that. I mean, where I come from, it's not so much about doing the thing that makes you happy. It's more about doing the thing that takes care of the family. Responsibilities and all that."

"Are you telling me that you wouldn't have chosen this? Doesn't every little girl dream about being a movie star?"

At once, Phoebe felt the familiar twinge of guilt at the thought that not only had she never wanted to be a star, but that she'd almost turned it down. And she would have, too, if it weren't for the responsibility she felt to her sister. It wasn't something she'd mentioned in the *Star* article. How could she? She'd be labeled as a stuck-up, spoiled little celebrity who had everything she wanted even though she didn't really want it. No. That would not go over well.

"Phoebe?"

She shook her head, and pasted a smile on her face. "Sorry, I got lost in a thought for a moment."

"No worries."

His smile was so genuine and disarming, Phoebe couldn't help but want to open up to him. In fact, the mere idea of telling him the truth and letting him in a little actually seemed like a good idea. As though he might understand.

"So, you didn't spend your childhood dreaming of seeing your name in lights?" he asked with a smile.

She laughed and shook her head. "Not this little girl."

"Ever?"

"No. Well, unless you count when I was six years old and I really wanted to be one of the girls in *Bring It On*."

"*Bring It On?* That was the cheerleading movie?"

"Not just any cheerleading movie." Phoebe pretended to be offended. "It was *the* cheerleading movie. Everyone I knew wanted to be Kristen Dunst in that movie." She laughed as she thought about it. "Come to think of it, that might have been more about being a cute cheerleader in high school than a movie star. And I also wasn't one of those."

"Still," he said. "That counts."

"I don't really think it does." She smiled at him and when he winked back, her stomach fluttered. "But hey, here I am now. And it's a pretty incredible opportunity, even if I did sort of fall into it."

"Some would say that makes it even more special."

She nodded and looked at her bare toes in her sandals. "Can I tell you a secret?"

"Of course."

She focused on her toes. "I totally feel like an imposter here." The moment she said the words out loud, a weight lifted from her shoulders. "Like someone else probably deserved this more than I did. I mean, I didn't really even want it and here I am." She waved her arms around to encompass the true paradise she was in. "This is like a dream come true for so many people, and I..."

"You maybe don't fully realize it yet."

His voice was soft and, to her surprise, there was no trace of judgment in it. Phoebe turned to look at Dean as he continued talking.

"But from what I hear, you're pretty damn good at this. And maybe you didn't dream about it, or ever think it was an option for you. But the fact is, you're here now and this *is* happening to you. Enjoy it, Phoebe. You don't owe anything to anyone but yourself."

She let his words sink in. Maybe she didn't really owe

anything to anyone. But Kate…she owed her sister a lot, didn't she?

Sometimes it was hard to tell.

Dean saw the moment Phoebe drifted away into her own thoughts. It surprised him how much she'd opened up to him in such a short time. And more so, how she made *him* want to open up.

He'd only been sitting with her for a few minutes, but something about her made him feel as if he'd known her a whole lot longer. It was rare for him to feel that way with anyone, especially a woman. Dean had never felt close to his past girlfriends. Not in the way that he'd ever felt like he could talk to them about anything important.

Which was probably why they hadn't worked out.

That, among other things. Many other things.

Not that it mattered. Not now anyway, because he had no intention of being anything more than a friend and costar to Phoebe Flynn.

He gave her another minute to sort out her thoughts before he reached out and lightly touched her knee. "Hey. Sorry, if I said anything that upset you," he said softly. "It's really none of my business how you ended up here."

Phoebe turned and looked at him with a soft smile of surprise. "I don't mind." She shrugged a little. "And you didn't say anything wrong. I was just…well, the truth is, I've never told anyone that before."

Dean felt a little thrill of happiness run through him.

She'd confided in him? Only him?

The idea that she'd trusted him with her feelings, especially so quickly, made him unreasonably and ridiculously happy. No one had ever confided in him in such a way.

"I actually feel a little stupid that I said anything," Phoebe continued. "I mean, I just met you, and you're a big star and everything."

"So?"

She raised her eyebrows. "So? I'm just a nobody newbie coming in here, complaining about how I didn't want to be a movie star. And I'm complaining to a big-time movie star. It's completely—"

"Honest," he interrupted her. "Never apologize for your feelings, Phoebe." His hand still rested lightly on her knee, so he squeezed a little before withdrawing it. "And if I'm being truthful, I'm really honored that you told me all that."

Her smile was both sweet and sad at the same time. "Thank you for listening, Dean. I don't really know anyone here very well and it's nice to have someone to talk to."

That was the truth. Dean couldn't remember the last time he'd ever had someone to talk to who wasn't on his payroll.

He nodded in understanding.

They sat in companionable silence for a few moments, listening to the parrots chattering in the jungle behind them before Phoebe spoke again. "So obviously you know I didn't have the Hollywood dream, but I read somewhere that it was always your dream to be a star."

She'd done her research.

"It was."

She may have done her research, but there was a lot she wouldn't know because Dean had always been particularly careful to keep certain truths out of the media. They knew what he wanted them to know. Which was that he'd had stars in his eyes since he was a little boy.

The truth was a little darker, fueled by the misguided hopes of a hurt little boy.

It may as well have been a lifetime ago when he'd laid in his childhood bedroom, daydreaming about what it would be like to be a famous movie star. He was ten years old when the fantasy had really begun to take shape. His mother had just left and his dad was either working extra hours at his mechanic shop, or drinking to forget about it all. It was just Dean most of the time. Alone, with the television or a stack of his mother's gossip magazines that she'd left behind, to keep him company. She'd been obsessed with the glossy pages of *Star* and *Celeb* and all the others, with their photos and articles about the latest hottest movie stars and celebrities. She'd spend hours poring over the details of their lives, what they wore, and where they went for vacation.

Dean didn't have a lot of memories of his mother anymore, but the ones he still did have centered on the way she'd talk to him for hours about the people she'd read about in the magazines and the look in her eyes as she'd tell him all about their lives as if they were friends of hers. More than anything, Dean remembered feeling that Leslie Harrison wouldn't be happy until she herself had that lifestyle.

When she left without any explanation—at least not to him —ten-year-old Dean knew deep down that she'd gone to Hollywood. And that's when his own dreaming had begun in earnest. If he could become a big-time movie star in the pages of those magazines, his mother would come back. He could give her the one thing she'd wanted more than him. And she'd love him enough to stay.

"And now your dreams have all come true." Phoebe smiled innocently because she had no idea that she couldn't have been further from the truth.

He'd never told anyone, and for the life of him, he didn't fully understand why he was doing it now, but before he could change his mind, Dean opened his mouth. "Can I tell you something that no one knows?"

To her credit, she didn't seem surprised at all. Instead, Phoebe turned her body in toward him. It was just a little move, but he noticed and in that one instant, Dean was drawn tighter toward her in a way he couldn't have begun to understand.

Before he could change his mind, he gave Phoebe the abridged version of how and why he'd wanted to be famous. She listened without judgment, the slightest trace of a kind smile on her face. She nodded a little from time to time, but to his surprise—and appreciation—she didn't feel sorry for him. When he was finished, she reached out and took his hand.

"Thank you for telling me that."

They sat quietly for a moment. Dean felt lighter than he had in years. The weight of his secret evaporated in the telling of the story, and despite the fact that there wasn't a happy ending to his story, a smile crept across his face.

Their beers were long finished, and Dean couldn't help but wish he'd brought more.

He'd enjoyed his time with Phoebe a lot more than he'd expected and he wasn't ready for it to end. Not that he had any actual expectations about how it would go. He'd just assumed she'd be like every other costar he'd ever had—consumed with fame and maximizing it as much as possible. As it turned out, most women in Hollywood were completely obsessed with all that stuff. It was hard to find someone who was actually real.

Like Phoebe.

And someone who he could actually talk to.

Like Phoebe.

A good listener, interesting, sweet, smart, and gorgeous? Never mind the way his body reacted in her presence. *She was—*

No. Dean shut down the thought before it could take root in his brain. She was his costar. The exact wrong person to be attracted to. Not this time. He'd made himself a promise, and he planned to keep it. No matter how perfect this woman was.

"We should probably get back," he said reluctantly. "I'm sure you have things to do."

"Just some lines to go over. Again. I have an early call in the morning." She laughed. "But you would know, since it's our first scene together."

Her laughter was infectious and it drew him to her like a magnet. "That's right." He got to his feet in an effort to break the connection before it got too strong to fight. "I won't keep you then." He offered his hand as a help up. When she took it, he lifted her to her feet easily, but hesitated before releasing her. Just like the first time they touched, there was a heat between them that kept his eyes locked to hers.

It was probably just the heat of the day. The Panamanian sun was next-level hot.

They walked in companionable silence off the grassy hill and back toward the Dockside and the busy marina. As they reached the crushed shell pathway that would take them back into the chaos, Phoebe paused. "You know what? I think I'm going to head back to my room. I don't want to get caught up in another water fight." Her laugh was easy and natural. "I did just finish drying off."

"Good point." He looked over her shoulder to the buildings in the distance. "Your room, is it…"

"Oh." Phoebe turned to see where he was looking and then spun to face him again. She pointed over her shoulder. "Yeah, it's just over there in those condos. Did you know all those old buildings were used ages ago for the US military when they were stationed here to protect the canal? It's really cool. The main buildings have all been redone and modernized, but if you go back a bit into the jungle, you can see some of the old roads, and ruins from when this was an active base. It's actually pretty neat."

Her eyes sparkled with excitement and Dean couldn't help but get caught up in it. "I had no idea."

"What?" She was genuinely appalled. "How could you not know? How long have you been here? I swear, it was one of the first things I did. I love to explore a new place, and…sorry. I'm rambling." She pressed her lips together.

The last thing Dean wanted was for her to quit talking. It was cute. *She* was cute. Which was a strange thing to think about such a strikingly beautiful woman. But there was no other word for it. When Phoebe Flynn got excited about something, she was cute. *Really* damn cute.

"No," Dean insisted. "You're not. And I am ashamed of myself that I didn't know about this. It sounds really cool."

"It is."

"Maybe you could show me sometime?"

Instantly, her face transformed from warm and open to completely shut down. She nodded slightly, but Dean could see it was forced. She had no interest in showing him the ruins she was only moments before describing with so much excitement.

Once again, she pointed behind her. "I really should go. Are you heading this way, too?"

He swallowed hard and shook his head, feeling like a privileged ass as he told her, "I'm actually staying on a motor yacht out in the bay."

"Right." She nodded. "Of course. You're Dean Harrison. That makes sense."

Dean knew she didn't mean anything by her words, but each one felt like a shot to his spirit.

"Okay," she said before he could reply. "I guess I'll see you tomorrow." She moved to go, but before she did, Phoebe held up her empty bottle. "Thanks again for the drink. It was good to meet you."

He stood for a moment and watched her walk down the path toward the condos where most of the cast and crew were housed.

Belatedly, he raised his hand to wave and even though she

couldn't hear him, he said, "It was nice to meet you, too, Phoebe Flynn." He shook his head and grinned because he was going to need more than a minute to process everything that had just happened. "*Really* nice," he said aloud before turning and heading to the Dockside, and the boat that would take him to his yacht.

Chapter Four

PHOEBE FELT as if she could sleep for days. The last few days of shooting had completely drained her. If someone had tried to tell her how exhausting it actually was to star in a major action movie, she would have laughed at them. After all, how hard could it really be to pretend to be someone else, run around dodging a few bullets, and make out with one of the hottest stars in the world?

Okay...put that way, it actually did sound like a lot.

And she hadn't even had the make-out scene yet. Let alone the bedroom scene or the boat scene.

The boat scene.

That was going to be the sexiest scene in the entire movie. At least that's what everyone was saying. Sexier than the bedroom scene somehow. Phoebe still hadn't figured out how that was, but when she'd heard that it was also going to be a closed set, that pretty much cinched it. Apparently they only closed the set when there was a lot of nudity and they needed to foster a really intimate environment.

The idea of getting intimate with Dean, let alone *nude* and intimate, sent a rush of conflicting emotions through her. She didn't want to, and she'd had absolutely zero intention of doing it, but despite herself, Phoebe had actually started to like the man. A little bit.

At the very least, he wasn't at all the way she'd expected him to be. Which, to be totally honest with herself, was a judgment based almost entirely on his reputation online and in the tabloids. She knew better than to form an opinion on other people's views.

Still.

They'd been filming together for a few days already and it had gone really well. Wes Reacher, the director, seemed happy with their onscreen *chemistry*, whatever that meant. Phoebe didn't know about chemistry, but Dean did make it easy to work with him, and despite the early morning calls and long days, Phoebe had enjoyed herself.

Maybe the whole acting thing wasn't so bad after all.

In an instant, she felt guilty for even thinking such a thing. She didn't mean to come off as ungrateful, or even allow her thoughts to take her there, but she'd never wanted all this. She'd never once considered a life in the spotlight. It had been Kate's dream. One she'd never likely see come to fruition, which was why Phoebe should try a little bit harder not to be ungrateful for her opportunities.

She laid back on her bed and sighed. She was just tired. *Maybe a nap…*

The vibrating of her cell phone put an end to any thoughts of a nap before they could take root. Without sitting up, Phoebe reached around the bed until her hand landed on her cell. She answered it without looking at the caller ID.

"Hello."

"Pheebs! Finally!"

It was as if just thinking about her older sister had conjured her. Phoebe grinned. "Hey, Kate. What's up?"

"What's up?" Her sister laughed, but there wasn't any

humor in it. "Just livin' the dream, sis. The girls have colds, it snowed again, and I think the heater in my van is shot. So ya know…tell me about Panama!" Her voice shifted in a flash. Kate didn't have the easiest circumstances with two kids under six, from two different fathers, each of whom had turned out to be deadbeats and were largely uninvolved in their children's lives. Especially when it came to helping out financially. Kate did her best, and Phoebe had to admit, it was pretty damn good. No one worked harder than Kate. She had to drop out of college when she was pregnant with Olivia, the oldest, and had ended up waiting tables at Heartland, one of the nicer restaurants in their hometown. After Ally had come along, she'd ended up getting promoted to a manager. How she juggled it all was always a miracle to Phoebe, especially now that she wasn't there to help out. But if Kate complained, it wasn't for long and it was never seriously.

"Have you met him yet?" Kate fired questions at her before she had the chance to answer any of them.

"Met who?"

"Dean!" Kate all but screamed through the phone. "You know exactly who I meant. Have you met Dean Harrison yet? What's he like? Really like? Is he as sexy in person? There's no way he is, right? I mean, who can be that sexy in real life? It's not fair for one man to have that much yum factor."

Phoebe shook her head and laughed. "Do you want me to actually answer any of that? Or are you just talking?"

She could picture her sister pressing her lips together and glaring at her, but just as she knew she would, Kate groaned and said, "Spill."

There would be no nap. Phoebe sat up and grabbed a bottle of water from her bar fridge before falling into the wicker chair on her veranda. She had a view out over the pool with the ocean behind it. The pool was often full of cast and crew cooling off and blowing off steam on their downtime, but like her, they must all be exhausted from the last few days because it was currently empty.

"I've met him," she said, after waiting long enough to drive her sister crazy. "We actually had a drink before our first scene. But that was days ago now."

"You waited *days* before telling me?"

"I've been busy, Kate." She took a deep drink from her bottle. "The schedule has been insane for the last few days, and —" She stopped herself from complaining about how busy she'd been. Not to Kate. No way. "Anyway, Dean's actually…" She hesitated. How should she explain her costar? "He's nice."

It was lame, and Kate said as much. "Nice? Um…good? I need more."

Phoebe laughed. "It's hard to explain. I think I expected him to be kind of stuck up, but he's actually really down-to-earth and normal." She refrained from telling her sister the secret Dean had let her in on. She'd done a lot of reading on Dean Harrison, and not once in anything she'd come across had she seen anything about his mother. She was honored he'd trusted her enough to tell her. Then again, she'd trusted him, too. It had been so natural and easy to talk to him. He'd been completely different than she'd ever expected. There was something about him…

"And hot?"

Phoebe almost spat out the sip of water she'd just taken. "Yes," she answered when she recovered. "He is definitely hot."

Over the line, Kate squealed. "You are totally going to end up dating him. Just like Emma Dennis, remember? She was his—"

"No." Her laughter dried up completely as she stopped her sister from going down that road. Because despite what she may have thought about their chat the other day, there were the facts to keep in mind. Dean Harrison had a reputation.

One she had absolutely no intention of getting caught up in. "There is no way. I've read all the articles, too, Kate, and I have no intention of hooking up with a man who's only interested in the publicity of his relationships. Dean Harrison might be a nice enough guy, but that doesn't change the fact that he's still a total player who uses women, his costars in particular, for more media attention. No thank you."

"But Pheebs, it could be——"

"No, Kate. It's not happening. Never."

"Don't make me get on a plane, Dean. You know how I hate the humidity."

Dean had put Bruce on speakerphone less than five minutes ago, and he was already regretting it. His manager hadn't stopped harping on the fact that Dean still steadfastly refused to get involved with Phoebe. Even though he himself had second-guessed his own decision more than once since actually meeting her. Never mind the fact that their chemistry on camera was incredible. Wes had pulled him into his trailer to look at the dailies after their first day of shooting together, and could barely contain himself.

And Wes was right. They *did* have chemistry. Both on and off film. At least, if their brief conversation a few days earlier over a beer had been anything to go on. And as far as Dean was concerned, it was. He couldn't get the dark-haired beauty out of his head.

"Hello? Deano? Are you there?"

Reluctantly, Dean forced himself to focus on the conversation with his friend.

"It's pretty nice here, Bruce." He decided to change the subject. "Sure, it's humid. But it's absolutely gorgeous and when you get on the boat, the breeze cools things off nicely.

Speaking of boats, thanks for hooking me up with this one. It's pretty nice." That was a massive understatement. Dean was currently sitting on a multi-million-dollar superyacht, which Bruce had arranged as his personal accommodation while he was on location in Panama. He had his own chef, a gym, a private viewing room, and pretty much anything else he could want. But despite his luxury accommodations, he couldn't help but wonder what it was like back on shore at the condos where almost everyone else was staying. Where *Phoebe* was staying.

"If you don't seal the deal with Flynn soon, I'm going to have to find out for myself pretty soon, Harrison. Lock it down."

"I told you, Bruce." Dean sighed and leaned over the railing. "Not this time. It's time for a change. With all of it. The movies, the—"

"No." Bruce cut him off sharply. "I already told you, Deano. This is not the time for *change*. You're at the top of your game right now and you need to stay there. Do you have any idea how quickly this industry will forget about you if you don't stay current? You only have a few years to make your mark."

"It has been a few years." Almost ten, in fact. "I don't think it would hurt to—"

"Have I ever steered you wrong, Dean?" Bruce's voice lost a little of its edge. "Look. I know you're going through something right now, but I only have your best interests at heart, Dean. You know that. We've been through it all together. You wanted to be a big deal—you are. You wanted fortune and fame—you got it. Just keep at it, okay? They're casting for the next *Supers* movie in a few months, and that's the prize. The Max Silver franchise is huge, but *Supers*? Once you land a role there, you've got it made. You'll be able to write your own check and get exactly what you want."

Dean nodded, even though Bruce couldn't see him. Exactly what he wanted? Sure, he *did* want the role in *Supers*. But he also wanted more…maybe a little more time off between films. A ranch or property somewhere. Somewhere to settle down with a family. With *someone*. More than anything, that's what Dean wanted.

But maybe Bruce was right. He needed to push a little bit more.

"Okay." He turned around and walked back to the table where he'd left his phone. He picked it up, and clicked off the speaker function, holding it to his ear instead. "Maybe you're right."

"You know I am." Dean could hear Bruce's joy. "This will get you there, Deano. Everything you've ever wanted, okay?"

"Okay," he agreed. "But I'm not forcing anything with Phoebe. She's different than the others. It's not going to be like that with her."

"Whatever you say." Bruce laughed. "It's like that with all up-and-coming actresses, and Phoebe Flynn won't be any different. Besides, you're Dean Harrison. The sexiest, most successful movie star around. She'd have to be crazy not to be tripping all over herself to get to you."

"Seriously." Dean shook his head. Despite himself, he couldn't help but wish that was in fact the case. "She's different, Bruce."

But Bruce wasn't listening. He'd already moved on to talking about some interviews and appearances he was lining up for Dean.

It wasn't until Dean finally managed to get off the phone and was once again leaning over the railing of the boat, gazing out across the bay to where he knew Phoebe's condo was, that he let his mind drift back toward his costar. "She's different," he said aloud. "Different from anyone I've ever met."

Chapter Five

PHOEBE LOOKED AGAIN at her reflection in the mirror. It didn't matter how many times she'd sat in the hair and makeup chair, she still couldn't get over the complete transformation that took place at the hands of Susie and Louis. She blinked again and turned to the side a little. "I seriously don't know how you do this."

"It's pretty easy when I have such a beautiful canvas to work with."

He was humble, but Phoebe didn't miss the pleased look on the man's face. She'd learned early on that Louis thrived on compliments. Not that it was hard to give them; he truly was a genius. Somehow the man made her look high-level glamorous, but also natural at the same time. It was incredible.

"And your hair…" Susie, her hair stylist, chimed in. "All I have to do is put a bit of product in it and you shine."

She was exaggerating—Susie had to do a whole lot more than that to tame her long locks to give her those soft waves—but Phoebe didn't push it.

"You two are both way too humble." Phoebe pushed up from the chair and tightened her robe around her waist.

"And you are way too sweet." Louis pointed at her with a makeup brush he was tucking back into a case. "What are we supposed to say when the tabloids come sniffing around for some dirt?" He put a hand on his waist and tipped his head dramatically. "Huh? You're not a diva. You don't pull hissy fits because of the color of your lip gloss and—"

"You're not involved in any drama on set," Susie jumped in with a laugh. "Seriously, what are we supposed to say?"

Phoebe stared at them, horrified. "Is that a thing? Do they interview you guys about—"

"No. Silly girl." Louis shook his head. "Even if they did, our lips are sealed." He mimed the gesture with a flourish. "I'd like to keep my job, thank you very much."

Susie nodded in agreement, and added a wink. "But it wouldn't hurt to give us a little something to gossip about."

Phoebe shook her head. "Thanks, but—"

"Knock knock." Behind her, Kristen popped her head into the trailer. "Ready? It's almost time, Phoebe."

She looked in the mirror one last time at the face that was hers, but not hers at all, sighed, put a smile on her face and lied. "I'm ready."

"Ohh." Louis giggled as she walked to the door. "I wish we could watch."

"That would give us something to talk about," Susie added. "Can you sneak us on set?"

Phoebe turned around and grinned. "You'll just have to wait for the movie to come out." She stuck out her tongue and followed Kristen out and onto the set.

They were shooting in one of the hotel rooms upstairs from the Dockside Inn. Wes Reacher liked to stay out of an actual sound stage as much as possible to keep things *authentic*. Which also meant that there wouldn't be many people on this particular set because it was such a small space. And that was perfectly fine with Phoebe, given the intimate nature of this particular scene.

She didn't want to be nervous about it, but it was hard not to be. Sure, it helped that she'd gotten to know Dean even more over the last week or so of filming with him. Although she'd come to realize he actually was a really nice guy and way more down-to-earth than she'd expected, making it really quite easy and natural to act with him, there was a whole different problem.

She was insanely attracted to him and not just in that *you're a really hot guy* kind of way, but in the way that her entire body reacted every time she saw him. And to complicate matters further, in a few minutes, she was going to be expected to take off her clothes and perform a dirty striptease for the man.

Phoebe swallowed hard.

"You're going to kill it," Kristen said, obviously recognizing her discomfort. "Dean is a total pro. And you're absolutely nailing every scene. This one won't be any different." Her smile was genuine.

Phoebe was thankful for her friendship. She nodded and smiled.

"I'll be right outside here in the hall, okay?"

Phoebe nodded and let out a breath she'd been holding. "It's no big deal," she said, mostly to herself. "It's just acting." She closed her eyes for a moment and channeled her character, Misty Falls, a trick she'd recently mastered.

I'm a sexy siren. I'm an international spy. I'm totally in control.

When she opened her eyes again, she was ready.

Damn. Damn. Damn.

Dean struggled to keep his focus. A near impossible task when Phoebe walked through the door wearing nothing but a slip of a silk robe. Her dark hair hung in shiny waves over her shoulders, and her eyes had been made up with a smoky, heavy lid that Dean could only describe as *bedroom eyes*. Her lips were a deep red and just knowing that in a few moments he would have his own lips on them sparked a flame of desire deep in his gut.

But he needed to focus. Because the reality was, this was *not* reality. It was a scene and he was Max Silver, international spy, who needed to save the world. And she was Misty Falls, his not-yet-discovered enemy, who was determined to seduce him in order to obtain classified information.

This scene was to be a seductive dance between them. A sexy push and pull. It would be hot—*very* hot. But it wouldn't be *the* scene. That was coming later. On a closed set. On a yacht at sea.

Dammit, Dean. Focus.

He couldn't afford to let his imagination go there. Not yet. Not now. He needed to focus on the present and the incredibly sexy woman in front of him. She winked, and he knew she was already in character. It continued to astound him that this was Phoebe's first movie. She was more of a pro than a lot of the seasoned actors and actresses he usually worked with.

"Places, everyone."

The camera zoomed in on Dean. He closed his eyes for a brief second, opened them, and gave a slight nod. It was his cue that he was ready.

"And...action."

Music that would be dubbed over in the final cut started to play. A sexy, slow beat. And then Phoebe—or Misty, as he needed to think of her—appeared in the door of the adjoining bathroom.

She put one arm up the doorframe and leaned seductively against it. "What's it going to take, Silver?"

Dean stayed where he was, in the chair by the window, one

leg crossed over the other, a careful mask of indifference on his face. He shrugged ever so slightly, a tiny move he knew would be picked up on camera. "What are you proposing?"

Slowly, she walked across the floor until she stood directly in front of him. She was only inches away. It wouldn't take anything for him to reach out and touch her tanned bare leg. To wrap his fingers around her thigh and pull her into him so he could kiss the Misty Falls right out of her and have Phoebe Flynn in his arms.

He swallowed as her fingers slowly traced the edge of her robe until they reached the knot around her waist. "I have a few things in mind." Her voice was husky, with an edge that made his pulse race. Her fingers worked the knot until the silk slipped free. Her manicured fingers held it teasingly closed. "Do you like to dance, Silver?"

"I'm more of an observer myself." He twitched his lips up into a smile, playing Max Silver perfectly. He tipped his head in a nod that instructed her to go ahead.

Misty took a step back, turned her back to him and then, with painstaking slowness, let her robe slip off her shoulders, where it landed in a puddle on the floor beneath her stilettos.

Dean allowed himself a moment to drink in the perfection that stood before him. He'd read the script. He knew what she'd be wearing. But somehow, seeing the black leather corset pulled tight, creating an impossibly perfect hourglass figure, the laces tight down her back, leading to only the tiniest piece of material running between the plump globes of her luscious ass, was an entirely different experience. And she hadn't even turned around.

Two circles of lace and leather wrapped each of her toned thighs, with garter clips attached to sheer black stockings.

Dean watched as Misty raised her arms, and lifted her hair from her bare back. She held it up on her head for a moment, while the music pulsed and she swayed to the beat.

His breath came fast, and he worked hard to control it. Max Silver would hardly be affected by the vision in front of him. She dropped her hair and, in the same move, bent at the waist, so that her ass was directly in front of his face. Still, he kept a bored expression on his features. She'd have to do better to affect Max Silver. He was trained for this kind of thing.

The beat of the music changed, and Misty stood and took a few steps away from him, waving her behind in a way that would make any normal red-blooded male crazy with desire. But when she finally spun and faced him, Dean sucked in a breath. Character break or not, there was no way he couldn't not react. And it wouldn't matter how many takes they did. He knew in his heart, he'd react every single time.

She was a fucking smoke show. Her full breasts had been lifted and pushed until they were almost but not quite spilling over the cups of her corset. The tiny scrap of fabric of her panties only barely covered her, another test of Dean's willpower. With her dark curls hanging over her bare shoulders, and the way her heavy-lidded eyes were focused on him, her red lips pursed in a sexy pout, Phoebe was every bit the sexual temptress.

Damn was an understatement.

She once again walked toward him; this time, her eyes locked on his. He knew what was coming next and he was ready for it. Acting or not, every fiber in his body was ready for what was about to go down.

"Like what you see, Silver?"

Dean shrugged and slowly uncrossed his leg, inviting her into his space. "Not much of a dance."

Her lips twitched up into a barely perceptible smile as she bent her knees and dropped into a perfectly timed squat directly in front of him. She flipped her hair forward, letting it fan out over his lap before looking up at him. Once again, she made and held eye contact as she moved her body to the rhythm of the music.

Where had she learned these moves?

From the vantage point he had, he knew if he broke eye contact and let himself look, he would have the perfect view of her breasts and the deep cleavage the corset was presenting for him. He forced himself to stay in character, because not only was it his job, but it would be the only way he would be able to keep from doing what he really wanted to do—which was kiss Phoebe Flynn and tell her that not only was she the sexiest woman he'd ever laid eyes on, but he was also starting to fall for the woman he'd been getting to know.

No. He had to stay in character. Kissing her senseless was not going to accomplish anything.

Dean feigned disinterest as she finally, mercifully touched him. She slid her hands up his thighs, until they'd almost reached his groin. That was his cue.

He moved with lightning speed as his hands clasped over her wrists and in the same motion, he jumped to his feet, pulling her up with him.

She gasped. He growled.

Two quick steps later, Misty Falls was up against the wall, her hands on either side of her head, pinned by his strong arms. Her breath came fast and hard, her breasts straining against the tight leather as they rose and fell. His gaze bore into hers. Misty Falls was definitely one of his tougher adversaries, but she was still no match for Max Silver.

Not yet.

She narrowed her eyes in a challenge that he accepted when his mouth crashed onto hers in a passionate kiss.

Breathe. Breathe.

Up until that moment, Phoebe had no problem staying in character. It was all part of her job. As soon as she was Misty Falls, she took over. Despite the fact that she was wearing a ridiculously slutty—but admittedly sexy—outfit, dancing like a stripper in front of Dean Harrison, it hadn't been a problem. Not when she was Misty Falls.

But when he'd kissed her....

It was a hard, hot kiss. He pressed his body into her, not releasing her arms so her breasts were pushed up into his chest as his tongue slipped between her lips. She heard a low moan, and was equally terrified that it might have come from her *and* that the camera had picked it up. But no one yelled cut, not that she would have heeded the call, anyway.

Her body responded naturally and she responded to the kiss.

Never before had she kissed a man like that. Acting or not.

Holy mother of—

Her thoughts were ripped from her as Dean's mouth left hers. He was still only inches away when she opened her eyes, forcing herself back into character as she did so.

"I don't dance with traitors." Dean delivered the last line. "And I definitely don't tell them anything." With a shove against her, he released her arms and took a step back, leaving her up against the wall, trying and failing to catch her breath.

Her arms dropped to her sides as he reached into her cleavage and plucked out the microchip that contained all the secrets, and then he was gone, the door to the room slamming behind him.

"And...cut!" Wes yelled. "Fuck! That was fire, everyone! One take. It's perfect."

The room became alive. People she hadn't even seen before the shoot started now appeared out of nowhere. Dean came back in, a wide grin on his face. Max Silver had been left outside; it was all Dean Harrison now and Phoebe couldn't help but like Dean Harrison. She'd really enjoyed working with him. But even more so, she'd liked the moments between takes when they'd chatted and laughed and started to get to know each other. She'd made a vow to stay away from him, but... that was before she'd gotten to know him better. And that kiss.

That was...*acting,* she reminded herself harshly. *Acting. It's the entire reason they were there, in Panama, and she was dressed like...well...*

"Damn, Phoebe." Dean had joined her. "That was...well, you look..." He laughed and ran a hand over his face. "Wow. All of it. That was just—"

"Fucking magic, is what that was!" Wes stood between them, clapping his hands together with a huge grin on his face.

Reluctantly, Phoebe shifted her attention to the director.

"Phoebe, are you sure this is your first film? Where have you been my entire career? You are an absolute star!"

Phoebe couldn't keep the smile off her face at the praise. Sure, she'd never wanted to be an actress and definitely had never dreamed of being a star. But despite all of the misgivings she'd had when she'd started, she was really starting to enjoy herself. "It was good?"

"Good?" Wes slapped his clipboard against his thigh dramatically. "No," he said with a straight face. "It wasn't good at all. It was fire, Phoebe. Fire! After watching this movie, every single man in America is going to go to bed, dreaming about you. Holy shit."

She blushed. Phoebe never blushed, but she'd also never been told she was about to be America's next sex symbol.

"Is that really what you want, though?" Dean stepped forward and asked the question to Wes, not Phoebe, although she couldn't help but feel it was really for her.

"That's exactly what we want, Harrison. I know you're not new to this. That's the goal of a Max Silver movie." He pointed at Dean. "You are every woman's fantasy. And she..."

He pointed at Phoebe, who suddenly felt very aware that she was still dressed in only a leather corset. "Is every man's fantasy. Sex sells. And you two...fire," he said again before turning to leave. "That's a wrap for today," he added. "Good work today. Get some rest. Or better yet, go have some fun. You deserve it. Both of you."

Phoebe shook her head with a laugh. "He's hilarious." She turned back to Dean, but the smile fell off her face when she saw how he was looking at her. "What?"

"He's right, you know," he said seriously. "You're going to be a star. That scene was—"

"It was fun," she interrupted him. "And...I'm still a little underdressed here." She could tell Dean was trying not to look at her, likely out of respect considering he definitely didn't seem to be interested in her at all. A fact that she had to admit was more than a little puzzling because he had such a strong reputation of dating his costars. And that kiss. *No. That was acting.* It wasn't going to be the last time, she reminded herself. He was a damn good actor. It wasn't as though Phoebe didn't have any experience with men; she did. But even her hottest relationship hadn't given her feelings like that kiss just had.

"Right," Dean said quickly. "You must be cold."

She raised an eyebrow. It was far from cold in the little hotel room that was starting to clear out. But she didn't say anything and instead scanned the room in search of the robe she'd dropped in the scene. But it was gone. The props and costuming crew were too efficient.

"Here." Dean shrugged out of the black leather jacket that was Max Silver's trademarked look and handed it to her. "Take this."

They walked off the set together. As soon as Kristen saw them, she moved discreetly away, and let them walk past without interruption, as did Dean's assistant, Kyle. The sun had long disappeared, leaving the marina shrouded in darkness, with only the lights along the path to guide their way back to the condos.

"Are you going to take Wes's advice?"

Dean's question confused her. She shook her head.

"What advice? About being America's next sex symbol? I don't even want to think about that. It's so strange." She laughed, but Dean watched her intently, his dark eyes fixed on her.

"There is nothing strange about that." His voice was low and gruff and for a moment, Phoebe thought he might say something more about it, but then a switch flipped. He grinned and laughed. "But no, that's not what I meant. I was referring to his advice about going to have some fun. Maybe we could—"

"Phoebe!" Layla, her stunt double, who'd also become somewhat of a friend on set, interrupted them. "Sorry to interrupt. I heard you killed it on set today. Too bad I couldn't be your double for the more fun scenes, right?" She turned to wink at Dean, who shook his head with a laugh. "Anyway." She returned her focus to Phoebe. "The van leaves in thirty minutes. We're going out."

"Out?" It was Dean who asked.

Phoebe did vaguely remember hearing something about the cast and crew going into the city for some dancing.

"The city," Layla answered. "Rumor has it that there's a hot club with sick beats." She swiveled her hips in a sexy dance. "And I don't know about you, but I could really stand to blow off some steam. Especially if that includes a sexy Latin lover to show me some new moves."

Phoebe groaned. "Thirty minutes? I'm not even a little bit ready. I need to—"

"Change nothing." Layla held out her hands, framing Phoebe in them. "You are perfect."

She laughed. There was no way she was going to any club,

no matter how sexy, wearing nothing but a corset. Her makeup and hair were pretty hot, though. "I'll put a dress on."

"Perfect!" Pleased with herself, Layla spun on her foot and headed in the opposite direction. "I'm going to spread the word. You come too, Dean!"

"I guess I am going to go have some fun after all," Phoebe said when Layla was gone. "What about you? It'll be fun."

Chapter Six

ITLL BE FUN.

Phoebe's words played on repeat in Dean's head, taunting him. Because it *would* be fun to go to a club in Panama City and let loose a little. Especially if letting loose involved Phoebe in any way. But he'd said no. He'd made up some stupid excuse about needing to run lines and getting a good night's sleep, even though he didn't have an early morning call the next day. It was lame and, judging by the look on her face, she knew it, too. But she'd accepted his reasoning; he'd said his good-bye and left her to get ready.

That had been three hours ago. They would be in Panama City by now. It was at least a two-hour trip by bus. No doubt they were already in the club, dancing and having a good time. Blowing off steam, Layla had called it. She'd also mentioned finding a Latin lover. He wasn't an idiot, and just because he wasn't a partier didn't mean that he didn't know what went on at the clubs. He also knew that Phoebe, looking the way she had—or hell, even if she were wearing a paper bag—would have no shortage of attention on her.

And the very thought of that made him crazy.

He wanted to be the only one giving Phoebe attention. And dammit, he *did* want to be giving her attention. Lots of it. He'd sworn that he wasn't going to get involved with his costar. Not this time. But that was before he knew his costar was Phoebe. And it was definitely before he knew that Phoebe was *Phoebe*.

Not only was she the sexiest woman he'd laid eyes on for a very long time, she was also smart, funny, and...*shit*.

It didn't matter that he hadn't gone to the club with everyone else. It wasn't going to keep him away from her.

Dean paced to the edge of his stateroom and onto the balcony. He could hear the water below slap against the hull of the boat, but the yacht was so big, it hardly moved in the swell. It really was a gorgeous boat. But it didn't matter how amazing the boat was if he was all by himself on it.

He stretched his arms out along the brass rail and dropped his head down, contemplating his options. It was too late to drive into the city. But that didn't mean he couldn't get there. He lifted his head and inhaled deeply as the decision was made.

Dean slapped the brass rail and pushed off it, and went back into his room, where he grabbed his phone.

"Kyle," he said the moment his assistant answered. "I need to get into the city. Now."

Thirty minutes later, Dean, who'd changed into a fitted black button-down shirt and black pants, walked through the doors of the club.

"Hola, señor."

The man who greeted him had obviously been prepped for his arrival, and although Dean was sure he'd been recognized, he appreciated the way the manager downplayed who he was. He slipped the man a bill that he tucked discreetly into his pocket before leading Dean through the pulsing nightclub.

"Right this way, señor."

The club was packed, and the music beat a pulse in his chest. Beautiful people danced and gyrated all around him. But he didn't see Phoebe. And then, as they reached the roped-off area the cast and crew had secured, he saw her. She was turned away from him, but there was no mistaking her long, dark hair that cascaded over her bare back. She'd changed out of the corset. A fact that he was both disappointed by and pleased with, because the thought of any other man seeing her in such a risqué outfit made him a little crazy. A detail that wasn't lost on him. He was protective over her. Maybe even a little jealous. Which meant—

"Harrison. You made it." Mike, who played an assassin, greeted him first, followed by a host of others who waved and called out to him.

He made his rounds, but Dean didn't take his eyes off Phoebe, who was moving to the music and sipping a drink and had yet to notice him. But he'd definitely noticed her.

She may have changed into something *more appropriate* for the club, but there wasn't much to it. A deep-green halter dress that was made of a flowy material, it was cut dangerously low in the back and there wasn't much more to the front. Two lengths of fabric fell over each full breast, only barely covering her before coming together into a tight, short skirt. The dress was sinful and sexy in a way that was beyond what she'd been wearing earlier.

A waitress appeared and handed him a drink. Phoebe still hadn't noticed he was there, but she was no longer dancing. Instead, she was obviously talking to someone Dean couldn't see. She flipped her hair back over her shoulder and laughed. He didn't want to be rude, but Dean was tired of waiting. There was only one reason he'd used his celebrity status to charter a helicopter to take him into the city, where a private driver had picked him up and whisked him to the club, and she was standing right in front of him.

He wasn't going to waste one more moment of his night.

Dean crossed the space and, taking a chance, slipped his hand to the small of her back, touching her with the slightest glance of his fingers. "Having fun?" Out of the corner of his eye, he recognized his stunt double, Eric, purse his lips. No doubt he'd been hitting on Phoebe, and Dean didn't blame him. But he also wasn't interested in standing around and watching it happen.

"Dean!" She spun to face him and her face lit up in a dazzling smile. "You made it after all. How did you get here?"

"Let me guess," Eric said, not bothering to hide his annoyance. "A private jet."

"Close." Dean spared the other man a quick look. "A helicopter." He focused his attention back to Phoebe. "I thought about what you said. And it did sound like fun. So here I am."

"Well, I'm glad you're here." She raised her glass to both men. "Cheers, guys."

Both Eric and Dean clinked glasses with her. But as far as Dean was concerned, that was the limit of how much sharing he was going to do. He took a sip of his drink and put it down on a nearby table. "May I have this dance?" He reached for her hand.

She tilted her head and gave him a flirty smile. "Oh, but I thought you didn't dance with traitors?"

Desire tore through him. "Then I guess I'm going to have to spend a little more time deciding if I can trust you."

She winked and set down her own drink before she took his hand. "You definitely have your work cut out for you."

Without another glance to Eric—he could find someone else to dance with; Phoebe was all his—Dean led his costar out to the dance floor.

The minute he pulled her into his arms and stared into her eyes, he knew with no uncertainty that he was in trouble. His pulse raced, and the need to kiss her again, this time for real, almost consumed him.

She looked at him with heavy lids, desire and need radiating from her, too.

But he needed to stay in control. As much as he wanted her, he also wasn't a complete moron. And there was no way he was going to kiss her in public. Dancing was one thing. Almost everything else crossed a line, and the tabloids would have a field day with any inch of gossip he gave them.

Dean swallowed hard and, with a flick of his wrist, spun Phoebe out onto the dance floor. Her hair whirled around her before he once more pulled her into his arms and began moving his hips, leading her around the floor with ease. Earlier in his acting career, he'd taken intense dance lessons for a role that had been one of his breakout roles. And besides being a huge boost to his career, it had also given him mad dancing skills, which more than paid off all night as he led Phoebe, spinning and dipping and holding her closer until their feet ached and the lights were ready to come on.

Chapter Seven

PHOEBE'S EYES fluttered open as the helicopter landed with a thud that jarred her awake. She blinked and lifted her head that had been resting on Dean's shoulder. "Oh, I'm sorry," she said quickly. "I didn't mean to fall...oh no! Did I miss it?"

"Miss what?" Dean grinned at her, as if she were the cutest thing he'd ever seen. "And what are you sorry for? You're exhausted."

She spun around and looked out the window. There was nothing but blackness outside. "The helicopter ride? I missed it, didn't I? Are we back already?" She turned back to Dean, who was unbuckling his seat belt.

"It is over," he said, sounding genuinely apologetic. "I'm sorry. You did miss it but you were so tired, I couldn't stand to wake you up. Besides," he added. "I kind of liked you sleeping on me. You snore. It's very cute."

She smacked him playfully on the arm. "I do not snore."

Phoebe unclipped her own seat belt and gathered up her small purse and her shoes. They were killer heels—the sexiest shoes she owned—and they made her legs look amazing. But after dancing in them all night, there was no way they were going back on her feet. "I can't believe we got here so fast. How long did it take?"

"About twenty minutes." The door opened from the outside and Kyle, Dean's assistant, appeared to offer her a hand down. "A little bit faster than the bus, right?"

"Way faster." She stepped down to the ground and straightened her dress. Dean had all but insisted that she take him up on the offer to ride in the helicopter with him back to the marina, and she had to admit, it had been a good decision for so many reasons.

"Thanks, Kyle." Dean joined her on the ground and a moment later, put a pair of flip-flops in front of her. "I had Kyle bring these for you. I figured maybe your feet might need a little break."

Phoebe sighed as she slid her feet into the sandals. "Thank you. That was..." In the dim light, she could just make out his face, and the tenderness in his features as he looked at her. "That was really thoughtful," she finished.

He held her gaze a moment longer before touching her arm gently. "It's late. We should get you home."

They walked in silence down the crushed shell path that would lead them to her condo. On the horizon, the sky was just beginning to lighten. Phoebe couldn't remember the last time she'd stayed up all night and was even more grateful that she'd accepted the helicopter ride instead of taking the bus with the others. A few extra hours in her bed would definitely be welcomed after such a big night of dancing.

"Thank you," she said again as they reached the door that would lead to her second-floor condo. "I'm really glad you came. And not just because of the helicopter ride, although that was pretty sweet, too. Even if I did sleep through it."

"We'll have to do it again."

"The dancing or the helicopter ride?"

"Both?"

"I think it might take my body a little while to recover from tonight." She chuckled. "I don't think I've ever danced so much before. But the helicopter—I would love to do that again one day and stay awake for it."

He took a step toward her and despite the fact that they'd had their bodies pressed up against each other all night, his nearness made her breath hitch. "Anytime you want," he said softly. "Say the word."

They'd literally been inseparable all night on the dance floor, only occasionally breaking to grab a drink and chat with the others, and then only for a minute or two. Their moves had been intimate and sensual, but standing in the quiet pre-dawn by her front door, with no one around, was so much more.

Dean reached out and cupped her cheek. Instinctively, she leaned into the touch and let her eyes close for a moment. When she opened them, he was leaning in.

"Phoebe, I've been wanting to do this all night."

Yes. She'd been wanting him to do that much longer than just one night. Her body lit up, every nerve ending responding to his proximity and what was about to happen. Finally.

Phoebe and Dean. Not Max and Misty.

But…

Crap.

It was the last thing her body wanted, and her heart…that was too soon to tell. But her mind knew better, and moments before Dean's lips connected with hers, she slipped a hand between them and pressed on his chest, forcing him to take a step back.

Confusion filled his eyes and took over his handsome face.

"Sorry, Dean." She shook her head and tried to keep it light. "I don't think that's a good idea."

He took a step back and ran a hand through his hair. "I think it's a very good idea. I really like you, Phoebe, and I'm sorry if I misread the situation, but I was pretty sure you felt the same way. Did I get it wrong?"

Oh, he did *not* get it wrong. Far from it. He got it exactly right. Never in her life had Phoebe been more attracted to anyone. Never before had she felt such an insane attraction to a man. And that kiss...sure, it had been acting. But...*damn*. Had it?

No. He had it exactly right.

But still...

"It's just...you have a bit of a reputation with your costars, and I'm not that kind of woman." She saw the moment her words registered on his face. He shook his head, but before he could say anything, she picked her keycard out of her clutch and said, "Thanks again for the fun night, Dean."

Her card beeped against the lock and she put her hand on the door right as Dean grabbed her arm.

"Wait."

She took a breath and turned around, expecting him to be upset about what she'd said, but she wasn't prepared for what he said.

"Give me a chance."

"What?"

"Look, I know that it doesn't matter what I say right now, because you're right. I do have a reputation for dating my costars. I get it. But this is different, Phoebe. Getting to know you and talking to you and...it's different."

She bit her bottom lip. She wanted to believe it. She wanted to trust what her heart was saying and what her body was screaming. But she couldn't risk it. She refused to be like all those other women—famous because of their relationship with Dean Harrison. No. She may not have chosen this life, but if she was going to do it, she was going to do it on her own.

She started to shake her head again, but he stopped her. "It is, Phoebe. This is different. And I'm going to prove it. If you'll give me the chance." He took a step back and grinned.

It was such a genuine, open smile. Boyish and so much more the Dean she was getting to know than the slick, movie star he presented to the world.

"Will you give me a chance to show you that this is different? I've never opened up like I did to you with anyone else. That's how I *know* it's different. Never mind the way I feel when you're near." He let out a puff of air. "How I feel about you and getting to know even more about you is so different than anything I've ever experienced before."

Her heart clenched and Phoebe had to work hard to stay strong with her convictions. Sure, he was saying all the right things, but…

"Phoebe?"

Before she knew what she was doing, she nodded. "Okay. I'll give you a chance."

It was all he needed. One chance to show Phoebe that his feelings were genuine. Every new thing that he learned about her just concreted that in his head *and* his heart.

She was different. Phoebe wasn't like the other women who were only interested in using him for his fame. Okay, maybe that wasn't fair. Maybe they had genuinely cared about him. *Maybe.* But in hindsight, it sure didn't feel like it. Hell, even at the time he'd been dating those women, he'd known.

Everything about his past relationships had been cold, distant, superficial. Everything that Phoebe Flynn was not.

As Dean made his way back to the marina and the speedboat that would take him back out to his yacht for a few hours of sleep, a plan began to formulate in his head. He'd asked for a chance. One chance to show her that his intentions were pure, and he wasn't going to waste it.

He didn't have to be on set until later that night, which was a very good thing, because there was no way Dean was going to be able to sleep. He had too much to organize. Details to sort out and plans to put into place, and he was definitely not going to waste any time sleeping. He knew he could get Kyle to organize the most phenomenal date Phoebe had ever seen, but that was a cop-out. He needed to do it himself. Phoebe had to know without a doubt in her mind that he had planned every single detail, because she was worth it.

She was so worth it.

When Kyle knocked on his stateroom door hours later, he still hadn't slept, but he did have almost every single detail of his date planned. Including the timeline. Tomorrow night. He'd spoken to Wes and he had a two-day window while they broke set and got ready for the next action sequence. And Dean planned to take full advantage of it.

"Are you ready for this?" Kyle handed Dean a much-needed cup of coffee. "Because you look like shit. Did you sleep?"

He shook his head and grinned as he gratefully accepted the coffee. "Ready for what?"

"Today is stunt day. Eric's ready to run through things with you. Don't tell me you forgot."

He *had* forgot. It wasn't long ago that doing his own stunts had been the most pressing thing on his mind. Things changed.

A lot.

"You forgot." Kyle shook his head. "Drink up. You're going to need the caffeine. And I'll have the chef make you some sort of energy smoothie. The last thing you need is to get hurt doing this. Wes will never let you forget it. And, so help me...if you kill yourself, Harrison, I'm out of a job."

Dean laughed. "I won't kill myself, Kyle. It's a simple stunt. Some jumping and dodging and diving, if I remember correctly."

"And fighting," Kyle reminded him. "There's a fight scene. A few punches. A kick or two. Then you dive off the boat."

"Right." Dean stood, rolled out his shoulders, and jumped up and down a few times to get the blood moving. He was in excellent shape. But still, his body protested after a night out dancing. Not that he was going to tell Kyle that. "A bit of a fight and a dive. No problem. Besides, today is just practice."

Chapter Eight

PHOEBE LOVED her tiny hometown tucked into the Montana mountainside thousands of miles away, but at that particular moment, as she let her body be warmed by the hot Panamanian sun in the middle of February, she was not missing the snowy, frigid temperatures they were experiencing.

Not even a little bit.

She rolled to her stomach, reached around, and unclipped her bikini top so to avoid tan lines. Not that she should get any color at all with the massive amounts of sunscreen she'd applied. She'd been told by Louis in no uncertain terms that if she *insisted on being out in the sun*, she could get *some* color, but no sunburns.

He'd seemed to be pretty serious about it, and she liked having Louis on her side, so she'd dutifully slathered on a thick layer of cream before lying out by the pool. And she had a timer set on her phone to reapply or get inside in exactly twenty minutes. She should be fine.

Phoebe groaned with satisfaction as the heat washed over her and a slightly evil grin played on her lips when she thought of her sister, Kate, stuck at home in the snow. She knew she shouldn't, but she couldn't help herself.

She picked up her phone and lifted her head off the chaise just enough to show her grinning face and the pool and palm trees in the background. She took the selfie and quickly tapped in a message.

Missing you.

She laughed as she hit Send. She was definitely the bratty little sister. But she couldn't help herself. And she knew that Kate would laugh. Despite the three-year age gap, they were close. They always had been. They had to be. They were only seven and ten when their parents died and they moved in with Uncle Benny. He'd done his best, and his best was pretty great. It had been a home full of love, which was all they could have asked for. Spending most of their time at the car dealership when they weren't at school might not have been the most orthodox upbringing, but Phoebe had enjoyed it. Kate, not so much. And where Phoebe had turned to school and her studies, Kate turned instead to partying and boys.

It wasn't until she was much older, and a mother of two, that she finally settled down. But by then, as far as Kate was concerned, it was too late to go after her dreams. She knew it shouldn't bother her, but it still made Phoebe sad that her older sister seemed so unhappy with her life and worked so hard to keep everything and everyone going. More than anything, Kate had dreams to travel and see the world.

Maybe, one day soon, Phoebe could help make those dreams come true for her. If she could help out with some of the bills and expenses, it would ease her big sister's stress, and that was enough motivation for Phoebe to keep working. And then, when she was a big star, Phoebe could take them all on vacation. Kate deserved all of that, and more. Still, the idea of her being a big star made Phoebe laugh and shake her head. No matter what Wes and the others said, it was hard to wrap her head around it all.

Shit head.

Kate's response came through and Phoebe laughed.

You know I really am missing you, right? You'd love it here.

The bubbles that showed Kate was typing a response appeared and then disappeared. Phoebe waited. The bubbles appeared again and then once more were gone. Finally, impatient, she typed.

Hello? You there?

Phoebe propped herself up on her elbows. It wasn't like Kate not to take the bait when she dangled it. A flicker of worry lit in Phoebe's gut.

Kate? You're worrying me.

.   .   .

It occurred to Phoebe that her sister was screwing with her. But it wasn't Kate's style. She was about to pick up the phone and call her when the text bubbles reappeared.

Sorry. Can't talk. Stuff going on.

The flicker sparked into a full-on flame. She knew Kate too well. Something was definitely going on. *Stuff?* What the hell? Before she could reply, Kate texted again.

I'll call you later. Gotta go.

For a moment, Phoebe contemplated pushing the issue, but Kate was too stubborn. If she wasn't going to tell her what was going on, there was nothing more she could do. Thousands of miles away, there was *really* nothing she could do. She dropped her head to the chaise and breathed in deeply. Suddenly, the sunbathing didn't feel so decadent. It seemed selfish.

She reached around her back and had just refastened her top when Layla sat down next to her.

"Where are you going?"

Phoebe sat up. "In. I just—"

"You're not going anywhere," she interrupted her with a grin as Mason sat down next to her. The two of them together were an incredible sight. Layla, in her string bikini, and Mason, with only his swim bottoms on, were both lean with muscles so defined they looked as if they could be models.

"You're not going anywhere," Mason repeated and looked at Layla with a wink.

"Not until you tell us everything about Dean Harrison."

"Dean?" Phoebe sat up and grabbed her bottle of water from her bag. "There's nothing to tell."

"Bullshit." Mason crossed his arms and looked pointedly at her.

"Exactly," Layla jumped in. "Bullshit. Everybody saw you two out on the dance floor last night."

"Never mind the fact that Dean *never* comes out."

"Never." Layla shook her head.

Phoebe didn't know who to look at. The two of them were like a well-rehearsed comedy duo. But Phoebe wasn't laughing. Nothing had happened between her and Dean, and already rumors were starting. It only concreted her resolve to keep things professional with him. This was exactly the type of thing she'd been trying to avoid by keeping Dean at a distance. Something that was getting harder and harder. It had been practically impossible for her to push him away the night before. But she'd done it. And this exchange with Layla and Mason was exactly why.

"Nothing happened," she repeated. "And nothing will. We're coworkers. That's it."

"Coworkers don't dance like that," Layla insisted with a shake of her head.

"That was some dirty dancing-level shit."

They nodded at each other and Phoebe groaned.

"I don't know what to tell you two. But he's one hell of a dance partner, so we danced. And I got a ride home with him. He walked me home. End. Of. Story."

She grabbed her bag and stood. There was going to be no pleasing the two of them until they heard something that she wasn't prepared to tell them. Even if it was true. Which it was not.

"It's only a matter of time, Pheebs. Dean always gets his lady."

"Not this time."

"Dammit." Mason dropped his arms and leaned forward on his knees. "You're serious, aren't you?"

Phoebe nodded. "'Fraid so. I'm not like the others. It's not happening."

"Dean can be pretty persuasive," Mason said. "I've seen him in action more than once."

Phoebe laughed. "I'm sure he can. But I'm not interested in dating someone just because he's the lead in the movie I'm in. It's not my style."

Mason nodded, but Layla shook her head and narrowed her eyes. "I don't buy it. There's something you're not saying."

Was there? Only the fact that she was so attracted to him that it was starting to cause a physical pain in her chest. And worse, she actually *liked* him as a person.

"I have to get out of the sun." She pulled her bag over her arm. "I'll see you guys later."

Fortunately, at least for the time being, they were going to drop the subject and let her go. Which was a very good thing, because Phoebe didn't know how long she'd be able to put them off. Especially considering she'd received a text from Dean only an hour earlier confirming their plans for the next day. She'd promised him she'd give him a chance and he wasn't wasting any time taking her up on the offer.

Maybe it was a bad idea. No. It *definitely* was a bad idea. But she couldn't seem to stop herself.

Besides, one date couldn't hurt.

Just practice, my ass.

Dean worked to catch his breath from his position on his hands and knees where he'd landed *again* after Eric had kicked him in the ribs. He pulled himself up from the deck and faced his teacher—or should he say adversary—once more. "I didn't think you were supposed to make contact, Eric?"

"You're supposed to dodge it," the stunt double said matter-of-factly.

"Dodge it?" Not one to back down, Dean took a step toward him. "You want me to *dodge* it?"

The other man straightened his shoulders and stared him down. "That's the idea, Harrison. Don't let yourself get hit." Without warning and before Dean had caught his breath fully, Eric came at him again.

Dean had seen what the man could do and despite the fact that he'd been getting the shit kicked out of him, he knew that Eric was capable of more. A lot more.

This time, Dean dodged Eric's punch, spun the way he'd been taught, and braced himself for the kick he was meant to block. The kick didn't come. He had the timing right. Dean turned to look, and in that moment, the kick came, sending him once again backward onto the deck.

"Dammit, Eric. Your count was off."

He grabbed his side and winced. Wes would lose it if he hurt himself, even if it wasn't his fault.

Eric appeared and looked down at him. "My count is never off. It's how I keep from being killed."

He didn't offer a hand up, and for a moment, Dean thought the other man might actually kick him while he was on the ground.

Something was going on.

"Enough already," he said as he once again got to his feet.

Eric grinned, but there was no humor on his face. "You've had enough, huh? Not as easy as you thought to do your own stunts?"

Dean shook his head. "Is that what this is about? Stunts?" Something flashed in the other man's eyes.

No. It wasn't about stunts.

"We haven't even gotten to the actual stunt yet," Dean said. "So far, you're just beating the shit out of me and if I didn't know better, I'd say that you're actually enjoying it."

Eric's lips twitched.

Fuck. He was *enjoying it.* "What's this about, Eric?"

They'd worked together for years and although Dean wouldn't have ever considered him a *friend*—he didn't have many of those—they'd always gotten along and enjoyed an excellent working relationship. This was a different side of Eric than he'd seen before. But why? What had—

Phoebe.

He chuckled and shook his head. "You've got to be kidding me. That's what this is about, isn't it?"

"What?"

"You're kicking the shit out of me and getting off on it because you're jealous."

It was quick but Dean didn't miss the flash of acknowledgment on Eric's face.

"That's it." He crossed his arms. "Was all this because of—"

"Phoebe? Yes."

Dean hadn't expected him to be so upfront. But he appreciated it.

"You like her?" A flicker of jealousy he had no right to flashed through him.

"It doesn't matter if I do or don't." He turned and started to walk away.

Dean caught up with him in a few steps. He grabbed the other man's arm to stop him. "What the hell does that mean?"

Eric exhaled hard. "It means that Phoebe's different. She's not like the others, Dean. She hasn't been hardened by Hollywood. She's...not innocent." He laughed. "She's far from that."

Dean bristled at the comment but held himself in check.

"She just doesn't deserve to be used," Eric finished.

It took him a moment to realize what Eric meant but when he did, he laughed. "So you were taking the opportunity to beat the crap out of me because you're feeling protective of Phoebe? You think I'm going to use her?"

Eric shrugged and nodded. "Frankly, yes."

"I'm not." The laughter died on his lips. "It's the last thing I want to do. Besides, I'm sure this will make you feel better, or not. But there's nothing going on between Phoebe and me." It wasn't a lie. "Furthermore, she seems to be very aware of my history and wants nothing to do with it." Also not a lie. He didn't need to know that Dean had been working on some major plans to change her mind about him and his intentions with her. It wasn't an important detail to the matter at hand.

"She doesn't?" Eric chuckled. "You struck out, huh?"

Dean swallowed hard to keep from defending himself. Another detail that didn't seem very important at the moment. What *was* important was that Eric stop using him as a punching bag to make his point and actually start teaching him what he needed to know so he didn't kill himself in the upcoming shoot. Or worse, injure himself and screw up the filming schedule, in which case, Wes would take care of the killing him part.

He nodded.

Eric laughed again. He slapped his thigh. "Good for her."

"Right?" He flashed a smile. "Now, can we get back to this, please, before you break one of my ribs, if you haven't already?"

Eric slapped his back, causing a wince of pain that Dean covered with a cough. "Absolutely. And, just so you know, I am sorry about that. I wasn't trying to…well, okay, I was. But I'm glad to hear that Phoebe's smart enough not to get involved in the tabloid gossip machine, you know what I mean?"

He did. Together, they started walking toward the pool,

where they would practice the basics of the dive Dean would have to perform. As they walked, Dean realized that Eric had a point. Even if he could convince Phoebe that what he was starting to feel for her was more than a publicity stunt, would anyone else see it any differently?

Chapter Nine

"THIS IS NOT A DATE." Phoebe shook her head with a laugh when Dean picked her up the next morning as planned and led her back down the path they'd walked a few nights earlier, to a waiting helicopter. When she saw it, she stopped walking, dropped her head, and started to laugh.

Dean pretended to look offended. "You don't even know what it is yet."

"I know that a *date* that starts with a helicopter ride is most definitely *not* a date." She turned to look at him. He was dressed in cargo shorts and a simple T-shirt. His thick hair looked soft, free from the slick, polished look that his character preferred. Phoebe had the undeniable urge to reach out and touch it to see just how soft it really was. She tucked her hand in the pocket of her cut-off shorts instead. "This is ridiculous, Dean. Dates don't include helicopters."

Dean lifted his sunglasses from his face so he could look at her clearly and winked. "Dates with me do." She laughed again as he took her free hand and led her toward the aircraft. "Besides, you fell asleep last time and didn't get to enjoy it. Not that you would have been able to see much. It's way better in the daylight."

She couldn't argue with that logic. Besides, she *was* excited by the prospect of another helicopter ride. Never mind the excitement about actually going on a date with Dean. Her imagination had run away from her the night before and had made it very hard for her to sleep. Even so, she hadn't imagined a helicopter.

She wasn't surprised to see Kyle holding the door open for them.

"Does he ever give you a day off?"

Dean's assistant was a young, freckled redhead who, due to his fair complexion, always wore a large brimmed hat to protect him from the blazing sun. Not that it actually worked, because the man seemed to be perpetually sunburned. Phoebe felt sorry for him, and his pale skin. He didn't seem to mind though, just the way he didn't seem to be bothered by almost constantly working.

"He's about to get the entire day off." Dean grinned.

"Well, you should, Kyle." She focused her attention on the young man. "You shouldn't be organizing all of this for Dean. It's too much. Really."

"Oh no, Phoebe." Kyle gestured toward his boss. "I didn't organize any part of this date. This is all Dean."

She looked between them, unbelieving.

"It's true," Dean affirmed. "It's too important. *You* are too important."

His choice of words caused a rush of warmth in her chest.

"Are you ready to go?"

His smile was so genuine, Phoebe couldn't help but fall a little harder for him. The man really was disarmingly charming. It was going to be a bit of a problem.

"I can't wait to show you what else I have planned."

She couldn't wait either, so she climbed into the helicopter, tucking her beach bag with a change of clothes inside. Dean had texted the night before and requested that she also bring a bathing suit, which she wore under her tank top and shorts. But beyond the casual attire, she had been given no further details.

The mystery was starting to add up as part of the excitement of the date, and she couldn't wait to tell Kate all of the details.

Thinking of her sister brought a fresh wave of concern to the forefront of her mind again.

After her brief text from Kate the afternoon before, Phoebe had spent the rest of the day worried and waiting by her phone for more news from her sister.

News that never came, despite her multiple texts and phone calls that went unanswered, all except for one response that simply read:

I'm fine. Don't worry and enjoy yourself. And get me some juicy gossip!

It was so typical Kate that, despite her worry, Phoebe had to laugh. Ironically, she would happily have told her sister all about her hot night out dancing with Dean, followed by the helicopter ride and the almost kiss plus the impending date, if only she would talk to her. No matter what Kate said, something was going on and most definitely there was something for her to worry about.

But Phoebe also knew that if Kate wasn't ready to say anything, she wouldn't. Especially if she thought it might interfere with Phoebe's time in Panama. She was always putting others before herself. Especially her little sister. There was nothing to do but wait until she was ready to talk. Still, it didn't stop her from pulling her phone out and trying one more time.

. . .

Kate! Talk to me. I need to know what's going on.

The text didn't go through. She checked. No service.

"Hey." Dean touched her arm. "You okay? You look a little...worried about something? Does the helicopter make you nervous in the daylight?"

She put a smile on her face and forced herself back into the moment and her time with Dean. "Sorry," she said. "I'm excited to see what this *date*," she used air quotes, "of yours is going to entail." He didn't look like he was buying what she said. She didn't want to darken their time together, but just as she'd felt it before, Phoebe had the urge to share with him. She took a breath. "It's just my sister is acting strange, like something's wrong. She won't answer my texts and now my phone isn't working and—"

"I have a satellite phone." He took her hand and squeezed. "You can call her when we get—where we're going." He grinned. "Maybe she'll answer?"

She nodded, feeling a little relief, even if it was only from sharing her concern. "Thank you."

Maybe Kate would answer if it was a Panamanian number? At worst, she could leave a teasing message for her with some gossip. That might be enough to get her sister to call her back.

Phoebe glanced over at Dean, and her heart swelled. Even with everything he'd planned, he was worried about her. That didn't seem like the way a player would behave. Not at all. And that was only complicating things.

He could see the concern in Phoebe's face, and it pulled at him. The satellite phone wasn't a solution, he knew. But it was something. And if he could do even the smallest thing to help her reach her sister, he would. Hell, he'd go a lot further than that if need be.

He knew that instinctively. He'd do whatever needed to be done for her.

"Here. Put these on. Then we can talk." He handed her a headset. "Last time you couldn't keep your eyes open long enough to try it out."

She tipped her head and gave him a look. "Hey, I had a very determined dance partner who wore me out."

His thoughts instantly went to a dirty place. A *very* dirty place.

It took some effort, but he cleared his mind and swallowed hard. "Well, there'll be no dancing today. That's a promise."

Her smile dipped. "Despite being completely exhausted, I did really enjoy myself the other night."

"Oh, of course." He spoke quickly. "So did I. I was just saying that...I have other things planned for today that you'll enjoy, too. Promise." Besides, there was the fact that he could barely move after his *training* with Eric the day before. But he didn't need to mention that his stunt double had schooled him on basic fighting techniques. *Or* the reason for it.

"Ready?" he said through the headset as the helicopter fired up and they lifted off the ground.

Dean had been on dozens of helicopter rides before, but he never tired of them. There really was something pretty incredible about being able to experience the world from the air. Especially when the world you were experiencing was as stunning as Panama.

They flew over the container ships anchored out, waiting for their turn to go through the Panama Canal. Phoebe pointed out each of them, wondering what might be held in the thousands of containers that were piled on each ship, and then, just the way Dean had instructed him to, Lee, the pilot, flew over the locks of the famous canal.

"Oh my God! Look at that." Phoebe pointed and bounced in her seat. "Have you seen the way the doors open? That is *so* cool."

It was cool. And even though he'd taken a private tour of the canals when he'd arrived in Panama, seeing it this way, with Phoebe, was a totally different experience. So much better.

They circled around the canal system for a few minutes, before Lee steered away and back toward the coastline and their real destination: the San Blas Islands.

Dean knew they were going to be shooting a few scenes later out in the islands—including the much anticipated boat scene—but being there surrounded by cast and crew would be a very different thing than what he planned.

"What do you think?" he asked into the microphone. "Have you ever seen anything like this?"

Below them was the bluest water he'd ever seen, and he'd seen a lot of gorgeous places. And the beaches...pure white sandy islands with a smattering of palm trees on them. They were remote and private and absolutely perfect for spending a day alone with Phoebe.

"It's amazing," she said. "Are we going down there?"

"We are." He scanned the horizon and pointed to the island they were headed for. "That island, in fact. It's called Barbecue Island." He'd done a little bit of research and had learned that although most of the San Blas Islands were either occupied by Kunas, the indigenous people, who still lived with the traditions of their culture, or were completely empty, there was one island that was occupied by a North American woman who'd made some sort of arrangement with the Kunas so she could live there. Not only did Josie live on Barbecue Island, she ran a bit of a rustic Aribnb experience that operated in conjunction with some of the locals of Shelter Bay Marina and their yachts.

Dean had first heard about it when he met Archer and Cass, the couple who owned and operated a charter yacht experience out of Shelter Bay. Archer showed him around their beautiful yacht. It would be the same yacht that they were to shoot the *boat scene* on.

"Barbecue Island? That's a strange name."

Dean shrugged. "I couldn't even begin to guess."

"It's absolutely beautiful." Phoebe shook her head in wonder and Dean knew it was going to be a great day.

The island was far enough away from civilization, and most importantly, prying eyes of all kinds, that they'd be able to really be themselves. He'd rented out all of the accommodations for the next two days, not that he necessarily planned to stay that long. But if the opportunity presented itself, he was not going to object. He wanted to spend as much time as possible alone with Phoebe, away from all the expectations and rumors and opinions of who he was and what it was that he wanted from her. Because the truth was, the only thing he really wanted from her was to get to know her better and prove to her that he was not only interested in her for the publicity. Nothing was further from the truth.

All he had to do was convince her.

He reached over and squeezed her hand. "Ready?"

Chapter Ten

THE HELICOPTER COULDN'T LAND on Barbecue Island, but instead stopped on a nearby, larger island were Dean and Phoebe took a small wooden boat on the short ride to their piece of paradise. They climbed out of the boat in knee-deep water, and the driver handed them their bags before zipping off, leaving them alone.

"I stand by what I said earlier." Phoebe waded through the turquoise shallows and watched the tiny fish dart around her toes as she moved. "This is *not* a date."

"It is!" Dean kicked at the water a little as they walked together away from the boat. "I told you I was going to take you on a proper date, and that's exactly what I'm doing."

She tipped her head to look at him. "Well, it's unlike any date I've ever been on."

"Hey. It's not my fault you've never been taken out properly. Maybe it's just the quality of men you've been picking?"

She couldn't help but laugh. Phoebe was enjoying this more relaxed version of Dean. He was playful and less guarded like this, away from the set and everyone else. She liked it.

"Maybe that's true," she said more seriously.

Dean caught the shift in her voice because he stopped walking for a moment before smiling softly at her and when he reached for her free hand, she took it. Together, they walked hand in hand up the beach toward a woman who'd appeared.

"That must be Josie," Dean said. "Let's go say hi."

Phoebe let Dean lead her toward the woman who wore a long flowing skirt covered in an intricate embroidery of some kind. Her arms and ankles were covered in delicate strands of colorful beads, and a large floppy hat shaded her deeply tanned face from the hot sun. When they grew close enough, the older woman's broad smile welcomed them. Her eyes crinkled in the corners with joy and a genuine warmth and friendliness that was rare to find. Phoebe liked her instantly.

"You must be Dean and Phoebe." She held out her arms. "I'm Josie. Welcome to Barbecue Island. My own little piece of paradise."

"Thank you." Dean reached out to shake her hand, but Josie pulled him into a hug.

"We hug here." She winked at Phoebe over Dean's shoulder and when she was done hugging him, Phoebe moved straight into her arms.

She smelled like coconuts, sea, and sun. Her strong arms instantly made Phoebe feel good, as if she'd finally come home.

"I like hugs," Phoebe said when they stepped apart. "And your island is absolutely beautiful. Thank you."

"It's my hope that you both enjoy the peace and beauty that we have to offer here." She looked between them. "I live right over there in the hut with the little garden next to it. If you need anything at all, please let me know. Otherwise, I'll have a lunch laid out for you about noon and then dinner at seven?"

Dean nodded, as they'd obviously made some previous arrangement.

"Great," Josie continued. "Over there, through the trees, you'll find some paddleboards on the beach, as well as some snorkeling gear if you're interested. There's an absolutely gorgeous reef right off the beach where you can see all kinds of colorful fish and even some rays. There's a volleyball net, if you have too much energy." She pointed through the trees. "And if you don't have much energy, I have hammocks in the shade, too, and there are daybeds placed all around, so you can explore every corner of the island."

All of it sounded amazing to Phoebe.

"Feel free to use the huts to change or rest or whatever you like." Josie finished up her tour. "The island is yours to enjoy. Have an amazing day."

Dean once more reached for Phoebe's hand and squeezed.

She liked the feel of her hand in his. It felt right. But as much as she liked it, she also didn't want to give Dean the wrong idea. Sure, she'd agreed to the date, but Layla and Mason's words rang in her ears. *Dean always got his lady.* Which was why the tabloids were full of stories of his exploits.

She wouldn't be one of those stories.

As soon as Josie retreated and left them to their day, Phoebe pulled her hand away and busied herself with pulling her hair into a ponytail.

"So?" Dean asked. "What do you think?"

"I think it's pretty amazing," she answered honestly. "But you know how I feel, Dean. I'm not going to—"

"Don't say it." He held up one finger. "You said you'd give me a chance, right?"

She nodded.

"Okay then. Before we go and have some fun, here." As promised, he handed her the satellite phone. "Call your sister. You can leave a message for her to call back if she doesn't answer and we can check it later."

Phoebe took the phone, looked up at him, and smiled.

"I'll wait over there."

As promised, Dean walked to the shade of some palms while Phoebe made the call. He didn't want to intrude, but he couldn't help noticing the way her shoulders slumped in release.

Her sister must have answered.

He looked away with a small smile and kicked at the sand while he waited.

Dean didn't have to wait long before Phoebe appeared and handed him the phone. "Thank you. She answered."

"And?"

Her smile dipped a little. "She's fine. Well, I think she's fine. She's so frustrating because she won't tell me what's really going on, but she did admit that she was getting some tests at the hospital. I just wish I knew what was going on. I feel so far away right now."

Dean didn't hesitate to reach out and take her arm. "Phoebe, I don't know what to say."

She shrugged, but he could see the worry in her eyes. "It's okay. I don't think there is anything to say right now. She didn't want to tell me anything until there's something confirmed. And she insisted it was probably nothing. Just routine tests."

"You don't believe her?"

"Not even a little." She shook her head, but there was the trace of a little smile, too. "Big sisters are so infuriating. But she's even more stubborn than I am, so she's not going to tell me anything. Still, it was good to hear her voice. Whatever's going on, she didn't *sound* too worried, so there's that. Thank you."

"Of course."

Phoebe smiled fully when she added, "She freaked out

when I told her where I was. She wants all the pictures so she can pretend she was here, too."

"Did you tell her you were here on a date?" He wiggled his eyebrows.

The smile fell from her face. She shook her head and Dean instantly regretted teasing her.

"I told you, I was—"

"You know what," he interrupted her before they could go down a line of thought he wanted to avoid. "Since we're here, why don't we go have some fun?"

"I can't argue with that," Phoebe said, her gorgeous smile returning to her face. "Can we start with snorkeling? I've only ever done it once before as a kid, and I don't think it counts because it was in a cold mountain lake with nothing to see but seaweed, freshwater clams, and an occasional trout. I have a feeling this will be different."

Dean couldn't help but laugh. "I have a feeling it will be *very* different." He took her hand and they started to walk down the beach. "Very different."

Even with a mask stuck to her face and a snorkel distorting her mouth, Phoebe was the most gorgeous woman Dean had ever seen. The fact that she wore a crocheted white bikini that looked positively sinful against her tanned skin didn't hurt.

"Did you see that?"

They'd been snorkeling around the reef for at least twenty minutes, but Phoebe didn't show any signs of tiring of it anytime soon, which was perfectly fine with Dean. He'd always loved the water, and even though he'd been scuba diving in some of the most exotic locales in the world, this tiny little reef in Panama was probably his favorite experience.

"I think they call those King Angelfish," he told her. "They're beautiful, aren't they?"

"It's so crazy." They'd kicked their way over to a sandy area shallow enough to stand up in. Phoebe pulled her mask up and off her face. "I didn't know fish like that actually existed outside of a pet store." She laughed at herself. "I mean, I *knew* they did. But I'd never seen them. You know?"

"I do know. It is pretty incredible to think about the world that exists just below us, isn't it?"

She nodded in agreement. "I don't know about you, but I'm so thirsty. Do you think Josie has anything to drink?"

"I know she does. Time for a break."

Once they'd put away their equipment and found the solar-powered fridge where Josie kept an impressively wide variety of soft drinks and alcoholic options, they each selected a can of beer, grabbed a beach blanket, and found a sandy spot where they could lie out in the sun and dry off.

Phoebe was easy to talk to, and unlike a lot of the women he'd ended up dating, she was refreshingly open and honest about life. None of her answers seemed to be constructed, or written by a publicist. They were just…Phoebe.

"I still can't believe you are so covered in bruises." Phoebe turned to face him and propped herself up on an elbow. They lay close to each other, but not touching. As much as he wanted to, he would wait. Her hand reached out and waved over his rib cage, which was indeed covered in bruises.

"I can." He laughed. "Eric did his best to make sure I was ready." He grinned. It wasn't worth mentioning that his beating had been in large part because of the other man's feelings toward her. "But I think I'll be ready to go, so I guess he did his job."

"I think it's great that you want to do your own stunts." She turned and looked up at the sky before looking at him again.

"So it's no secret that you've always wanted to be a movie star, and it wasn't my dream at all."

"Right."

"So, if you had to convince me what the best part of being famous is, what would it be?"

Dean thought about it, but he didn't have to think long. "Seeing the world and meeting people you'd never have the chance to meet."

She looked surprised. "Really?"

"Absolutely. And it's funny, because I didn't even consider travel as a benefit of being famous, but now...it's really the only one."

She laughed. "No way. I mean, you have more money than you know what to do with. You have everything you could ever want. And—"

"Not everything," he answered honestly. "Not even close."

She tilted her head in question. "What else would you want?"

Dean hesitated. She wasn't the only one who had a little bit of trust issues. He'd never told anyone what he *really* wanted from life. That was probably because he'd been dating the wrong type of women. And Phoebe wasn't anything like those others. He swallowed down his doubt and took a chance. "You're going to laugh."

"I'm not." Her face was serious and he believed her.

"You were almost right when you said that I got everything I ever wanted. I mostly did."

"You still haven't found your mom." It wasn't a question, but he didn't expect it to be. "Are you still looking?"

Dean shook his head. "Not really. I figure, if she wanted to be found, she would have by now. And I started to think, do I really want her in my life if she's there only because of the fame?" He shrugged. "Things change over time, and wants change, and now..." He dropped his head and looked at the pattern on the blanket they laid on.

"Now you want something different."

"Yes." When he looked up into her eyes, they were full of understanding and, more importantly, no trace of judgment.

"So what is it that you want now?"

"A family."

The moment he spoke the word out loud, a dual rush of relief and fear washed over him. He'd never said it out loud before.

Phoebe sat up so she sat cross-legged in front of him. "A family? But not your mom?"

He shook his head and clarified. "A family of my own."

"That doesn't seem crazy at all. Why would you be afraid to tell me that?"

"It doesn't really fit with the movie star persona, don't you think?" He laughed, trying to lessen the importance of what he'd told her. It was a defense mechanism he'd used before. Undermine what was important to him, fit the mold that everyone expected him to squeeze into. He'd learned long ago that it was easier that way. "It's not very sexy to want to buy up a piece of land somewhere far away from the lights and glamour, and build a life away from the fame and photographers, is it?"

She shrugged. "Maybe it's not shiny and exciting. But I think it's pretty sexy. Why wouldn't it be?"

Phoebe looked so unaffected by his big *secret* that Dean couldn't help but feel foolish for making a big deal about it. And then she reached over and took his hand.

"But I can appreciate how you might be a little guarded about who you tell."

"You can?"

She nodded. "Hey, I haven't been around this industry very

long yet, but it's easy to see that everything is about image. *Everything.*"

"Which is why you didn't believe me when I told you I was interested in you for more than just the publicity."

Phoebe twitched her lips up into a sexy little smile. "You got it."

"And now?" Dean pulled himself to a sitting position so he was directly in front of her, but he didn't let go of her hand. If he had it his way, he'd never let go of her hand. Or her. He leaned forward until his lips were only inches from hers. "What do you think now?" he whispered.

Her breath was soft on his lips. Dean closed his eyes, ready to press his lips to hers; only moments before they touched, she jumped up with a laugh. "I think I want to go paddle-boarding. Come on!"

Chapter Eleven

SHE WASN'T TRYING to be a tease. And she definitely wasn't trying to lead him on or play hard to get, but she couldn't kiss him. Because if she let herself, she knew in her heart she'd be lost to it. And she did believe that there was more to him than just the playboy movie star that the media made him out to be. But…still.

Her resolve to keep her distance was starting to waver. A lot.

And when she let herself, Phoebe could actually imagine that Dean was exactly the authentic man he was trying to tell her he was. And what if he was exactly the man he said he was? And what if she was keeping herself from the opportunity to get to know him? *Really* get to know him?

She dug her paddle in the crystal-clear water and pulled so her board moved forward in a strong glide toward where Dean stood on his board. She couldn't help but take in a sharp breath every time she saw him without his shirt on. No matter how many times it happened. His body was absolutely perfect. Lean with defined muscles, he was strong but not in the bulgy way that Mason was. Dean's strength was quieter. More subdued, but intensely sexy. He dipped his paddle in the water, but only a little. His gaze was fixed on something down in the water.

"What are you looking at?"

"A turtle. Look."

She did. And saw it immediately. She did a little dance, forgetting she was on a wobbly board in the water, and almost splashed in next to the turtle before catching herself.

Dean laughed. "You okay?"

"Totally. And that is the coolest thing I've ever seen." Her eyes tracked the turtle's movement as his head popped up out of the water before quickly ducking down again. "Do you think he saw us? I don't want to scare him."

"He knows we're here." Dean maneuvered his board to be closer to hers. "They are pretty phenomenal, aren't they?"

"You've seen them before?" She looked up to see Dean nod and somehow it disappointed her that they hadn't experienced the moment as a first, together.

"I swam with turtles once in the Bahamas. They were all around. It was so peaceful. Almost meditative."

The turtle swam away and Phoebe felt oddly sad about it. "I'd like to do that one day," she said, almost to herself.

Her board bumped as Dean settled his next to hers, so he was facing her. She looked up as he stepped one foot on her board, joining them together.

"You can do anything you want now, Phoebe. You know that, right?"

She nodded, but only a little before she shook her head. "Maybe it's that easy for you, but some of us have obligations. We can't just do whatever we want. My sister..." She trailed off. "Anyways, you make it sound so simple."

He stepped forward until they were only inches apart.

Despite the heat of the day, Phoebe shivered. Her resolve was definitely wavering.

"It is simple." His voice was low, his eyes focused on her in a way that was causing all kinds of tornados to rip through her body.

Oh yeah. She was wavering.

After all, what harm would one kiss cause? She was a big girl, fully in control of her decisions and her actions. She knew what the media said, and she knew what she was getting into with him. She also knew the Dean she was getting to know. And...*dammit.*

Before she could talk herself out of it again, Phoebe closed the distance, wrapped her free hand around his neck, and pulled Dean toward her. Their lips crashed together, and instantly, Dean's hand found her cheek and cupped it as they explored each other. She groaned as his tongue slipped between her lips and—

She was moving. The board slipped out from under her feet and an instant later, she hit the ocean with a hard splash. She came up sputtering and coughing. Dazed, Phoebe spun herself around to see Dean swimming after the two boards that had shot out from under them and were headed out to sea. She couldn't help it; she laughed. And was still laughing when Dean returned to where she was now standing in waist-deep water.

"What's so funny?"

"You...me..." She couldn't formulate words between her fits of giggles. "I just—"

Her laughter was cut off abruptly and perfectly with a kiss. Dean wrapped his arms around her and lifted to pull her close in the water. By reflex, Phoebe wrapped her legs around his waist and deepened the kiss. The magic they'd experienced on set a few days earlier had definitely not been a fluke. Their connection was electric.

Despite the cool water, Phoebe's entire body was on fire and yearned for more.

When finally they pulled apart, Dean hadn't released his hold on her, and Phoebe wasn't in a hurry to move.

"So does that mean you're giving me a chance?"

"Against my better judgment..." She kissed him again. "Yes. At least a small one."

He grinned against her lips before kissing her again. "That's good enough for me."

The rest of the day was spent between splashing in the ocean and lounging in the shade of the palms. They ate a deliciously simple meal of a fresh ceviche that Josie prepared for them, and spent the afternoon napping and cuddling in a hammock. As far as Dean was concerned, it had been the perfect date. And it wasn't over. Not if he had anything to say about it.

"Today was pretty awesome," Phoebe said. She was tucked up against him, her head on his chest.

He'd been working his fingers through her salty hair and tracing lines up and down her back. It was the most relaxed Dean had felt in years. In fact, he couldn't remember the last time he felt so comfortable and at peace.

"It doesn't have to be over." He dragged a finger up her spine to the base of her neck. She groaned and cuddled closer.

Oh no. It definitely didn't have to be over.

"What do you mean? Isn't Lee waiting on the island, to take us back to Shelter Bay?" She lifted her head a little so she could look at him. "You didn't forget, did you?"

He chuckled. "No. I didn't forget." Lee wasn't exactly waiting for them. He was on standby to come and get them, but that could be changed with a quick text message. "But I wasn't sure if we were going to be ready to go back to civilization, so I booked the island for two full days. There's lots of huts," he added quickly. As much as he'd like to spend the night with Phoebe's body tucked into his arms, he was a gentleman. No matter what the press said. "I wasn't thinking that... well. I wasn't thinking anything."

She laughed and sat up, causing the hammock to swing dangerously. "Despite everything, I didn't think you had any ill intentions at all." She swung her legs over the edge of the netting.

"Where are you going?" Dean reached out for her and pulled her back down into his arms. She squealed, but didn't protest as he kissed her again. "There's no rush," he said between kisses. "We can stay here until the sun goes down."

"We could."

"But?" Unfortunately, Dean could feel the *but* coming.

"But I feel like a salt lick." She wriggled from his grip again. "And I need to shower or rinse off or something if we're going to stay." She managed to get away and jump to the ground next to him.

"So, we're staying?" He didn't even try to hide his grin. "At least overnight?"

Phoebe nodded. "Two days, you say?"

Dean's grin grew wider as he held up two fingers.

She winked. "Let's see how it goes." She turned to search for a shower.

Dean watched her go before collapsing back into the hammock. *She didn't say no.*

Sun-kissed and exhausted from the day, Phoebe was revitalized by a freshwater shower and a quick nap in the hut Josie had directed her to so she could change. She'd been impressed with the shower, not that she knew what to expect from the island— not really. But it was surprisingly luxurious and with the water warmed by the sun, it was refreshing against her skin.

She spent a few minutes taking pictures of the beauty that surrounded her. Kate would never believe such a place existed. Barbecue Island was just like all those places they'd read about as kids, or seen on TV. But they didn't actually believe they existed in the real world. Kate would lose her mind to see it. Never mind hearing that she was there on a *date* with Dean Harrison.

Phoebe still had to pinch herself to believe that one. And more, to believe that he was actually a good guy. She had to admit that she'd gone into the day with some biases. One, she'd done her research. She knew everything that was ever published about Dean and his *history* with women. Two, she was incredibly attracted to him. *Almost* to the point where it didn't matter what she'd read. And, three, she knew from experience that it was best to make up your own mind about things that concerned other people. Particularly when you were so intensely attracted to that other person.

So, she had gone in with an open mind, and it had been changed. Maybe she was making a huge mistake, but she didn't think so. When Dean opened up to her about wanting a family, she'd seen that familiar look in his eyes, the same one she'd seen in her own reflection. He had a deep need for belonging to something bigger than himself. A family, he'd said. But she could see there was more to it.

He was lonely. Just like her.

She'd let her hair air dry into soft, loose waves before changing into the simple sundress she'd brought with her. She didn't have much in the way of makeup except for a little lip gloss, which she applied in the little mirror that had been affixed to the hut wall.

The huts were remarkably well-appointed. *Glamping.* And it didn't get any better than *glamping* on a deserted island in the middle of paradise.

At least that's what she thought. But when Phoebe left her

hut to go in search of Dean, and dinner, she was proved wrong.

It *did* get better.

She followed the path toward the beach, where she saw tiki torches had been lit.

The sun was just starting to set and the sky was lit up with streaks of pinks, purples, and vibrant oranges. The sight took her breath away and a hand fluttered up to her chest. "It's gorgeous."

"I was just thinking the same thing."

Phoebe turned to see Dean, who'd changed into khaki shorts and a white linen button-down shirt, standing next to her, looking not at the horizon, but directly at her.

"You look amazing, Phoebe."

She couldn't help but smile as he kissed her on the cheek. "But the sunset, Dean…" She gently tilted his face away from her, toward the sunset that was just starting to disappear.

Together, they watched the sun slip away with one final flash of light and when it was gone, Dean spun her gently to face him. "That was gorgeous, but it had nothing on you." It could have been an incredibly cheesy line, but he delivered it with such sincerity that it was nothing but genuine. "Dinner's ready." He waved his hand toward the table she'd been too preoccupied to notice before.

It was set on the beach, with a heart made of shells encircling it. Tiki torches cast light over everything, and a bottle of wine and two glasses waited for them.

"Wow."

"Does it feel like a date now?"

Phoebe laughed. "Only the best one ever."

"I aim to please."

Dinner was grilled, locally caught lobster with a risotto and fresh salad. Simple and delicious. But it wasn't the food that had Dean's attention. Dressed simply in a sundress, with her hair falling over her shoulders and a fresh, sun-kissed face, Phoebe had never looked so beautiful. And now that she'd loosened up with him—which hopefully meant she was starting to trust that his intentions were good—she was visibly more relaxed and whatever walls she'd had in place had come down, or at least, were in the process of coming down.

"Tell me about your family," Dean asked as they lingered over another glass of wine. "You don't mention them much."

Phoebe took another sip of her wine before she spoke. "Remember how I told you about the dealership?"

"The one you'd quit working at so you could fulfill your lifelong dream to scoop frozen yogurt?"

"That's the one." She winked. "It's my uncle's dealership. He raised us. My sister and I. My parents died when we were just kids. It was a car accident. I don't really remember them, though, and my uncle did a great job with us. I think that's why Kate and I are so close, too. We kind of only had each other when Uncle Benny was working. Which was a lot. I mean, he never intended to have a couple of kids to raise. I think it was a lot financially for him. But he never complained. Not once."

"He sounds like a good guy."

"He is." She smiled, her face lighting up at the mention of her family. "I couldn't have asked for better. And Kate, too. She has two little girls. Olivia and Ally. They're amazing and so busy. I don't know how she does it, and…" Her smile dipped.

"Phoebe?"

"It's nothing."

Obviously, that wasn't true. He reached across the table and stroked the back of her hand with his thumb. "You're worried about your sister." It wasn't a question, but she nodded.

"I know she said there's nothing to worry about, and logically I know that's true, but..."

"It's still a worry."

She nodded again, and Dean saw the glisten of an unshed tear in the corner of her eye.

"Is there anything I can do?" In that instant, Dean knew he would do anything he possibly could. All she had to do was to say the word.

"I wish there was." She shook her head. "I just hope she tells me the truth when she does get the results."

"She'd lie?"

"She's just trying to protect me because I'm so far away and there's nothing I can do about anything from here. No matter what it was, she wouldn't want me to come home. Not for anything. This is her dream."

Phoebe's choice of words startled him. "It was *her* dream? To be in Panama or to be a Silver Starlet?"

She looked into her glass for a moment before looking up. "Both, I guess."

"But not yours?"

She chuckled a little and swiped her hair off her shoulder, behind her back. "I already told you that it was just dumb luck that got me here. I was hardly auditioning, remember?"

"I do." Dean nodded. "But still...you're here. If you didn't want to be an actress...I don't understand."

Phoebe paused for so long, he wondered whether she'd heard him.

Finally, she spoke. "Honestly?"

"Always."

"The only reason I'm here is because of Kate. She was so excited when I went home and told her about Lorilee that she did all this searching on the internet just to make sure it was legit. Obviously, it was, and when Lorilee called the next day, Kate was sitting right there. I couldn't say no. It would have crushed her. And she's so convinced that she'll never be able to follow her own dreams because she's a single mom with two kids, I think I felt like I kind of owed it to her. She'd been such a great sister and had always been there for me growing up. The least I could do was give her this. Never mind the paycheck that comes with it. It'll really help her and the girls out. It's the least I can do after all she's done for me."

Dean listened with amazement. She'd uprooted her life, taken a chance in an industry she'd known nothing about, and she'd done it entirely for someone else.

"You're kind of remarkable, did you know that?"

She laughed then, and Dean let the sound wash over him and fill the night as he watched her. He liked her before, but the more he learned about her, the more he realized that he was falling and hard. Phoebe Flynn was special.

"I think I've had enough wine," she announced abruptly, yanking him from his thoughts. "Let's walk."

Chapter Twelve

SHE DIDN'T KNOW whether it was the wine, or her sun-soaked brain, but Phoebe never usually opened up the way she had with Dean. It had left her feeling a little off-kilter. She probably just needed to get the blood moving to clear her head. She'd been sitting too long and the wine and... She knew it wasn't either of those things.

It was Dean.

He was unlike any other man she'd ever met before. Never had she felt as if she could open up to a guy the way she wanted to with him. Which was crazy, because he was exactly the *wrong* person to open up to. He was a celebrity. A movie star. A...he wasn't real.

But when he reached out and took her hand as they walked down the beach, letting the moonlit water wash gently over their feet, he sure felt real.

Everything about being with Dean felt *real*.

Maybe she'd just been overthinking it all. Maybe there was more to him than the tabloids reported. Maybe she should just follow her heart. To hell with what anyone else thought.

Why not?

Phoebe stopped walking and stared out over the ocean as her thoughts swirled around in her head, looking for a place to settle. Without speaking, Dean moved behind her, wrapped his arms around her waist, and held her close to him. His support and strength flowed through her, making her decision an easy one.

"Today was amazing." She leaned back into him and tipped her head up a little.

"It was," he agreed. "I have to confess, I don't want it to end."

She smiled wickedly, despite the fact he couldn't see her face, and spun around in his arms. Dean's hands moved to her hips, and her hands reached up to his neck. "It doesn't have to." She pulled him down to meet her lips in a kiss.

They'd been kissing all afternoon, but those kisses had been flirty and fun.

This kiss held heat. And the promise of the night ahead.

"Damn, Phoebe, you do things to me." His words were a husky breath against her lips before they once again crushed hers.

She groaned, her body shivering under his touch, as his hands left her hips and traveled down her body to cup her ass.

Phoebe worked her hands down, gripping the muscles in his back as he moaned against her neck. "The feeling is more than mutual." His need pressed up against her stomach, urging her on as their kissing and grabbing became more urgent.

Phoebe had never felt a need like the one she was experiencing with Dean. He was different, all right. In all the right ways.

"Dean." She broke the kiss. "I need—"

"We can stop." Dean took a step away. "I'm not trying to—"

"No." Surprised by her own vehemence, she laughed. "I mean, no, that's not what I was going to say."

His lips twitched upward a little. "Oh? And what were you going to say?"

Suddenly, a little shy, she tipped her head coquettishly. "I was going to say..."

"Please tell me it is what I think it is." Dean took a small step forward, closing the distance between them. "Because I have to tell you, Phoebe, I want you so badly right now that I don't think I'll be able to stand here for one more second without picking you up and throwing you over my shoulder and I *really* don't want you to think I'm some kind of neanderthal."

Heat blossomed in her core. "I definitely won't think that." She reached out and unbuttoned his top button, and then the next. "In fact, I'd think it was pretty—"

She couldn't finish the thought before he'd done exactly what he'd threatened. He lifted her easily and with one hand splayed over her ass to hold her in place, he carried her up the beach. The huts were on the opposite side of the island, but they'd passed a chaise daybed lounger on their walk, and Dean had obviously noticed it, too. A few moments later, he deposited her on the chaise and stood over her, his body silhouetted by the moonlight.

Phoebe's body shuddered with desire. And although there were probably a million reasons they shouldn't be doing what they were about to do, there were a million and one reasons they should.

And that's all she needed.

Phoebe leaned back on her elbows and used her finger to beckon him to her.

Dean didn't need any further invitation. He finished unbuttoning his shirt and dropped it to the ground before climbing up onto the daybed, where he let his hands slide up Phoebe's long, lean legs, pushing the thin material of her dress up as he went until he was hovering over her and close enough to once again press his lips on hers.

"You are absolutely delicious, Phoebe."

It was a massive understatement, but he couldn't seem to formulate words adequate to describe everything she was. He would just have to show her.

Her hands slipped over the muscles of his back, exploring the planes of his body, and Dean released a low moan of pleasure. No woman had ever touched him that way, and if they had, the sensation hadn't even come close to what Phoebe was making him feel.

His need throbbed between his legs as Dean once more let his hands slip under her dress, this time pulling the fabric up and over her head to reveal her completely naked body. The sight of her curves, glistening in the moonlight, took his breath away. "Phoebe, you—"

"I didn't pack much," she said by way of explanation for her lack of panties.

Not that any explanation was needed. He loved the way she was comfortable with her body, displayed for him.

"You're so incredibly perfect." He kissed her again, hungry with need. Her body rose to meet his, her need matching his.

Unable to help himself, he let himself explore her. Her breasts were full and heavy, filling his hands. The groan that escaped her lips when he pinched first one nipple, and then the next, was almost his undoing, but he wasn't finished yet. From the moment he'd laid eyes on her, he'd imagined this moment. His fantasies only grew stronger with each passing day. But this, the reality of actually having his hands on her, feeling her body respond under his touch—it was far better than any fantasy could ever be.

She wriggled underneath him. "Your shorts are starting to get in my way."

He chuckled, but it only took him a second to shed the extra clothes, so he, too, was naked. And then there was nothing between them.

Dean gasped as her hands wrapped around the length of him and squeezed.

"Mmm. Better."

Their kisses came hot and fast then. Their hands were all over each other—exploring, squeezing, and teasing before finally, Dean wasn't sure he could take much more. He reached down to find the condom he'd left in the pocket of his shorts— just in case. He sheathed himself quickly before slowly sliding himself inside her. Phoebe groaned as he entered her. He paused, giving her body a chance to adjust to the size of him before moving again.

"Dean." His name was a breath on the air as she tilted her head back and wrapped her legs around him, drawing him closer.

He embraced her, pulling her closer to him with every thrust until they were both groaning from the waves of pleasure that began to build. She came first, her head back, crying out her ecstasy. Moments later, his own orgasm took over and he, too, cried out his release into the night air.

Chapter Thirteen

PHOEBE HAD no idea what time it was when her eyes fluttered open, but the gray of the pre-dawn washed over the beach, putting a muted filter over everything. She rolled over, away from Dean, so she didn't wake him. Her body protested as she stretched out first one leg and then the other—sore from the uncomfortable sleeping arrangement, but also, and more likely, from a night full of intense lovemaking. Not that she would change a thing.

Definitely not.

She tried to slip from the bed, but Dean's arm shot out and wrapped around her waist, drawing her back to him. He spooned up against her, holding her hip with one hand while his other cupped her breast lazily. "Good morning, gorgeous." He kissed her neck, a move that sent an instant shot of heat between her legs. He had the most incredible effect on her. Never before had she been so turned on, so easily and completely by a simple kiss. But Dean...even with only one shared night together, he knew how to bring it out in her. And he did.

Phoebe moaned as he lazily massaged her breast and continued to leave kisses on her neck. She felt his hardness once again against her back and reflexively wriggled her ass against him.

"Hmmm, it *is* a good morning."

"It certainly is." Dean slipped his hand down her thigh as she opened her legs a little to allow him access. She moaned as he entered her. "I can't think of a better way to—"

They both heard the distinctive sound of the helicopter at the same time.

"Shit." Dean pulled away and rolled backward off the daybed, into the sand.

Phoebe jumped up. She grabbed what she thought was her dress and sprinted for cover in the trees. There were a few shrubs that provided a bit more privacy, but not enough. Lee would be able to see her wearing nothing but—Dean's shirt, she realized belatedly as her eyes found the crushed material of her dress lying in the sand next to the chaise and the white linen of Dean's shirt in her hand.

"Dammit." She slipped the shirt over her shoulders, and quickly buttoned it to give herself some measure of decency.

From where she stood, she could see Dean, who'd donned his shorts, wave off the helicopter. A few minutes later, the sound faded, and they were once again left in the silence of the dawn. Still, she didn't move.

"Phoebe?"

"I'm here." She stepped from the inadequate shelter of the palms.

"I'm so sorry about—damn. You look sexy." Dean's grin spread across his face as he approached. "I've never seen that shirt look so good." He opened his arms, and as if they'd been dating years, not hours, she moved right into them.

He kissed the top of her head before lifting her chin gently away from his chest to kiss her lips. Her body responded with a sigh and a familiar moisture between her legs. There was no denying what the man did to her. And he did it so very well. But as much as Phoebe would like to give in to his kisses, she wasn't about to let go of the fact that only moments ago they'd almost both been discovered lying out naked, twisted up in each other's arms for all to see.

The shock of it and the complete violation of her privacy was enough to kill any desire.

"What was that…" She wriggled from his arms and attempted to tame her wild hair. "Why was Lee here? I thought…that *was* Lee, wasn't it?" The idea hit her hard. *Could it have been paparazzi?* That was ridiculous, though, because they were in the middle of nowhere and no one knew where they were. "Wait. Who knows we're here? Why was—"

"Ssh." Dean once again wrapped her up in his arms and held her tight. "No one knows we're here but Kyle and Lee. And yes, that was Lee. I don't know why he was here so early. I'll text him when we're ready to go."

Ready to go?

Was she ready to go already? Their time on the island had been so special. So private. So…invaded. She couldn't help but wonder how or why that had happened? Was it a coincidence or had Dean set it up? He hadn't set that up, had he? *No.* He was a good actor, but he wasn't *that* good. They had a connection. It was real. What they'd shared last night was real. She couldn't bring herself to think it was anything else.

Dammit.

She pulled her dress from the sand and shook it out.

"Phoebe, I promise…" Dean came up behind her and squeezed her shoulder. "I had no idea that Lee was coming." He turned her gently so she was looking at him. "You believe me, right?"

She looked into his eyes, searching for some kind of indication that he'd set it up for publicity. But there was nothing but sincerity reflected back at her. More than that, she *wanted* to believe him. She nodded. "I do."

He was going to kill someone.

Dean had to force himself to take a deep breath and breathe it out slowly before he picked up his phone. He dared not call Lee directly. Instead, he dialed Kyle. He'd let his assistant deal with it. After all, that's why he paid him.

He needed to calm down. Especially before he saw Phoebe again. She'd gone to her hut to shower and freshen up. He was to do the same before they met for breakfast. But he wanted to offer her something else when they met again: an explanation for what exactly had just happened. *And* a reassurance that it wouldn't happen again. He *needed* that.

He'd worked too hard to convince Phoebe he wasn't a player. That he didn't date for publicity. At least, he didn't want to date *her* for publicity. And then… "Fuck."

He wasn't going to calm down. Not until he spoke to someone and they were held accountable for the helicopter showing up.

Dean took the satellite phone and left the little cluster of huts behind. He didn't want anyone, especially Phoebe, overhearing his conversation. As soon as he was on the other side of the volleyball court, he dialed Kyle's direct line.

He picked up on the first ring.

"Dean? Everything okay?"

"No. Everything is *not* okay. What the hell? Why would you send Lee out so early? He wasn't meant to come until I gave my word. What the hell, Kyle?"

"Whoa. Dean, I don't know what you're talking about. I

didn't send Lee. I was waiting for your call. The way we arranged. Total privacy until you gave the word." The other man spoke quickly, and Dean knew he was probably texting Lee from his cell phone in his other hand as they spoke. "Lee was there? What happened?"

Dean filled him in on their abrupt wake-up call. He trusted his assistant. They'd worked together for years, and had developed a friendship of sorts. But also, Kyle had signed the same watertight nondisclosure agreement Dean had all his employees sign before they started working for him. It was to protect him and his privacy in just this type of situation.

Shit.

"Kyle, did Lee sign the agreement?" Had the helicopter pilot been looking to make a few dollars with some particularly sensitive photos? He didn't want to think so, but he couldn't help but be paranoid. Plus, he wasn't stupid. Photographic evidence that Dean Harrison was once again dating his Silver Starlet would fetch more than a few bucks. They'd also destroy any chance he had to prove to Phoebe that he was *not* just out for one thing.

Fuck.

When Kyle didn't answer right away, he pressed. "Kyle. Tell me Lee signed an agreement. Tell me you *gave* him one to sign."

"I did," Kyle answered quickly. "I definitely gave him one. It was in the standard papers I give….shit."

"Shit?" Dean shook his head and paced the sand. "Don't say shit. What? What's shit?"

"It's nothing, I'm sure. I have all the papers back, but that one's missing. It probably just got misplaced, Dean. I'm sure it's nothing."

"It better be nothing." He took a deep breath in and let it out slowly, grounding himself through his feet into the sand.

"I'll sort it out, Dean. And I'll find you a new helicopter pilot, okay? I'll handle it. When do you want pickup?"

Pickup?

Never. Was never an acceptable answer? If he could stay forever on that little island with Phoebe, he'd die a happy man.

Sadly, he knew it wasn't an option. No matter how badly he wanted it.

"Just before noon."

He ended the call without waiting for Kyle's response. He'd handle it. Because that's exactly what Dean paid him to do. He turned around so he was facing the cluster of huts at the other end of the island. He'd handle things with Phoebe. At least he hoped like hell he could.

***

By the time she'd rinsed off and changed into a tank top and shorts, Phoebe was feeling a little less startled, and a whole lot more awake. Her body was still heavy with the aftermath of a night of lovemaking, but she relished it. As she did the memories of the night before. She sipped on the coffee that Josie had brought her from the shade of the dining shelter that opened up to the beach, but protected her from the sun that was already high in the sky and sizzling hot. She wasn't sure she'd ever get used to the intense heat of the Panamanian sun.

"You look a little more awake now." Josie appeared with a plate full of freshly cut tropical fruits and more coffee. "Mind if I join you?"

"Not at all." Phoebe liked the older woman. It would be nice to have the chance to spend more time talking with her. She got the feeling that Josie had some stories to tell. "Please, sit."

They sat in silence for a few moments, enjoying the peace

of the morning. When she'd gone to the outdoor shower, Phoebe had noticed Dean on the other side of the volleyball court, talking into the phone. Even from a distance, he'd looked pissed. No doubt someone was getting an earful about their early morning wake-up call. Phoebe inhaled and blew out the breath. She didn't want to think about that anymore. At least, not if it meant ruining the peace of her morning.

"It looks like the two of you discovered the magic of the island." Josie didn't look at her while she spoke, but smiled over the rim of her own coffee mug. "It always has a way of finding those who need it."

"The magic of the island? What do you…" She let the question trail off because she already knew the answer. "Maybe we did." She grinned to herself.

Josie chuckled. "It certainly did. But I knew it would. I saw the way he looked at you when you arrived."

"Really?" Phoebe put her mug on the table and looked at the other woman. "What do you mean? How did he look at me?"

Finally, Josie looked at her. The deeply tanned skin next to her eyes crinkled as she smiled. "He looks at you as if he's been searching his entire life for you and now he is home."

She closed her eyes and let Josie's words roll around in her head.

"You have your doubts."

It wasn't a question, and Phoebe once again opened her eyes to stare at the woman.

Josie waited and finally, Phoebe nodded. "I do," she said honestly. "It's just…he's…" She sighed. "It's hard to know what to believe in this world. I'm not sure it's for me." Phoebe couldn't be sure whether she meant the situation with Dean, or the career of acting. Or both.

The older woman reached across the small table and put

her hand over hers. Phoebe focused on the rows and rows of tiny colorful beads that were strung up her arm while she spoke. "Don't be quick to judge," Josie said softly. "Sometimes things are not at all what they seem on the surface. The only way to know is to look inside and feel it in your heart. If you can't trust your heart, you will always be disconnected. Stay in touch with it. Your heart will never steer you wrong if you listen closely."

She held her hand for another moment and Phoebe let the words sink in. *Did she listen to her heart? Did she even know how?*

"Good morning."

At the sound of Dean's voice, she sat up abruptly and turned to see him dressed in a fresh T-shirt and shorts. Her body reacted at the sight of him with a low shiver that ran from the tips of her toes to the top of her head.

He moved directly to her and kissed her softly on the lips. "You look gorgeous. And much more relaxed."

On the other side of the table, Josie stood.

"Oh no," Dean said. "Stay. You don't have to—"

"Nonsense." She waved her arm. "The two of you must be hungry." She winked and Phoebe couldn't help but laugh. The magic of the island had definitely worked. "I'll bring you a cup of coffee, Dean. Sit."

With no further protests, she was gone, and Dean sat in her vacated seat. "I'm really sorry about everything this morning. I dealt with it and I want you to know something."

He waited until she turned to look at him. His dark eyes held hers. She could feel the intensity in his gaze. She nodded and he continued.

"I would never do anything to jeopardize your privacy. *Our* privacy. And I didn't know anything about Lee coming by this morning. We're dealing with it, and we'll have a new pilot later. But there's nothing to worry about because we make everyone sign a nondisclosure agreement. Do you believe me?"

She wanted to believe him without hesitation, but there was a tiny piece of her that wasn't sure. She tried to focus on what Josie said. *Trust your heart.* But Phoebe had no experience listening to her heart. Still, he looked so sincere and he'd been just as shocked when the helicopter had disturbed them. She nodded.

"You do?"

"I do."

A tiny smile of relief played at his lips. "I'm glad. Because I really like you, Phoebe, and I had a really good time with you out here."

Her body flushed at just how good of a time they'd had together. "So did I."

They sat in silence for a few moments, just enjoying each other's company, and it was the most relaxed Phoebe had felt in months. Comfortable and easy.

"I think when we go back, we need to play it cool."

Dean's words caught her off guard. Her sense of peace shattered. "What? You don't—"

"Oh, no no no." He moved quickly from his chair until he was on his knees in the sand before her. "I meant what I said. I had a *really* good time with you here, Phoebe. Every second I spend with you is some of the best time of my life. And I don't want that to end. But..." He took a breath while Phoebe held hers. "I don't want to get caught up in gossip, and I think the only way to do that is to pretend like nothing happened out here. That we're not together."

He kept talking, but Phoebe focused on one word.

Together. Were they together? An item? Dating?

"Wait. *Together?*"

His lips flicked up at the corner in a sexy grin. "I don't know if we need a label or anything. But...yes. Together. I'd like that. I mean..."

She laughed. "Okay. I get it. But what do you mean, you want to pretend like nothing happened?"

His face grew serious. "No hand holding. No kissing. No... well...just coworkers. Otherwise, the tabloids will—"

"I get it." She nodded. "And I agree." That flicker of worry and uncertainty rekindled inside her. She refused to allow herself to be used. Not by anyone.

Chapter Fourteen

IT WAS HARDER than Dean expected it to be.

Pretending that he didn't want to spend every spare second in Phoebe's presence, in her arms and in her bed, was almost impossible.

It had only been two days since they'd left the island and returned to Shelter Bay. Shooting had resumed as normal, and everyone was getting set up for the big boat stunt scene in the marina, where Dean would finally be able to do his own stunts. He'd been practicing his dives with Eric out in deeper water, having finally nailed down the fight scene without any more damage to his ribs. He was thankful for the busyness of his days and something to keep his mind off Phoebe, not that it was nearly as effective as he'd hoped it would be. But anything was better than nothing.

Not for the first time, Dean second-guessed his plan to keep Phoebe at arm's length.

But as soon as he'd convinced himself he was overthinking things, Bruce would send him a text reminding him to *seal the deal* or some other equally vulgar terminology that was evidently supposed to encourage him to date Phoebe for the sake of his career.

Bullshit.

What he was going to do for his career was nail this stunt. It was frickin' ridiculous that his worth as an actor should be based even a little bit on who he was dating. He'd let it go on far too long already. It was time to take charge.

"Ready in ten, Harrison."

A production assistant walked past him and waited for a thumbs-up, which he gave.

Ten minutes.

He took a breath.

In ten minutes, it was going to happen. He was finally going to do his own stunt *on* camera.

Duck, dodge, punch, jump.

It was the jump he was nervous about. Not the actual dive, but the timing. What if he got it wrong? What if he was too slow? Or missed his timing?

Explosion.

That's what would happen.

The boat he was due to jump from was rigged with explosives. Stage explosives, but still. If he didn't get off in time, there could be damage. Or injury. It had been impressed upon him that a serious injury was a definite possibility. No one had actually used the word death, but it likely wasn't completely off the table. There was a reason stunt professionals did these things.

That was also the reason Dean wanted to do it.

He closed his eyes and inhaled deeply.

"Ready for this, Harrison?" Eric slapped him on the back, causing him to jump a step forward.

"Dammit, Eric. I'm trying to get in the zone."

The stunt double grinned, but there was very little humor

in it. "There is no zone, Harrison. This isn't just reading some dumb lines. This is serious. You get that, right?"

He knew the other man was just trying to get under his skin. He had a problem with Dean for some reason that had never been there before in all the times they'd worked together. Surely the man wasn't that jealous of Phoebe. Especially, because as far as anyone was concerned, there was nothing going on.

Dean brushed it off. He wouldn't let Eric get to him. "Well, if you coached me properly, it shouldn't be a big deal." He slapped his hands together and walked toward the set.

Dean was to drive the speedboat through the marina while the bad guy, stunted by Mason, chased him in a boat of his own. Dean's boat would be driven by Eric, who would be concealed by a dummy section under the steering wheel. So at least he didn't have to worry about the actual navigating of the watercraft.

The chase would weave through the docks and finally, when they entered the bay where sailboats were anchored, Mason's boat would get close enough for him to jump onto Dean's boat. That's when the fighting would start.

Dodge, duck, punch.

The fight would take place while the boat continued to weave and speed through the marina before finally clearing the anchored boats and head toward the shore. That's when Dean would dive into the water. Moments before the explosives fired.

If all went to plan, they'd get it in one shot.

Wes had impressed upon them his desire to nail the scene in one shot as apparently the setup and rigging of the explosives was *money*.

Dean wasn't worried. Well, not much.

He had just enough adrenaline flowing through him to nail it.

"Ready?" An assistant offered Dean a hand to get onto the

boat, but Dean ignored it and jumped on the deck, followed moments later by Eric.

"Let's do it."

Eric lifted the hatch for his concealed steering compartment but before he got settled inside, he turned and gave Dean a fist bump. "You've got this, man. Your coach knows his shit."

Dean nodded his thanks and turned to scan the docks and shoreline, where a number of people had gathered to watch the scene play out. He didn't expect to see Phoebe. Not really. But he couldn't help but wish she had come out and watch. Seconds before he turned away to focus on getting into character, he spotted her. She sat on the grassy hill where they'd shared their first beer together.

She'd come.

Phoebe couldn't believe how nervous she was. Dean had told her all about the stunt and how Eric had coached him the night before over the phone. They'd been spending so much time on the phone and video chatting, it was starting to cut into her sleep. Not that she cared. She didn't. Not at all. She felt like a teenager again, with a new crush.

All she wanted to do was see Dean. She'd started going out of her way to find him on set, or casually walk by his trailer before he had a call. She'd even popped in to hair and makeup under the ruse that she'd wanted to ask Louis and Susie a question.

And what was even cuter was that Dean was doing it too. She'd caught him a few times on set of one of her scenes that he wasn't in. He was casually talking to Wes about something, or pretending to keep an eye on production. But she knew he was there for her.

It gave her butterflies.

She was totally acting like a teenager. Hell, even when she *was* a teenager, she hadn't behaved this way.

Kate would tell her it was love.

Love. Ha.

The idea made her laugh, but only for a second before it died on her lips at the thought of her sister. Kate still hadn't told her why she'd been at the hospital. She kept dodging Phoebe's questions and when they did talk, she conveniently had to get off the phone to help one of the kids, or get dinner out of the oven or something that was suddenly very pressing, right before it was her turn to talk. Phoebe knew what she was up to. And if she was right, it meant that whatever news Kate had to give her wasn't good. Which was why she was holding off on telling her. No matter what, Kate didn't want anything to ruin Phoebe's experience with the movie.

She settled into the grass, in the exact spot she'd been with Dean those weeks ago, and pulled out a beer before checking her phone again. She'd told Kate there was going to be an exciting scene to watch. She'd even offered to video chat it for Kate on the condition she finally told her what was going on. But still, she hadn't heard.

Phoebe twisted the cap off her beer and raised it in a cheers to Dean and the stunt he was about to perform. She knew he couldn't see her. Or if he could, he likely wasn't going to be looking for her. And she hoped he wasn't. He needed to concentrate and focus. This was a big deal. A *very* big deal, and not only because she didn't want him to get hurt. But she could see in his eyes and hear in his voice how important it was to him to be taken seriously and advance in his career. And for a mega superstar, the only way to advance was to do *all* the things. Including stunts.

At least that's how he saw it.

She took a sip of her beer right as her phone rang. Phoebe almost spat out her beer when she saw it was Kate video chatting her. She took another look to the docks, where Dean was hopping onto the boat. Everything was about to start.

She answered the call.

"Kate, are—"

"If I tell you one thing, can I watch?"

"Kate. I—"

"One thing, Phoebe. I'll tell you quick and then we can watch and then I promise I'll tell you more, but…"

"You don't want to miss it." She finished for her sister because despite how much she wanted to hear what Kate had to say, Phoebe also didn't want to miss the scene. But she would. In a heartbeat if it meant finally knowing what was going on with her sister.

"I don't."

Phoebe nodded. "If you promise."

"I promise."

She nodded again. "Okay. It's about to start. Tell me."

Kate nodded and opened her mouth.

A second later, the roar of the boats' engines and the hollering from the production crew as everything got moving on set was enough to jar her back to reality and became a welcome distraction, even if a temporary one, from the information her sister had just shared with her.

"I found a lump in my right breast."

The boat swerved, and Dean expertly squatted down and leaned into the turn the way he'd been taught. He turned the steering wheel, as beneath him, Eric steered the boat, all the while keeping the intense smoldering Max Silver expression on his features. This was his big getaway scene. Having secured it from Misty Falls, Max finally had the microchip in his possession. His mission was to get it back to headquarters without getting killed along the way.

The plot was largely all the same in the Max Silver franchise, but the writing was witty and the movies action packed, with just enough sex scenes to keep everyone coming back for more. It was a formula that worked.

But only if Dean managed to execute the scene and escape the bad guys who were hell-bent on chasing him—and the microchip—down.

The boat hit a wave and Dean almost lost his footing, but he adjusted quickly and looked over his shoulder as scripted. Right on cue.

The bad guy's boat was coming up fast and then—bam! Mason was on board.

It was go time.

Mason threw a crate. It landed with a smash next to Dean. He spun around as Mason's leg swung out in a roundhouse kick.

Dodge.

Dean bounced upright again, in time for Mason's left hook.

Duck.

So far so good. He glanced around. The boat was swerving through the anchored yachts. Right on schedule. He turned as Mason picked up the empty barrel and lifted it high over his head.

This was it.

He counted in his head the way Eric taught him.

Five…

Dean turned his back on Mason again.

Four…

He put his foot on the wooden edge of the boat.

Three…

He sighted his jump. All clear.

Two…

Jump!

With one quick motion, Dean launched himself up and over the edge of the boat. He put his hands over his head and executed the dive perfectly. In the split seconds as he moved through the air, he heard the explosions behind him, and felt the heat on his back. And then he was in the water. He pulled his arms back and into a slick glide before finally popping his head out and into the air.

It was quiet.

Too quiet.

He kicked and treaded water while one hand smoothed the hair from his face. And then he heard it.

One single whoop of joy that had to have come from Wes.

Moments later, the spectators and crew broke out into a cheer.

He'd done it.

"That was so freaking awesome!"

It *was* awesome. He'd done it. And he'd made it look easy. Phoebe released the breath she'd been holding and blinked. She shook her head in wonder, only belatedly remembering that she was holding the phone for Kate.

Quickly, she turned the phone around to see her sister, who was still gushing over the scene she'd just witnessed.

"That was so cool," Kate said. "You said that was Dean doing the stunt? I didn't know he did his own stunts."

"He doesn't. He didn't. He…" She grinned, proud of him and unable to hide it. "He was so incredible."

Her sister wasn't stupid. She noticed the shift in Phoebe immediately, subtle as it was. "Is there something you want to tell me, little sis? Don't tell me you've fallen for him. You have, haven't you? He does have a way of—"

"No." She didn't want to hear it. She didn't want to hear her sister, of all people, tell her that Dean had a reputation for seducing his costars. She didn't need to hear it. Besides, Kate had things that she *did* need to hear. "You're not getting out of it that easy, Kate."

Her sister's face changed, the glee of a moment earlier gone. She shook her head, but Phoebe wasn't going to let her off so easily.

"You found a lump?" she pushed. "What did the doctors say? The tests? What's going on?"

"I don't want you to come home." Kate's face was lined with seriousness. "I mean it, Phoebe. You're almost done there and what you're doing, it's...well, it's so incredible."

It wasn't. It was a movie, not a peacekeeping mission. But Phoebe was very aware that she'd come off sounding more than a little ungrateful for her opportunity if she mentioned that.

"Promise me you won't come home until filming wraps."

Phoebe took a deep breath. She knew without hearing it that Kate wasn't going to give her good news. But they only had a few more weeks of shooting. She could make it. Probably.

"I promise."

"The results came back malignant."

One word and Phoebe's life froze. Nothing was important. Not the movie. Not Dean. Nothing but her sister.

"Malignant?"

"Cancer."

"I know what malignant means."

"You just didn't sound like—"

"What does that mean?" Phoebe's mind raced and a barrage of questions flooded her. "Are you having surgery? Is there chemo? When? How are the girls? Do you need me to—"

"No!" Kate cut her off sharply. "You promised you would not come home. We're fine. The doctors said they caught it early and they're very optimistic that a lumpectomy will take care of it. We'll know more after that."

"A lumpectomy?"

"They'll take it out. Next week, in fact. I didn't want to tell you because I didn't—"

"I'm coming home." Phoebe pushed up from the grass as if she were going to leave at that exact moment, which, if she had her way, she would. All she needed to do was find Kristen. She'd book her a flight and then she'd go talk to Wes and—

"I told you," Kate's voice once again broke through her mental lists. "You're not coming back. Uncle Benny is going to take care of the girls, and I have a friend driving me to the hospital. I'll be fine in a few days. It's not really a big deal."

Not a big deal?

"Kate! It's a huge deal. You have *cancer.*"

On the other end of the line, Kate laughed. She *laughed.*

"What's so funny?" Nothing about what was happening was funny. She said as much.

"Phoebe." Kate finally caught her breath and spoke again. "Calm down. Seriously. You promised me you weren't coming home, and you're not." Her voice had shifted to that big sister tone she reserved for particularly intense moments.

"But Kate…you need—"

"I need you to stay there. You have a contract, Phoebe. A big one. And that's the best way for you to help right now."

Realization washed over her. Of course. Kate's illness was going to be expensive. Childcare. Hospital bills. Her lost wages. Phoebe took a deep breath, inhaling through her nose. *That's how she could help.*

"You get it now."

She refocused her gaze at her big sister on the phone screen and nodded. "I get it."

Kate's eyes shone but she blinked quickly. Her big sister only very rarely cried in front of her. "I miss you, Pheebs."

"I miss you, too, Kate. I'm so sorry you have to go through this." Phoebe sniffed back tears of her own. It wouldn't help Kate to see her break down, either. "And when I get home, I'm not leaving again until you're all better, okay?"

Kate nodded. "Now go enjoy the rest of your time there so you have lots of stories for me when you get back, okay?" Her bright smile was back. "And don't think I'm going to let you off without more stories of Dean Harrison." She wiggled her eyebrows, and Phoebe felt a flash of guilt.

She hadn't told Kate what had happened on the island, or how she was falling hard for the superstar, and it was both exciting and terrifying at once. They'd decided to keep things quiet, and Phoebe made the super hard decision to keep it a secret from her sister, too.

For now.

She'd tell her.

Just not yet.

Chapter Fifteen

DEAN WAS RIDING ON A HIGH. He couldn't remember the last time he'd felt so alive. The stunt had gone perfectly. He couldn't have asked for a better take. And Wes had said so.

When the divers—who were there for safety—escorted him to the shore, Wes had been there almost at once to pat him on the back and celebrate the success of the scene. They'd worked together for so long that the director knew how important the moment was for Dean. It felt good to get the kind of acknowledgment that he'd been seeking for so long. *Damn good.* He was more than a pretty face who could recite lines. He could do his own stunts, and maybe one day he'd dip his toe into production, too. The world was just starting to open up for him. He couldn't wait to celebrate with Phoebe.

He'd scanned the shoreline where he'd seen her before shooting began, but she was gone. As much as he wanted to, he knew he couldn't go after her. But only for a few more weeks. Then shooting would be done and they could spend some time together—some *real* time. He had plans to take her away some-where they could be alone. Maybe to the West Coast, or a ranch in Wyoming. Or…back to their island. It didn't matter where they went, as long as they were together. And alone.

But it would have to wait a little longer.

It wasn't until he got back to his yacht anchored in the harbor to shower and change that Dean had a chance to check his cell phone. There was a text from her.

Great job! You were amazing and made it look so easy.

He smiled to himself and tapped in a reply.

I saw you watching. I couldn't screw it up! See you later to celebrate?

There was no doubt she'd heard about the impromptu celebration planned for the Dockside later that evening. It wouldn't be the private celebration Dean would have preferred. But if it meant seeing her, he'd take it.

Before he had a chance to call him himself, Dean's cell phone rang with an incoming call from Bruce. He grinned and answered it. "I take it you heard the good news."

"I heard you nailed it, Deano! Hell ya. I almost wish I'd been there to see it for myself. Almost."

Dean laughed.

"Do you know what this means?" Bruce continued. "Doing your own stunts. This opens things up for you and that super-hero gig…I can feel it, Deano. Look in the mirror, buddy, because if everything goes to plan, you could be looking at the next *Supers* hero. I'm reaching out as we speak."

Dean laughed, because he had no doubt that's exactly what Bruce was doing. Still. He did look in the mirror. The

Max Silver franchise had been good to him. It had set up his career and shot him to stardom. But a *Supers* film? That was the end all, be all. Every actor who'd landed a role in the popular franchise had been able to write their own ticket for success. Some had gone on to star in more films, each one bigger than the next. But others had taken their success and the royalty checks that came with it, and had retired to live their dream lives.

For Dean, that could finally mean a piece of property in the country and a family to raise on it.

Phoebe.

Just thinking of the possibility of finally getting everything he'd ever wanted filled him with a happiness he was unfamiliar with.

"Perfect," he told Bruce. "Make it happen, man."

"You know what would really seal the deal, right?"

The warm feeling of happiness vanished and Dean's blood ran cold. "I told you, Bruce. No. I'm not going to use her for your own agenda."

"And yours."

He shook his head. "More the reason not to do it." Dean pushed away from the mirror. "I told you, no. Now drop it."

"If you change your mind, I—"

"I won't." He ended the call and tucked his phone into the back pocket of his shorts.

The brief call had dampened his mood, but he wasn't going to let it derail him. Dean had a lot to celebrate and a future to look forward to. And he couldn't wait to get started.

The party was in full swing by the time Phoebe got there. The Dockside Inn had been taken over by the cast and crew, but a few of the yachters and locals were mixed in as well, and everyone was having a great time together. The music pumped through the speakers, and drinks were flowing.

The last thing Phoebe had felt like doing was celebrating after getting her sister's news. But Dean had texted and asked whether she'd be there, and the pull to see him was greater than her need to feel sorry for herself, or her sister. Besides, there was nothing she could do for Kate from Panama. Except keep her promise to have a good time and give her some stories to tell when she got back.

Phoebe looked but didn't see Dean as she wove her way through the crowd. Someone put a glass of champagne in her hand and she drank, letting the bubbles burst on the top of her mouth.

She took another sip, this time holding the liquid in her mouth to enjoy the tingle and pop of the bubbles on her tongue. Phoebe was about to have another sip, when an arm wrapped around her shoulders.

"Phoebe! You made it." Wes squeezed her tight before releasing her. "Come. We have a table over here."

She let herself be guided through the people to a table directly in the center of the room. Among a few of the other lead actors was Dean. He was deep in conversation with Brent Lowell, who played his adversary. Laughter erupted at something Brent said as Phoebe took the empty seat across from Dean, and Wes went to find another chair.

The laughter died off, but the smile remained on his lips as Dean caught sight of her. "You made it."

She matched his smile with one of her own. "Of course. Today was your big day. Congratulations."

Dean raised a glass. "Did you watch?"

He already knew the answer, but she nodded. "Of course I did. It was the highlight of the day. Everyone watched." Dean winked and Phoebe raised her glass to clink with his. "I guess this means you're a next-level celebrity now, hey?"

"Don't say that." Wes returned and sat next to her. "This is already all going to his head. He's going to be completely insufferable before long."

"You know it." Dean laughed and took another drink.

She was happy for him; she really was. And of course it was good to see him. But as exciting as it had been for him, it had been an emotional day for Phoebe. The last thing she wanted to do was be surrounded by so many others who were laughing and having fun when she'd just gotten such terrible news.

She hadn't realized until that moment what a bad idea it had been to go out. She should be alone, to let herself absorb the news about Kate. Not surrounded by a party.

Phoebe took a breath and forced her face to remain neutral. She'd finish her drink and go. She didn't want to ruin the festivities by making any kind of a scene.

"Next time, I'm going to be the one taking shots at you, Harrison." Brent raised his glass. "Maybe if I start doing my own stunts, too, I can—"

"Do not even think about it," Wes interrupted them both. "This was already almost too much for my blood pressure. I swear, if something happened to you and—"

"We had to delay shooting," Dean finished for him. "I know, I know. But nothing happened and I'm ready to go. How many shots are left?"

The hairs on the back of her neck stood up as Dean made eye contact with her. They both knew at least one of the scenes that was coming up.

The boat scene.

Arguably the most intimate scene that had ever been shot in a Max Silver movie. It was going to push all the boundaries. Phoebe had done little but think about it, go over the script, and picture it in her head. An act that had become a little more intense since their trip to the island, which had been pretty damn intimate in its own right.

Wes was talking, outlining the few scenes that were left, but Phoebe wasn't listening. Instead, she was focused on Dean. Without even saying a word, he was saying everything with his eyes and Phoebe's body was responding. She craved the warmth of his touch. His kiss on her skin, his fingers on her. His arms wrapped around her, holding her close. She craved it with an intensity that almost hurt. Suddenly, unbidden hot tears pricked at her eyes, startling her.

She pushed back from the table so quickly, the chair scraped against the floor. "Sorry," she said to the table. "I just need to get a little air. It's really hot in here all of a sudden." She didn't wait for anyone to respond before getting up from the table and pushing her way through the crowd until she got to the patio door and out into the fresh air where she could finally take a breath.

"What was that?" Wes looked at Dean as if he held the answers as to what had gotten into Phoebe.

He didn't. But he sure as hell wanted to.

"It's probably the heat and the intensity of an onsite shoot schedule," he said as casually as he could. "You know what, I'll just go pop my head out and make sure she's okay. I'll be back in a second."

No one questioned him, a fact he was grateful for as he took his leave. He hated acting like a teenager sneaking round so *Mom and Dad* didn't find out about his girlfriend. It was ridiculous. What he really wanted was to take Phoebe in his arms, dip her low and kiss her senseless in front of everyone so there was no question how he felt about her. But with Bruce's words once again ringing in his ears, he was reminded as to why exactly he was *not* going to do that.

"Phoebe?" He made it to the deck, where a handful of people were lingering, smoking and drinking in small groups. He scanned the dark space, and finally caught the movement of someone headed down the stairs at the far end of the deck. He moved quickly, reaching her right before she disappeared into the shadows of the night.

"Phoebe. Wait." Dean reached for her arm and spun her gently. He froze at the sight of her face. Her eyes were filled with sadness, and even in the dim light, he could see the shine of tears. This was more than just the stress of sneaking around and an intense shooting schedule. "What's wrong? Talk to me."

She shook her head and glanced around quickly.

There was no one around, but still, Dean grabbed her hand and led her into the dark behind the Dockside, where the kitchen doors were sheltered by a lattice enclosure.

"No one can see us here." He cupped her cheek and gently tipped her face up. "What's going on? Are you okay?"

She nodded. "I'm sorry." Her voice broke a little. "I shouldn't have come tonight. I didn't want to be a downer on your big day. You really were great today, and I know—"

"Don't worry about that." He cut her off gently. "And you're not putting a damper on anything. Just seeing you has made my day complete. Now tell me. What's going on?"

He was aware that he was starting to sound like a broken record, but he didn't care. He would repeat himself as many times as it took. Something was going on, and he was going to get to the bottom of it.

"My sister has cancer." She blurted out the words so quickly, they seemed to shock even her.

"What?" Dean shook his head in an effort to process what she'd said. "Cancer?"

"I just heard." She tried to drop her head, but Dean

brought up his other hand, and gently cradled it in his hands. "She just told me and there's nothing I can do about it. I can't go home and I know she needs help with the kids and everything, but I need to be here. And…"

A tear streaked down her face then and it broke Dean's heart.

He knew how important Kate was to her. She was Phoebe's family. Everything. The news must be killing her.

With no words that could possibly be adequate, he released her cheeks and pulled her in close for a tight hug. She cried then—full, body-wracking sobs—and he held her and tried in his own way to absorb the pain for her.

He rubbed her back and gave her the space to let all of her emotions out. Dean had no idea how long they stood that way, but when Phoebe finally lifted her head from his shoulder, her eyes were red, but her tears were dry.

"I'm sorry." She tried to pull away, but he held her fast. "I should go, Dean. I didn't want to—"

He silenced her with a kiss. It wasn't nearly long enough, but he couldn't *not* kiss her.

"I didn't think we were doing that." Phoebe looked up at him with a slight smile on her face.

A smile that *he'd* put there.

"We're not."

But damn, he wanted to do it again. And…there was no one around.

To hell with it.

Dean dropped his lips to hers again right as the kitchen door opened.

"Oh, excuse me. Lo siento."

Phoebe and Dean jumped apart like teenagers caught making out in school.

Maria, the wife of the dockmaster, stood in the doorway, lit by the kitchen lights behind her, with a baby on her hip. Dean had been introduced to her, but didn't know her. And really didn't know whether she could be trusted not to say anything.

"Maria." He put on his dazzling smile that never failed to work with women. "We were just—"

"No hay problema." Maria waved her hand. "It's none of my business."

"It's not like we're doing anything wrong," Phoebe chimed in. "We just really don't want anyone else to know right now and…"

"Esta bien." The baby on her hip fussed. "I won't say a word."

"May I?" Dean reached out and without hesitation, Maria put the baby in his arms.

It wasn't something a lot of people knew about him, but Dean loved babies. He loved kids. More than anything, he wanted one or two of his own. One day. Along with a little bit of property, away from it all. Just like that part of his dream, it seemed like nothing more than a wish and a hope.

He bounced and cooed, and the baby settled quickly. He looked up from the chubby cheeks with a smile on his face to see Phoebe watching him.

"What?"

She shook her head with a small chuckle. "I would never have guessed."

He winked. "There's a lot you don't know about me yet."

"It's sweet."

"Nothing better than a man with a baby, mi amiga." Maria nodded and smiled at them both before gesturing between them. "Bebes?"

"Oh my goodness."

"What? Oh wow."

They spoke at the same time, but Dean couldn't help but notice, she didn't say no.

Chapter Sixteen

THE NEXT DAY, Phoebe woke up to rain and a headache.

She'd only had the one glass of champagne, but the unexpected outburst of emotion had left her feeling ragged and worn out.

She'd slept in. A quick glance at the clock on the wall across from her bed told her it was almost noon. Phoebe couldn't remember the last time she'd slept so late. But she'd obviously needed it.

Phoebe wasn't needed in the makeup trailer for another hour. With any luck, her headache would be gone by then, and Louis could work his magic with her puffy eyes.

Until then, she might as well go back to sleep.

Phoebe had just closed her eyes again, when her phone buzzed with an incoming call.

With a groan, she reached out for her cell, but her annoyance was quickly replaced by worry when she saw Kate's name and picture on the screen.

Phoebe pressed the button to take the call. "Kate? What's wrong?"

"You need to tell me the truth."

"What?" Phoebe sat up and leaned against her headboard. "The truth about what?"

"Dean Harrison," Kate said simply. "Tell me the truth."

"About Dean?" Maybe her brain was still foggy from sleep, but Phoebe had no idea what her sister was saying. "I don't—"

"Something is going on between the two of you. I know it."

Phoebe froze. *How could she know? Was there a picture or something on the internet?* "What do you—"

"Phoebe." Kate's voice was serious. "Do you know what happened this morning?"

"Clearly I don't. What's going on, Kate? Is everything—"

"I was woken up by the doorbell at seven a.m. On a Saturday."

"I'm sorry?"

Kate ignored her. "Do you know who was at the door?"

The guessing game was starting to get old. Phoebe sighed.

"A nanny, Phoebe."

She moved the phone to the other ear, certain she'd misheard.

"A nanny," Kate repeated. "A real-life Mary Poppins."

"What? How? Why?"

"Right?"

Phoebe was fully awake now. "Oh my God, Kate. You aren't making any sense at all."

"Phoebe. A nanny showed up on my doorstep today and told me that it was *all taken care of.* And then, not even twenty minutes later, the doorbell rang and there was food there. Like, lots of food, Phoebe. Frozen meals that have literally filled my deep freezer."

Phoebe didn't even know that Kate had a deep freezer.

"Again," Kate continued. "All I was told was that it was *taken care of.*"

"I don't understand."

"Neither did I. But then my Mary Poppins finally explained it to me. She'd been hired by Dean Harrison. *Dean Harrison.*"

"Oh."

Dean. Dean had sent a nanny and food service to her sister.

"Exactly. Which is why I need to know—what is going on between the two of you? Because there is no way that a guy just does that for a random person he doesn't even know."

"He's a really nice person." It sounded lame, even to her. "That's just who he is. I'm…well…I was upset last night and I told him what was going on and…wow. I didn't think he'd do that. I mean…" She shook her head in an effort to make sense of what her sister had just told her.

"Nice people don't just send nannies and food for strangers."

Phoebe knew her sister wasn't stupid. She also knew she wasn't up for the conversation that Kate wanted to have. There wasn't time. She looked at the clock. Definitely not time to get into things with her. Not yet.

"Just be thankful, Kate. There's no agenda with this. Honestly. Dean is a really good guy and he just wanted to help." She swung her legs over the edge of the bed and stood with a stretch. "If I see him today, I'll thank him for you, okay?"

"*If* you see him?" Kate laughed. "You're not fooling me, Phoebe. I don't care what you say—something's going on between the two of you."

Phoebe couldn't help but smile, thankful that her sister couldn't see her face. She'd know the truth right away. She could always tell when Phoebe was lying.

"Don't make me pull the cancer card," Kate continued. "You wouldn't deny a sick woman the—"

"Bye, Kate," she interrupted with a laugh. "I've gotta go. I'll talk to you later." Phoebe pressed the button to end the call.

Before putting her phone down, she typed out a quick text.

You're amazing. Thank you.

Before hitting Send, she added a kissing emoji.

I just wanted to help somehow.

The reply came quickly. And before she could respond, another text:

I'll take that kiss in person.

More than anything, she wanted to give it to him. With a grin, she tapped her reply.

Tonight.

There was a chance they'd be caught. But…there was also a chance they wouldn't be. And at that moment, Phoebe was more than willing to take that chance.

Challenge accepted!

If the night before had taught Dean anything, it was that he couldn't let another day go by before he had Phoebe in his arms properly. And not just behind the kitchen door where anyone could catch them.

If she wanted to see him tonight, he'd make it happen.

"Mr. Harrison, I really do need you to look up."

Reluctantly, Dean looked up to see Louis in front of him, tapping a makeup brush impatiently against his hand. "Sorry, I just have a lot on my mind. I was…it doesn't matter."

Louis grinned, but didn't press the issue.

No doubt he'd heard all kinds of stories from those who'd sat in this chair. For a moment, Dean considered confiding in the man. He'd signed a nondisclosure agreement, too. Then again, so did almost everyone on set. It never seemed to matter. Secrets always seemed to have a way of getting out.

He swallowed hard and straightened up in his chair so Louis could do his job. "How's your day been?"

The other man smiled and did a little spin on his heel

before grabbing yet another brush from his table. "Living the dream, Mr. Harrison. Living the dream."

He laughed. "Call me Dean, already. How many movies have we worked on, now? I think we're past all the formalities, don't you think?"

"Three now." Louis swiped something on his face. "And how's *your* day going, *Dean*?"

The smile crept up onto his face before he could control it. It was only for a moment, but Louis noticed.

The other man took a step back and waved the makeup brush back and forth. "Woo-ie. Now that is the look of a man who has definitely had a very good day." He clicked his tongue. "There's a story in there somewhere."

Dean chuckled and ducked his head. "No story."

"Umm hmmm." Louis stepped closer, and again started to apply the makeup. "Say what you want, Dean. But I'll tell you what, I've been around for a bit and I've seen enough men—and women—in my chair to know what I know when I know it. And I know that you have a story you're dying to tell." He nodded knowingly and wiggled his head a little as he applied something to Dean's face.

"I'm not saying that you don't know what you're talking about, Louis, but...you don't know what you're talking about." He winked and immediately hoped he hadn't given too much away.

"That's no surprise." The hair stylist, Susie, chose that moment to enter the trailer and come up behind Dean in the chair. She looked at him in the mirror. "Louis rarely knows what he's talking about."

"That's enough out of you, girl." Louis gently smacked his partner on the arm. "I know exactly what I'm talking about, and you know it." Before Susie could ask, Louis told her. "Dean here," he emphasized the use of his first name, "has the look of a man who has had a *very* good day, if you know what I mean."

"Ohh." Susie took a step back and examined Dean herself. Presumably in search of the same *look* that Louis had noticed. "Yup." She nodded slowly. "You're right. He does have that look." She looked at him pointedly in the mirror. "Are you going to tell us, or do we have to guess?"

"You're both out to lunch." He'd been having fun, enjoying the playful banter, but it was starting to venture into dangerous territory. Dean refused to do or say anything that would jeopardize Phoebe's reputation. No matter what. "I'm sorry to say, I have no gossip for you." He shrugged, working hard to call on all of his acting skills. "I'm probably just a little hungover after last night's celebration." It was an out and out lie considering he hadn't had more than two drinks. He had a strict rule when he was filming. Almost everyone on set knew it. Judging by Louis and Susie's face, they knew it, too.

With any luck, they'd pick up on the fact that he had no intention of telling them anything.

Their line of questioning was cut off a second later anyway, when the door to the trailer opened and Phoebe walked in. Dean tried, and failed, not to react to her presence. He couldn't help it. His body had a completely visceral response to her.

"Hey, girl!" Louis greeted her. "I'm almost ready for—oh."
Oh?

Dean looked up and met both Louis *and* Susie's eyes in the mirror. They both wore wide, shit-eating grins and were nodding, almost to themselves.

Shit.

He didn't have a choice. "Hey, Phoebe. Ready for the scene today?" It was a basic shot with Max and Misty hunched over a computer, arguing and analyzing the data on the microchip Max was trying to steal from Misty. There was nothing particularly hard about it. Their banter would flow; the dialogue was easy and fairly intuitive.

"I am." Her voice was clipped and measured as she no doubt also worked hard to control her reaction to him. "Thanks, Dean. How about you?"

She sat in the chair next to him, and Dean worked hard to keep his breathing level and even as his senses went wild at her nearness and the intoxicating scent that was all Phoebe. "Yes." He went to nod, but then caught himself as he was in the makeup chair. Of course, it had also just occurred to him that neither Louis or Susie were actually doing hair or makeup. "I think I—"

"Enough!" Louis dropped his makeup brush to the table with a clatter. "You two are ridiculous."

"And for professional actors," Susie chimed in, "you're both doing a terrible job right now."

Phoebe cleared her throat and looked to Susie and Louis, whom she'd come to think of as friends. They both wore equal looks of humor and annoyance. "What are you...what are you talking about?"

"Girl, you are going to need to do better than that." Louis crossed his arms and next to him, Susie nodded.

They knew.

She risked a glance at Dean, whose face was blank of expression. He wasn't going to give it up. She looked back at the duo, who watched her closely.

Shit. They totally knew.

There was only one thing to do.

Deny. Deny. Deny.

"I don't know what you're talking about." She made a show of looking at the clock. "We need to be on set in twenty,

Louis." Phoebe leaned forward in her seat and poked at the skin under her eyes. "And these bags of mine—"

"Are you saying that if we left the two of you alone in here for more than thirty seconds, you wouldn't be going at it like two teenagers in the coatroom at church?"

"Church, huh?" Susie gave him a look, but Louis only shrugged.

"I grew up very Catholic."

She looked at him—and his flamboyant outfit of short shorts and tight tank top, reminiscent of something from an eighties music video—up and down. "I can tell."

"Don't bring my fashion sense into this," he shot back. "You wish you had as much style as I have in my—"

"If you two are done." Dean cleared his throat. "Miss Flynn needs the bags under her eyes touched up."

Phoebe's mouth fell open as she glared at him. *How dare he—*

Dean was laughing and then, in a move she didn't expect, he reached his hand out to her and took her hand. "I'm kidding." He squeezed.

Were they doing this? Were they coming out with their relationship?

Panic and joy fought for her attention.

Panic was about to win out when Dean squeezed again before releasing her hand.

"Oh." Susie did a little dance, wiggling her hips and shaking her shoulders. "It *is* like that. I knew it!"

"*We* knew it." Louis turned to give her a high five.

"Um, Dean?"

"I got this." Dean nodded and got up from the chair. "Listen." His voice was strong, and laced with authority that Phoebe hadn't heard from him yet. He faced Louis and Susie and waited for them to stop dancing in celebration of everything they thought they knew. It felt like it took forever, but they finally stopped and looked at him. "This isn't what you think it is," he started, and when they both made low whistling sounds, he amended, "Okay, it *is* what you think it is. But we don't want anyone to know." He waited and let it sink in. "*Anyone.* We're keeping it super quiet and so far that's been working out pretty well. You both signed NDAs?"

The mention of a legal document seemed to take some of the fun out of the situation and both Louis and Susie snapped to attention. "You know we wouldn't say anything, right?" Susie looked directly at Phoebe. "That's not what we do."

"Nope." Louis shook his head. "It doesn't take an NDA for us to keep our mouths shut. It's just decency." He looked offended that Dean would even suggest otherwise.

Phoebe stood so she was facing him. "I know," she started, despite the fact that she did not know. She also didn't know that they'd signed NDAs. If everyone was signing them, then why did they need to keep their relationship a secret anyway? It was a question she was going to ask Dean as soon as she got the chance. But one thing at a time. "It's just that...I wasn't sure at first if Dean was interested in me because of...well...I don't know...it's just..."

"It's just easier to keep the press out of our relationship," Dean finished for her. "And we really don't want it getting out." He looked pointedly at both of them. "To anyone. We're trusting you two."

No one spoke for a moment and finally, Louis used his fingers to mime a zipper and a lock against his lips. He dramatically threw the key over his shoulder and looked to his partner. Susie followed suit and did the same.

"Thank you." Dean exhaled and the stress he'd been holding released with his breath. He reached for her hand again, and Phoebe moved to stand next to him. "Because I've been dying to do this all fucking day."

He put one hand on either side of her face and, right in

front of Susie and Louis, kissed her, until she was gasping for breath of her own.

"Damn!"

"That's what I'm talking about!"

The duo let out a series of hoots and hollers, which only made Phoebe laugh against Dean's lips. And then she kissed him again. And again. Because the only thing better than kissing him in secret was kissing him out in the open. Or, at least, as out in the open as they were going to get.

Chapter Seventeen

FOR THE NEXT WEEK, Dean and Phoebe got creative with the ways they saw each other. It felt good that their relationship was no longer a total secret, but still, Dean wasn't convinced that it was safe to come out completely. In fact, he knew it wasn't.

Phoebe had asked him why it was a problem if everyone had signed NDAs. It was a fair question, but what she didn't understand was that more often than not, if someone was determined to sell their secrets to the tabloids, the payoff was greater than the potential consequences. People could be assholes. And, sadly for him, it was a fact that Dean had learned the hard way. More than once.

No. It was better to be safe than sorry. He'd meant it when he'd told Phoebe he was interested in her for her and not for the publicity that was sure to come from it. He was serious. And this was the only way to prove it. She would always question his intentions if he didn't do it this way. And he cared way too much about her, and what he hoped would come from their relationship, to screw it up.

Maybe it had been a mistake to come clean with Louis and

Susie. Dean liked to think he was a good judge of character, and his gut said he could trust the two of them. He hoped it wouldn't be a decision he'd live to regret. But he didn't think so. They didn't seem the type to sell secrets, or they would have done it a dozen times over with some of the celebrities they'd worked with.

Besides that, they'd guessed. And they were too smart to be deterred.

The added benefit of others knowing about them, though, was that Phoebe and Dean now had allies in their mission to steal a few moments together. More than once, Louis had called Dean into the trailer to touch up some makeup, only to find Phoebe waiting for him, for a few moments of stolen kisses.

He wanted more. He needed more. But he could be patient.

Mostly.

Besides their rendezvous in the makeup trailer, Dean had arranged on two occasions to have Kyle secretly pick Phoebe up with a boat and bring her out to his yacht.

Those were the best nights. To have her all to himself for an entire evening. Dinner, conversation, and...*damn*. He was never going to grow tired of Phoebe and her touches, her kisses, the way her body responded to him.

It was as if she were made for him. Every part of them just worked together. It was silly, and probably a bit romantic and ridiculous, but he couldn't help it. Something about Phoebe was just...right.

Never before had Dean been eager for a movie to wrap. He loved filming. Immersing himself in the experience and the character. It was in his blood and almost always when filming was over, he'd fall into a funk that could take weeks to come out of.

But that was before.

Now, he couldn't wait for things to finish up. He couldn't wait for it all to be over, so he could be with Phoebe properly. He knew now that his plans to whisk her away for an extended time were going to have to be put on hold. She was consumed with worry for her sister, and was chomping at the bit herself about getting home and being able to be with Kate.

He'd tried to assuage some of the guilt he knew she felt by being so far away by sending the best nanny money could buy, as well as more than enough food to get the family through the hard days while Kate was recovering from her procedure. And even though Dean's offers had been well received and welcomed, they were no replacement for Phoebe being there in the flesh.

Not that he minded. Not at all. The love and concern she had for her family only made him fall a little deeper and a little faster. Phoebe had already bought her ticket home for the morning after the wrap party, and she didn't plan on leaving her sister, until she was convinced she was through the hardest days.

Dean had already rented a private home on the West Coast for them to retreat to as soon as Kate was well enough for Phoebe to leave for a little bit. Until then, he would join her in her hometown. Anything to be close to her.

Besides, maybe he needed to start expanding his search for a piece of property to Montana. It had never been something he'd considered before, but he didn't know why. Now, he had a reason to look into it. A *very good* reason.

The sound of a boat pulled him from his thoughts. Dean jumped up from the lounger on the aft deck and moved to the rail just in time to see one of the deckhands of his yacht pull the tender up to the stern.

"My lady."

Dean was waiting for her at the back of the boat. No. She needed to stop calling it a boat. Dean was on a yacht. A mega superyacht.

Phoebe was never going to get used to the fact that she was dating a man who was wealthy enough to charter a super mega *fucking* yacht. Never mind the fact that he'd personally staffed her sister's cancer treatment.

She took Dean's extended hand and let him pull her onto the deck of the *yacht*.

"Hi, handsome." She stood on her tippy-toes and kissed him.

"Oh," he groaned into her lips. "I like hearing that."

"As if you don't have enough people telling you how handsome you are." She laughed. "You don't need to hear it from me."

"Oh." He pulled her back into him as she tried to walk away. "On the contrary. I *definitely* need to hear it from you." He kissed her then, and she all but melted into his arms.

Was it crazy that he had the power to make her feel so completely at his mercy?

Yes.

And also…

No.

Wasn't this what love was supposed to feel like?

The word scared her. But also, it calmed her. Phoebe had never been in love before. She'd never felt the thrill of seeing a man and knowing he'd been waiting for her and only for her. That just laying eyes on her was the high point of his day. She'd never before felt the rush of warmth that lit her body on fire when another's lips were on hers.

Not like this.

Not. Like. This.

But *love?* The word alone was heady and terrifying and, frankly, had her questioning her sanity.

Besides, it was way too early to think such things. What they were doing—it was fun. It was flirty and it was easy. Hell, it was a secret. It was too early for love.

"Where did you go?"

Dean's words shook her out of her internal monologue, which was probably for the best. *No.* It was definitely for the best. She needed to get out of her head and into the moment. For goodness' sake, she was with the most gorgeous man alive —according to *Celeb* magazine—and half the female population. And he only had eyes for her.

That's what was important. Not anything else. Not what they *might* be. Or *could* be. Or hell, even what they *were.*

They were having fun is what they were, and Phoebe needed to stop overthinking all the things and get right back into the moment and live it.

"Sorry." She shook her head clear of the thoughts and smiled. "I got caught up in a thought. But I promise you…" She took his chin between two fingers and pointed his face so he was looking directly at her. She lowered her voice, conveying all her desire in her words. "I am right here with you. Completely."

"Mmm." Dean murmured against her lips and kissed her thoroughly. It wasn't until the kiss started to heat up and her body started to liquify in his arms that one of the deckhands cleared his throat.

She jumped back and laughed, forgetting they weren't alone.

Were they really getting that careless about their relationship? And more importantly, did she even care?

Yes.

Phoebe looked over at the two deckhands who were trying to be as inconspicuous as possible.

Yes. She did care. She wasn't going to get lumped in with all those other women. She was different. She didn't use people for her own success. She wasn't going to use Dean. He was worth more than that. And if anyone at all, especially him, thought that was the case, she'd be devastated. Let alone how she'd feel if she thought for even a second that he'd been using her.

Phoebe took a step back and assessed him. *No. He wasn't using her.* She'd know. She'd feel it.

Besides, that's why he was going to all of these lengths. He was bending over backward to prove it to her.

And she couldn't help but kind of love him for it.

Damn. There was that word again.

Love.

"Phoebe?"

"No." She shook her head and forced a flirty smile to her lips. She really did need to pull herself together. "I'm good. Sorry. My thoughts are running away with me tonight." She laughed and focused on Dean. "We should get going and leave these poor guys to their work. I'm sure they don't need us standing around here all night." She took his hand and led him up the stairs to the back deck, where she could gaze at the magnificent Southern Hemisphere stars and lose herself both in them, and in the man she was with as long as she had the chance.

"You know how beautiful you are, right?" Dean regretted the words as soon as they were out of his mouth. Not because Phoebe wasn't beautiful. Damn. She was the most gorgeous woman he'd ever laid eyes on, let alone had the pleasure of spending time with. And it wasn't just her long, dark hair and piercing blue eyes that seemed to see right through to your soul. No, it was who she was. Fundamentally, the soul and spirit of who Phoebe Flynn was, was stunning.

She rolled over on the mattress, her dark hair spread out over the pillow, and smiled. "Has anyone ever told you that you're a smooth talker, Dean Harrison? I mean…" She wiggled her eyebrows and laughed.

"No." He shook his head with a laugh of his own. "But I mean it. You are…" He reached out and took a strand of her hair between his fingers, twisting the silky tresses as he wrapped them around and around before letting them go again. "I just mean…" He squeezed his eyes shut for a second and tried again. "I've never met anyone like you, Phoebe. You're…well. You're just something else."

She laughed, pushed forward, and kissed him on the nose before rolling back to her side of the bed. "You don't need to whisper sweet nothings to me, Harrison. You've already got me. I mean…" She waved a finger between them. "We just… you know." She laughed again and it was both so damn cute and at the same time, completely crazy making because she didn't understand what he was trying to say.

Hell. Even he didn't understand what he was trying to say.

But he needed to try.

Dean launched himself up until he was leaning over her, caging her in with his arms. "Woman," he growled. "You are not understanding me."

"Oh, I think I'm understanding you plenty. You're just trying to—"

"Tell you how I feel," he interrupted her. "And failing miserably." He swallowed hard, but was not ready to give up. "You are the most incredible woman I've ever met, Phoebe Flynn. Every little thing I get to know about you, I think I fall for you a little bit more."

She stilled beneath him. "Fall for me?"

Had he said too much? Had he opened up more than he should?

Dean nodded.

"What do you mean?"

"You know exactly what I mean."

When she didn't respond, he knew he had to elaborate. He knew he needed to speak what was on his heart. If he didn't… well, he couldn't even think about what it would mean if Phoebe walked out of his room, away from his bed, even one more time and he hadn't laid his heart out for her. He didn't think he could bear it.

"I'm falling in love with you, Phoebe Flynn." He spoke quickly, before he could chicken out and change his mind. How was it that he could even consider facing death-defying stunts and they didn't faze him, but saying a few tiny little words reduced him to a puddle of goo? It was almost laughable. *Almost*. That was the power this woman had over him.

She blinked. Once. Twice. Finally, she spoke. "You…what?"

Dean cleared his throat and spoke again, so there could be no doubt. For either of them. "Phoebe, I'm completely falling in love with you."

It took a second. A long, painful second.

But finally, slowly, her lips curved up into a smile. "I'm falling for you, too, Dean."

He didn't need to hear another word. Dean lowered himself so his lips were on hers, kissing her softly. He braced himself with one arm and used his other to gently cup her cheek.

They kissed slowly and tenderly as their hands began an exploration of each other's bodies. They'd already spent their night wrapped up in each other's kisses and touches, but that coupling had been hot and frenzied, as it always seemed to be in their stolen moments. This was different.

He felt it deep down as he moved his lips over her flushed skin. He left kisses wherever he went, sucking and nipping until she moaned softly. He took his time until he was once more over her, kissing her and looking deep into her eyes.

They were still completely connected by their eyes alone, when he shifted his body and pressed his length inside her. Phoebe groaned on an exhale as he entered her. They stayed that way, wrapped in each other's arms as they moved slowly. They kissed and she gasped into his mouth as she grew closer to the edge. And then they were both there. Crashing. Tumbling. Gripping tight together as they rode the wave.

Chapter Eighteen

TWO DAYS LATER, Phoebe still felt like she was floating. On that first day when she'd snuck onto the set and watched Dean —the biggest superstar in the business, the most handsome, with the worst reputation—running through the boatyard, she never could have imagined that in such a short time she would be having feelings like this for him.

Feelings that were completely consuming her and making it hard to focus. She was falling in love with him.

Maybe she was already *in* love with him.

She really had no idea, because she'd never before felt this way about anyone. The boys she'd dated back home were just that. Boys. They were nice enough, and some of them she'd even developed strong feelings for. But even if the question of love came up—which it never did—nothing she'd ever felt for those guys had been even remotely close to this full-body vibration she felt throughout every inch of herself. The pull to see Dean, to talk to him, to touch him…it was almost a physical yearning in her chest, and the only way to satisfy the urge was to see him.

Was that love? The intensity and distraction and—

"Phoebe! Over here."

She blinked hard and focused on Kristen, who was waving frantically at her from across the Dockside Inn. Right. She was meeting her assistant for breakfast.

Phoebe shook her head, smiled, and went to join her at the table.

"You okay?" Kristen poured her a cup of coffee from the carafe on the table and passed her the milk. "You look..." She tipped her head and examined her.

Phoebe pretended not to notice the way the other woman was looking at her, trying to figure out what was going on.

It wasn't until Kristen finally smiled, nodded, and sat back in her seat that Phoebe gave her any mind. "It's not what you—"

"It's exactly what I think."

Phoebe sighed, stirred her coffee, and stared into the milky liquid. First Louis and Susie and now Kristen. Everyone was going to know. For a couple of actors, they weren't doing a very good job of pretending they weren't involved.

Kristen must have seen something on her face, because she leaned forward and put her hand on Phoebe's. "It's not like that, Phoebe. I didn't—"

"It's okay. You figured it out and that's on me." She shrugged. "On us, I guess." She raised her cup and took a sip of her coffee, grateful for the caffeine. "And if you've figured it out, then you're probably not alone. I wonder how many—"

"Kyle told me." Kristen blurted it out, and immediately covered her mouth with her hands. "Shit. I wasn't supposed to say anything. He'll kill me. Dean will kill him. Oh no. Please don't say anything."

Her assistant's eyes flooded with fear for the man. It was more than just an innocent colleague's concern. And in an instant, it made sense why Kyle would break his employer's confidence. *Love.*

Phoebe's lips slipped up into a broad smile. "You and Kyle."

Kristen's brown eyes widened in surprise but she didn't deny it.

Maria, free of the baby who was usually on her hip, chose that moment to appear at their table. "Buoenos dias, mi amigas."

"Good morning, Maria."

Shit. Maria knew too. Which meant Joe knew, which meant... Phoebe pushed the thought from her head and focused on the breakfast specials that Maria was relaying to her.

They both ordered fruit with toast, and Maria disappeared back to the kitchen to put in their orders. It wasn't until she left that Kristen groaned and dropped her head to the table.

"So," Phoebe tried again. "You and Kyle, huh?"

Her assistant's head nodded against the table and after a moment, she sat up again and smoothed her hair back. "We were trying to keep it quiet because of work, but..." She looked up and, in that moment, Phoebe recognized on the other woman what she'd seen in her own face in recent days. "We're in love."

"I'm so glad." She put her hands over Kristen's and squeezed. "I'm so happy for you. Kyle is so amazing and the two of you...it really is great."

"Really? You're not upset?"

Phoebe laughed. "Why would I be upset? You have a right to live your life and you should be living it with as much love as you can find." She let her own words wash over her but ultimately shook her head in dismissal. Her situation was different. Very different.

"Thank you, Phoebe. Really. And I want you to know that

me and Kyle...it's not going to affect my work for you. I'm serious about my career, and I swear to you that—"

"Kristen. It's fine. You are amazing, and I know it's not going to affect anything. I mean, it hasn't so far, right?"

She nodded and finally her own smile took over her features. "And you and...I *love* it. You two are just so...it's really good. And I really respect how you're keeping it quiet." She shook her head and her ponytail swung back and forth. "Anything I can do to help. Just let me know, okay?"

"Of course." She nodded, but then shook her head. "You know what, though? I've been thinking more and more about that. I mean, why *are* we trying to keep it so quiet? What's the point? I mean, you know."

Kristen screwed up her face and shook her head. "But Kyle told me."

That was true. And Kyle only knew because he knew everything about Dean and frankly, he'd been instrumental in all of their sneaking around. "But if he hadn't told you, would you have seen it?"

"Here you go, mi amigas." Maria dropped a plate in front of each of them. "Enjoy."

When she was gone, Phoebe asked again. "Would you have seen it?"

Immediately, Kristen shook her head, but an instant later, caught herself and shrugged. "Maybe," she admitted. "But that's only because I spend a lot of time with you. It's kind of my job to *know* you and what you need. So..."

"You would have seen it," Phoebe finished for her. "Right. Just like Louis and Susie did, too."

The more she spoke it out loud, the more it made sense to her that they should just come clean about it all.

"I know what you're thinking, Phoebe. And I have to respectfully disagree with you."

"What?"

"Don't do it, Phoebe. Do *not* tell anyone about your relationship with…" She lowered her voice and looked around. "With *him*. It's a mistake."

She was no longer sure it was.

"It *is*," Kristen insisted. "I know this business. And they won't take you seriously if they think the only reason you're successful is because of who you're sleeping with. Or worse, you'll be labeled." She looked around to see whether anyone was listening in, but everyone else in the restaurant was minding their own business. "Look at Emma Dennis and Ashlyn Bay. What do you think when you hear those names?"

Phoebe swallowed hard. She knew exactly what she thought. The same thing most of the world did.

"Exactly." Her point made, Kristen sat back in her chair and crossed her arms. "Besides, I think it's incredibly romantic that he's going to so much effort to keep it a secret, too. I mean, if he did…never mind." She shook her head, and picked up her coffee, taking a long drink.

"Kristen? What?"

"I shouldn't have said anything. It doesn't matter."

It obviously did *matter.*

"Kristen," Phoebe said pointedly. "What doesn't matter?" She focused on her until finally Kristen cracked.

"It's just that Eric mentioned that Dean's getting a lot of pressure from his manager to up his publicity quotient so he can secure the *Supers* role. And the fact that he's not going public with, well…" She waved her hand between them. "I think that's super romantic."

Phoebe couldn't help the smile that took over her face. It *was* romantic. And it had been *his* idea to keep things quiet. "Maybe you're right," she said after a minute. "We should keep it quiet for a bit longer."

Kristen picked at a piece of pineapple from her plate and popped it in her mouth with a wink. "Of course I'm right."

———

They were almost done. Only one scene stood between them and wrapping filming. Normally at this stage of a movie, Dean would start to feel a sense of melancholy settling over him. He loved filming and being on set. The camaraderie, the sense of family—all of it. But this movie was different. It had been a lot of fun to shoot, sure. And he still had all of those other things. But this time he also had something else.

Something better.

Phoebe.

He sat back against the mast of the boat and let himself watch her and Cass, the captain of the *Cassiopeia*, the gorgeous sailboat they would be using to film the last scene. The much anticipated *boat scene.*

At least Wes had been anticipating it, and probably all the crew, too. It was set to be an intense and incredibly intimate scene and definitely at the beginning of filming, when he'd first laid eyes on Phoebe, he, too, had been anticipating it. But now, Dean knew the real thing. He knew what it was like to kiss her, feel her lips on his skin and move inside her. All of which was a thousand percent better than any scene they could possibly film.

That being said, it was still going to be a pretty hot scene and any excuse to kiss Phoebe in front of others, even if it was under the pretense of acting, he'd take it.

"Dean! Check this out!" Phoebe called to him from where she stood, a rope—or a *line*, he'd been taught—in her hand. "I'm going to hoist a sail!" She laughed as her long hair flew around her face, loose from the elastic that never could quite seem to tame her locks.

She looked so happy, so free and so completely gorgeous, Dean was once again pleased that he'd insisted on traveling out to the San Blas Islands on the boat together instead of riding with the rest of the crew on the power yacht.

Phoebe had never been on a sailboat before, and was thrilled to have the opportunity. Cass and her boyfriend, Archer, ran the yacht as a whole experience and they were more than happy to show them the ropes—quite literally. Wes opted out of the trip, claiming seasickness, so it was just the two of them.

Just the way Dean liked it.

"Take my picture!"

"Really?" Dean laughed but took out his cell phone and snapped a few pictures for her.

Before he tucked it away again, he flipped to his main screen and the green bubble that suggested he had unread messages.

Bruce.

The last thing he needed to deal with was more pressure from his manager about everything, so he almost put his phone away without looking at what he had to say.

Ultimately, he pressed the button to see the text messages, and he was glad he did.

Got us a meeting!

Dean knew exactly what the meeting was. The producers of the next *Supers* movie. Bruce had been working on it for a while now. And now....*damn.* He wanted to let out a little cheer, but he held himself in check and typed back.

. . .

When?

Bruce replied immediately.

Day after tomorrow. You'll have to leave after shooting.

Dean started to type in his reply, but stopped himself. *Day after tomorrow?* That would mean he'd miss the wrap party. He looked up and once again got lost in watching Phoebe. Maybe it was for the best that he miss the party, anyway. That way, Phoebe could enjoy her first big wrap-up, and have the spotlight all to herself. Which was well deserved, because the woman was a star. She needed to have this moment, where she could just soak it all in. Besides, Dean wasn't sure he would be able to get through an entire night of pretending it was no big deal for him to be in the same room with her when he couldn't kiss her.

He let out a slow breath as Phoebe successfully finished hoisting the sail and let out a whoop of excitement as the boat caught the air. His groin tightened in response to her. She was the sexiest woman in the world as far as he was concerned, but when she was laughing and smiling, she was simply electric with energy and he could not take his eyes off her. Not for anything.

"Isn't this amazing?" she yelled out, and held her hands up to the sky.

It was amazing, all right. Amazing that he'd been lucky enough to have her come into his life. It hadn't been very long, and he was definitely not the type of guy to rush into things. Not usually. But...*damn.*

"Dean! Look!" He looked to where Phoebe pointed. "Dolphins! Come see!"

He didn't need to be asked twice. Quickly, he typed his reply to Bruce.

I'll be there. Send me details.

The message sent, he tucked his phone away and went to join the woman he was very quickly losing himself to.

Chapter Nineteen

THE BOAT HAD BEEN ANCHORED in a quiet bay next to a deserted island in the San Blas Islands. It reminded Phoebe of *their* island. Of course, almost all of the islands they'd sailed past on their way to their destination had reminded her of *their* island. Seeing the area from above in a helicopter had been stunning, but seeing it from the water had completely taken her breath away in a new and different way.

The opportunity hadn't been wasted on her. Phoebe had enjoyed every moment. Fortunately, Cass and Archer had been immensely patient with her because she'd insisted on learning as much as she could. Hoisting the sails had been fun, but when Archer had let her stand at the helm and steer the boat, that had been a highlight. She couldn't believe she'd never been on a sailboat before. It might have been her first time, but it was definitely not going to be her last.

It had been a fun trip, but now that the sun was starting to go down, it was time to get set up for the shoot. The crew had been brought over on motor yachts, which was where Phoebe had gone for wardrobe and makeup. Upon her return, there were definitely more people on board the yacht, with camera operators, lights, and production assistants running around setting things up. But as promised, it was a skeleton crew. A fact Phoebe was thankful for because it was to be her first, fully nude scene.

First.

Would there be more?

She'd taken the role of Misty Falls more for Kate than herself, it was true, and she had no real intention of pursuing acting as a career. Not really. But…her feelings on that subject were changing. Or more accurately, they *had* changed. If Lorilee asked her now—which she was sure to be doing—she would definitely entertain other movies.

But first things first. She had to get through her first nude scene.

"Ready, Phoebe?" Wes put his hand on her shoulder. "You're not nervous, are you?"

"Absolutely not." She opened her eyes wide, and the director laughed.

"You have nothing to be worried about. You'll be great."

"She will." Dean appeared next to them and smiled at her. "You're a natural, Phoebe. I know it can be intimidating to… well." He laughed. "I guess I don't actually know since I've never done a fully nude scene."

"Would you like me to have the scene rewritten?" Wes raised his eyebrow but Dean just rolled his eyes.

"Are we ready to do this?"

Phoebe nodded at Dean's question. They all moved into position, got some last-minute instruction from Wes, and then it was time.

As she always did, Phoebe took a moment to close her eyes and channel Misty Falls. When she opened her eyes, she was ready.

"Action!"

The moon was full, reflecting off the calm water and illuminating the deck of the boat just enough to cast Phoebe as a silhouette as she slowly walked the length of the yacht. As she moved, she slowly worked the buttons that ran down the front of her dress. Max Silver stood silently against the mast, hidden to Misty Falls, who thought she was alone on the boat. Or did she? When she reached her mark, the buttons were all undone. With her back to him, Phoebe shimmied the dress from her shoulders and down over her hips, until it puddled to the floor.

It was a hot night, as most of the nights in Panama were, but as the breeze flowed across her bare skin, Phoebe shivered a little. Was it the breeze, or the knowledge that she was completely naked, being filmed for millions of people to watch?

She wouldn't let herself think about it.

Still in Misty's persona, Phoebe raised her arms above her head, tipping her head back. As she did so, her hair fell seductively down her back. Slowly, she lowered her hands and let them trail down her body. Her fingers traced the gentle swell of her breasts and dipped in at her waist, before she spread her fingers over the cheeks of her ass and then slowly, continuing the seductive dance with herself, she let her hands circle to her front.

Her back still to him, Phoebe started to move her hips in a silent dance. She kept her breathing slow and measured. She wouldn't break character. She wouldn't.

But she couldn't help but imagine Dean's reaction to watching the scene play out. Was he enjoying what he was seeing?

She knew damn well he was.

Three…two…one. She completed the mental countdown in her head before straightening up to her full height and speaking. "Like what you see, Silver?"

He didn't move at first, but then, slowly, Dean stepped from the shadows.

Their characters had been playing a cat-and-mouse game through the entire movie. The striptease had been a turning point, but this scene meant finally they'd come together. Even if their motives weren't pure.

Completely unlike in real life. Which was why Phoebe would have to rely even more on the acting skills she'd recently developed.

Dean nodded slowly as his eyes roamed her body in the half light.

Damn. There was a reason Dean Harrison had women falling all over him. He was straight up sexy. It was the tiniest of gestures, but Phoebe felt her entire body come alive under his watchful gaze.

It's not real. This is not real.

But dammed if it didn't feel real.

Dean had starred in almost eight feature films by this point in his career. He'd been in all types of dangerous situations. There had been times he would cry on demand, blow up in anger at some of the in-real-life-nicest people, kiss countless women, and perform dozens of sex scenes.

Arguably, he'd had much harder acting challenges.

But watching Phoebe, completely naked, standing in the moonlight, shimmy her hips and run her hands over her delicious body, was without a doubt the hardest thing he'd ever done in his career.

By. Far.

His mind raced in an effort to stay in character. This moment wasn't about Dean and Phoebe. It was about Max and Misty. He was a professional. He could do it. And the sooner he got it over with, the sooner they could wrap and—

"Like what you see, Silver?"

Focus!

He blinked and put himself into Max Silver's head. On cue, he stepped forward and with Max's signature smoldering gaze, let his eyes travel down every single inch of her glorious body.

Phoebe tilted her head and with a disinterested flick of her hair, she turned to face forward again.

The woman *was* good.

Misty Falls was playing hard to get.

Misty Falls was completely uninterested.

But Dean knew the truth. No matter how good of an actress Phoebe Flynn was, *he* knew that she wanted him just as badly as he wanted her. It was that private knowledge that fueled him.

Dean moved with his Max Silver swagger across the deck until he stood directly behind Phoebe. Close enough that he knew she'd be able to feel the heat from him, but not close enough to touch. Yet.

"I do like what I see." He spoke low and slow. "But I'm going to like this a fuck of a lot better."

She gasped a little when a moment later, he grabbed her hair, and in a quick move that was a lot gentler than it would look on screen, tugged her head to the side to expose her throat.

Still, without his body touching hers, he bent and slowly sucked her earlobe between his lips. She moaned again, and for a second Dean couldn't be sure whether that moan had been scripted or not.

He continued to work his mouth on her earlobe and the sensitive skin behind it before moving his kiss down her neck. Unlike Dean, Max Silver was a greedy lover, taking what he wanted, how he wanted, with very little care or concern for his partner. That was a detail that, through the magic of Hollywood, ended up coming off as intense, brooding, and incredibly desirable to almost every woman in America. And likely some men, too. Dean had never understood it considering he personally took pleasure by giving it. Especially with Phoebe.

His kisses grew more intense, more demanding and finally, Dean moved the half inch forward until the length of his fully clothed body was pressed up roughly against her soft, naked one.

She pressed back into him, only for a moment, with a totally unscripted move that immediately made him hard.

Focus, Dean.

His left hand still twisted in her hair, Dean's right hand came up to cup and squeeze one full breast. She groaned again, but only a little. Misty Falls was a strong character and she was working hard not to take control of the situation. It was a lost cause. Max Silver always got what he wanted. And in this particular case, what Max wanted was to take her right there on the deck of the boat with nothing but the tropical moonlight as cover.

And he'd get it.

As a brand-new actress, Phoebe obviously had never done a sex scene before, let alone one as vulnerable as this one was written. There were camera operators all over, strategically placed so they could shoot from all angles, meaning Phoebe's naked body was exposed at all times.

He unwound his hand from her hair and slipped it down her body roughly while his mouth worked the sensitive skin at her collarbone. She'd likely end up with a bruise from his attentions, and the idea of it thrilled him a little bit.

Still, he had to force himself to distance Dean from the actions of Max as he slipped his hand around her and between her legs.

It was his turn to gasp when his fingers connected with the wetness he found there. It wasn't unusual for actors to get turned on during a scene. After all, people were just people. But this was different. Very different.

Right on cue, Phoebe's knees buckled a little bit as he focused his attentions on her before he spun her around and kissed her hard.

"And…cut!"

Breathe. Breathe.

Phoebe used the scene break to drink a bottle of water, and take a breath. And then another. And another.

Fortunately, by some kind of freaking miracle, Wes was thrilled with that take and didn't need another. Thank goodness. Phoebe wasn't sure she'd be able to do it again. Hell, she wasn't completely sure she'd be able to make it through the next shot.

Because this time they'd be—no. She mentally corrected herself. *They* would not be making love. Misty and Max would be. And it wasn't *making love*. Not even close. What Max and Misty were about to do was much more carnal than what Phoebe and Dean experienced together. They had a connection. A closeness. There were feelings there. Real feelings.

Max and Misty—even if they were real people—were all about sex. Sure, it was hot and steamy. But it was about power and control. There was nothing intimate about it. Nothing *real.*

That's how Phoebe needed to keep thinking about it. It would be the only way she would be able to get through the rest of this.

"Okay, Phoebe?" Wes approached.

She nodded and took another sip from her water bottle. "Absolutely."

"I know these scenes can be a little…well, a little intimidating, I guess. But you're knocking it out of the park. Really, you and Dean have amazing chemistry. I can't remember the last time I was able to get away with one take in a scene like this." He nodded appreciatively. "Great work. I mean it. Really great work."

"Thanks." She couldn't help but smile with the compliment.

"Okay." He nodded abruptly and turned to his production assistant, who gave him a thumbs-up. "Looks like Dean's all set. Ready when you are, Phoebe."

She screwed the top back on the bottle and nodded. "Let's do it."

This time, the scene would start with them already together. It was a cutaway from standing on the deck, her naked and Dean fully clothed, to the next shot where they would actually be *coupled*.

Phoebe followed the assistant to where Dean was lying on his back, propped up on his elbows and completely naked. She did a double take, and almost laughed. He wasn't completely naked but had a skin-toned brief on. She bit her lip and grinned.

"Cute, right?"

Phoebe couldn't help it. She burst out laughing. "I don't know if cute is the word I'd use."

"Okay, Phoebe." Wes nodded to her. The signal it was time to go.

She looked directly at Dean when she dropped the robe she'd been using to the floor, which meant she didn't miss the way his nostrils flared and his pupils dilated at the sight of her. It was a small, silly thing, but it gave her the boost she needed.

She winked and wiggled her eyebrows before taking her position. On top of him.

"I'm not sure it's entirely fair that I'm naked, and you're not."

Dean grinned and put his hands on her hips, holding her in place. "Oh, I think it's plenty fair."

Beneath her, despite the tiny brief he wore, Phoebe could feel exactly what Dean thought about her lack of clothes. And the fact that she was straddling him in a position not unlike one they'd been in a few days earlier. For real.

"In five…"

Someone hollered, putting her back into the moment. She needed to focus.

"Four…"

She squeezed her eyes shut and took a deep breath.

"Three.."

She exhaled completely.

"Two…"

Her eyes opened.

"And…action!"

Right on cue, Phoebe threw her head back and moaned. Beneath her, Dean used his hands to guide her hips and imitate the motions. His hands were all over her, sliding over her breasts, her stomach, on her hips. As it always did, his touch felt positively electric. Still, she worked to stay in character.

For Misty, this was about power and control. She was on top. She was in control.

She lifted her head and let her hands slide under her thick, dark hair so she could pile it up on her head before letting it spill over her shoulders again. She moaned again and swiveled her hips on top of him.

Dean sat up a little and pulled her closer to him. This was about the control Max Silver needed to exert. Dean played it perfectly by looking in her eyes. "Not until I say so."

Presumably by this point in the scene, Misty Falls was to be too close to her climax to argue. She wanted it. She wanted him. And her need for control was quickly slipping away.

Phoebe bit her bottom lip and let Dean rock her in the

motion that, under any other circumstances, would have her very quickly approaching orgasm. Was it believable with Dean's arms holding her tight against him? Hell yes, it was.

Right on cue, Phoebe let out her *release*, and cried out in the night. She gave it a moment, counting to three in her head, before she lifted her head again to look into Dean's eyes.

His voice was low, barely controlled when he said his line: "I didn't say so." And then his lips crushed hers in a kiss that was possessive and hot and completely unscripted.

"Cut!"

It was after midnight by the time they were done with the shoot, and Dean was exhausted. It wasn't that it had been a particularly strenuous shoot, especially not compared to what he *had* done in the past. But he had completely underestimated how hard it would be to *pretend* to be with Phoebe and not actually be with her.

Never, in any of the sex scenes he'd ever done, had he felt even remotely like that. To say it had been exhausting to stay in character was a massive understatement.

"Good work tonight, Harrison."

Dean ran his hands through his hair as he turned around. He was aware that he likely looked as worn out as he felt.

Wes noticed it, too. "You look beat." He shook his head. "It wasn't that intense of a day," he continued. "Did you two get too much sun on your way over?"

He didn't say anything directly, and there wasn't any indication in his tone of voice, but still, Dean couldn't help but think that there was more to Wes's question than he was letting on.

"It was a fun day," was all he said. "Did some sailing, and

Archer and Cass showed us a few things on the boat. I think Phoebe really enjoyed it."

"Oh, I think she did, too." Wes gazed out over the edge of the sailboat to where three motor yachts were anchored. One was Dean's chartered boat; the other two were for the rest of the cast and crew. He'd thought about inviting Phoebe and some of the others to use one of his empty staterooms, but ultimately he'd decided it would be too tempting. So instead he'd pulled the diva movie star card and wasn't sharing.

They stood in silence for a few moments, both men with their hands on the brass rail, looking out to sea, before Wes spoke again the way Dean knew he would. "You went off script today."

Dean nodded. He knew the director would bring it up.

"I've gone off before. It's never been a problem before."

"I didn't say it was a problem."

"Didn't you?"

It was Wes who broke first and turned to face him. "No," he said plainly. "I didn't. Do you think it is?"

Dean shook his head once. "Only if you do. But you wrapped it."

He knew he'd been taking a risk kissing Phoebe the way he had at the end of the scene. And even though he could have ruined the entire thing and could have potentially had to reshoot—which would have been far more torturous—he couldn't *not* do it. It had felt right and for more than one reason. The least of which had been that he thought it fit the scene.

"I wrapped it because it worked." Wes chuckled. "Damn, Harrison. That scene was fire. *All* of your scenes together are fire."

Finally, there was something in Wes's voice that made Dean turn and face him. "Of course it was."

He should just shut his mouth and agree with the man; he

knew that. Dammit, he *knew* that. But something was making Dean defensive and protective, even. Which would be exactly why Wes was going to figure out that something was going on. He wasn't stupid. Still. Dean couldn't seem to stop himself.

"Of course?"

"All my scenes are fire, Wes." Dean smiled in what he hoped came off as cocky and nonchalant. "Especially the love scenes."

"Love scenes, huh?"

Shit.

"I've worked on how many films with you? Eight? They've always been sex scenes, Harrison. *Always.*"

Dean shrugged. "Same thing."

"You know it's not."

Dean swallowed and stared at the other man who'd become his friend over the years. Hell, he might even consider Wes a good friend. Could he trust him?

"You know what I think?" Wes asked.

"I couldn't possibly."

Wes turned again and placed both hands on the rail. He let out a long sigh. "I think there's a damn good reason the two of you light things up on screen." He nodded to himself and turned his head. "The two of you are—"

"I'm going to stop you right there." Dean held up a finger. "I'll tell you the same thing I've been telling Bruce. I absolutely refuse to have another public relationship that's nothing more than a publicity machine. It's not happening again. Not with Phoebe and not with anyone else. Ever."

He meant that last part, mostly because he couldn't imagine himself with anyone else but Phoebe. Not ever. She was it for him. He knew that in his soul. She was his person.

Which was why he was going to do his best to protect her from the media shitstorm that would inevitably happen if news about them got out. Friend or not, he couldn't tell Wes.

"Right." Wes nodded slowly, but Dean could tell he wasn't buying it. His next words confirmed it and made Dean's stomach roll. "But you didn't say you weren't with her. Just that it wasn't going to be public."

He had two choices. He could protest further, concreting what Wes already thought he knew. Or he could just walk away.

He chose the latter.

"It's late, Wes. Have a good night." He slapped his hands on the brass rail and turned to go in search of Kyle, who should have his tender ready to take him back to his yacht. Alone.

Chapter Twenty

HER TIME in Panama had gone so quickly. Three months had flown by, and Phoebe could hardly believe it was almost time to go home. At the same time, she felt like a completely different person than when she'd arrived. It felt like a million years ago that she'd watched Dean run through the boatyard with butterflies in her tummy. It was still hard to breathe around him, but for completely different reasons.

She smiled to herself and did a little dance around her room as she packed up her bags. She'd catch a flight in the morning that would take her back to Montana and her family. She was desperate to go. But at the same time, she wasn't in a hurry to end her time with Dean. Not even close. Even though it was ending all on its own.

The only downside of her last night in Panama, and the big wrap party that was sure to be an excellent time, was that Dean wasn't going to be there. He'd texted her earlier that morning to let her know he had an important meeting in LA and he'd have to leave. He promised to come by and say goodbye to her before he left.

As if she'd summoned him, there was a knock on the door of her room. He was early. Not that it mattered.

She all but skipped to the door and flung it open with a flourish. "I didn't expect you—Layla?"

The other woman raised her eyebrows in question. "Were you expecting someone else?"

"Yes." She shook her head. "I mean, no. I mean…hi. What's up?"

Layla gave her a look, but she laughed and pushed past her into her room, where she flopped on her bed and leaned back on her elbows. "I wanted to see what you were wearing to the party tonight."

Phoebe closed the door, and turned to give Layla a questioning look. It seemed a little out of character. No. It seemed *a lot* out of character for the stunt double, particularly because the friendship they'd developed early on in shooting had turned a little sour as of late.

"What?" Layla protested. "I was just wondering because it's your first big wrap party and you're the star and all. You want to look sexy."

Phoebe caught an edge to the other woman's voice, but she let it go. She'd long suspected that Layla was a little bit bitter toward actresses. When they'd first met, she'd been sweet and easygoing, and she largely still was. But as Phoebe had gotten to know Layla a bit better, she'd caught the edginess more and more. She wouldn't be surprised if Layla had started out in the industry working her ass off, with the goal to land the very same type of role that Phoebe had just fallen into. There could definitely be a little bitterness there. Either way, Phoebe had met enough women like Layla in the past to be wary of the shift in her personality.

"Okay," Layla continued. "Truth time."

Phoebe turned, with a stack of T-shirts in her hand, and narrowed her eyes in question.

Layla only shrugged. "Sometimes I get a little sad at the end of a shoot. It's like we've become a family, spending all our time together and then...gone. I was just trying to spend a bit of time with you before we go."

It still didn't make sense to Phoebe, but maybe Layla had felt a closer connection between them than she had. It was likely. After all, she and Mason and Eric had invited her on that trip to Bocas del Toro when they were all getting settled. Maybe Layla had considered their friendship to be a closer one?

Phoebe smiled and tucked her shirts into a duffel bag before joining Layla on the bed. "That's sweet," she said, making a decision to trust the other woman's intentions. "It is going to be strange to leave after all this. I didn't really know what to expect," she continued. "But it has been a little like a family. We've all gotten so close."

Layla sat up and grabbed Phoebe's hand. "Some closer than others, right?" Her nostrils flared a little, and once again, Phoebe's radar went up. "I mean, you and Dean. How do you *not* get close after shooting some of the scenes you have, right?"

Phoebe worked hard to control her breathing. The best thing about getting away from set would be to get away from the constant stream of questioning and defending herself against relationship allegations.

Allegations that were completely based in truth. But still.

It was no one else's business who she was dating, and the longer this questioning went on, the angrier she got with the status quo that had been set for celebrities. Did it really matter who anyone was dating?

She worked to keep her voice even. "It's called acting, Layla."

"But you guys spend so much time together."

Phoebe laughed, and hoped it sounded authentic. "Because

we shoot a lot of scenes together and we're friends." She pulled away from Layla's grip and walked to the other end of the room. "Don't read any more into it then there is. We're just friends."

Behind her, Layla made a grunting noise. "You can't fool me."

Phoebe knew the other woman was reaching. She wasn't going to fall for it or take her bait. She shrugged but didn't turn around.

"Dean *always* hooks up with his costars, Pheebs. We told you that when you first got here. It's not a secret."

It *was* a secret. And it was going to stay that way, no matter what Layla tried to get out of her.

"I don't know what to tell you, Layla." Finally, Phoebe turned around and shrugged in a way that she hoped was nonchalant. "I mean, this is all getting kind of old, and I'm sure you were hoping for some more gossip, but there's nothing going on between Dean and me. And," she added before Layla could interject, "I really don't give a shit what Dean's done with his other costars. Because *I* am not them." She couldn't seem to keep the edge of anger from her voice, and she no longer cared. Phoebe was done with playing the role of nice, sweet and naive, newbie actress from the sticks.

Screw that.

"Look, Phoebe. I'm not trying to—"

"Yes you are. And I'm done with it." She pointed a finger at the other woman. "What Dean and I do or don't do is none of your business, or anyone else's."

She realized her mistake as soon as it came out of her mouth.

Shit.

Layla's mouth twisted up into a smile that was anything but friendly.

"Not that there's anything going on," Phoebe added quickly. "But if there was—"

"Oh, I think I understand." She stood from the bed and straightened her shirt. "I understand better than you think I do." She moved across the room to leave. "Oh, and one more thing. Whether you admit it or not, there's a reason Dean has the reputation he does. I know that you're *new*." Her emphasis on the word was biting. "But you should know that pretty much nothing is what it seems in this industry, and whatever you think is happening, it's not. Everyone has an agenda." Layla opened the door to her room to see Dean standing there with his fist raised to knock.

Layla sneered, an unattractive snort coming from her before she turned and once again said to Phoebe, *"Everyone."*

Dean stepped aside to let Layla pass him out into the hallway. He watched her go and looked through the door to Phoebe. "What was that about?"

She opened her mouth as though she were going to say something, but shut it again and turned away. "It was nothing. She was just wondering what I was wearing to the party tonight." Phoebe looked at him again.

There was no indication on her face that she was lying. And why would she? But Dean couldn't shake the feeling that something else had happened. And knowing Layla the way he did, he wouldn't have been surprised. Still, if Phoebe didn't want to say anything, he wasn't going to push. Especially because he planned to enjoy every single moment with her before he had to leave. No way was he going to let Layla cloud it in any way.

He stepped into the room. "I am really sorry I can't be there tonight," he said as he crossed the room to her. He'd purposely left the door open. No doubt Layla was already running around telling anyone she could that he was just seen going into Phoebe Flynn's room. Alone. The bullshit was starting to wear on him. He'd be so glad when it was over. "But I am really looking forward to after."

"After?"

Dean grinned. "I know you're excited to go home and see your sister and family. But then I was hoping…" He hadn't told her of his plans. Or that he'd rented a little cabin on the coast of Washington, where they could be alone and out of the spotlight. "Will you go away with me for a little bit? Nowhere crazy," he added quickly. "I know you'll want to be close to your sister just in case she needs you, and we won't go for long, but just for—"

"Yes." She laughed. "I would love that. But you promise it's far away from people who want to stick their noses into our business?"

"As much as possible." He stuck a hand over his heart. "I swear, we will have complete privacy."

Some of the stiffness in her shoulders released. "That sounds amazing. As long as Kate's doing well, I'm all in."

"Good." He dared to walk closer to her. More than anything, he wanted to pull her to him and kiss her hard enough that his touch would stay with her until they could be together again. But he was also painfully aware that someone could walk in at any moment. He stood close enough to touch her and reached out his fingers to brush her arm.

To hell with it.

Before he could talk himself out of it, Dean reached forward and pulled her in for a quick but passionate kiss.

When he released her, she laughed. "Bit of a risk taker, are you, Harrison?"

"For you? I'd risk everything."

The sun was just starting to dip below the horizon as Dean and Kyle lifted off from the helipad behind the marina, headed to Panama City, where they would catch the plane to take them to LA.

"Sorry you had to miss the party, Kyle. If anyone deserves a night to cut loose, it's you." Dean spoke into the headset while they gazed out the window as the ground got smaller and farther away.

"It's not a problem," Kyle said. "Besides, I'll get a little holiday myself when you and Phoebe go to the coast. I'm not worried."

"You're a good man, Kyle. I've already spoken to Bruce about a raise. You more than deserve it. Thank you."

Kyle's mouth dropped open, but he recovered quickly and grinned. "I appreciate it, Dean. I really do."

He nodded his acceptance and thinking of Bruce, Dean pulled out his phone and fired off a quick text.

In the chopper. At the plane in ten.

As always, Bruce's response came in almost immediately.

Everything's on time. You should land in LA by breakfast. Then we'll head to the meeting.

It sounded exhausting. But hopefully he'd be able to sleep on the plane. There hadn't been time to secure a private charter, so he was flying commercial, which he didn't usually mind. It was a night flight, so hopefully he wouldn't be recognized and could sleep the whole way.

Good work, by the way. Producers will love it.

Dean rubbed his eyes, already exhausted. He *had* done a good job on the film, especially the stunt that had secured them this meeting. Not that it was normal for Bruce to notice or even acknowledge it. No doubt his manager was just excited they'd landed the *Supers* meeting and the role that should follow.

He shook his head and tucked his phone away.

It wasn't until an hour later, when he was safely seated in the first-class section of the airplane with Kyle next to him, and a beer in his hand, that he pulled out his phone again. This time to text Phoebe. She was no doubt already at the wrap party and he didn't expect her to answer it, but he still wanted her to know that he was thinking of her.

Have a great time tonight. Can't wait to see you.

He smiled at the thought of her all dressed up, looking sexy and soaking up every minute of her special night. Just the way she should be.

"Oh my God! Is that...it *is*!"

Travelers had started to file onto the plane, and just as he'd hoped they wouldn't, they'd started to recognize him. He'd been distracted. Normally, he kept his head down, his eyes adverted during the boarding process.

Shit.

Kyle discreetly handed him a ball cap and he tugged it into place, but the damage had been done.

"Dean Harrison."

"He just finished the Max Silver movie."

The whispers began.

"Who's his costar?"

"The one he's sleeping with?"

Dean worked hard not to react. It wouldn't serve anyone if he blew up at total strangers. Even if they were talking about him as if he wasn't sitting right there. If he said anything to defend himself, he'd give himself up and he'd never have a peaceful flight. Besides, he'd learned long ago that people were going to think what they wanted to and they were going to say what they wanted to, and there wasn't much he could do about it.

"I wonder where she is? Maybe it was just a hookup?"

"Did you see the pictures? It sure looked like a hookup."

Pictures? Ice ran down his spine and his beer soured in his stomach. *What pictures?*

Once more, he pulled out his phone. This time to text Kyle, but his assistant was already on it.

I'm looking now.

Dean focused on his breathing. He had to stay calm. It was probably nothing. Maybe some pictures of him and Phoebe on set had been leaked and were being sold as truth to fuel the fires of the rumor mill. That was probably it.

But in his gut, Dean knew that was definitely not it. He inhaled and closed his eyes, waiting for Kyle to text him that it was nothing. But Kyle didn't text. He spoke aloud.

"Shit."

His efforts at keeping a low profile forgotten, Dean jerked his head up and looked over to his assistant. Fortunately, the busybody women who'd been discussing him had moved on and taken their seats, and the people who were currently boarding didn't seem too concerned about who he might be.

"What do you mean, shit?" He spoke through gritted teeth.

Kyle handed him his phone. "This."

No.

Dean thought he might be sick. They weren't leaked pictures from the set. Not even close. The pictures he was looking at on the *Celeb* website, pictures that had already been viewed millions of times, showed quite clearly Dean and Phoebe wrapped in each other's arms on the beach of *their* island. There were some fairly innocent shots of them walking along the beach and playing volleyball. But those weren't the ones that were the problems and were certainly not the pictures that were causing the fuss. The photographer had also managed to catch them in an embrace in the ocean. They were kissing, and despite the distance the photo was taken from, it was very obviously both Dean and Phoebe. But it was the last picture that stirred up the most trouble: the one where they were tangled in each other's arms, completely naked, lying on the daybed. Dean was behind her, holding her tight and—*shit.* Someone had caught them in a very intimate moment. And although you couldn't tell for sure that's what was going on in the photo, it wasn't a reach to figure it out.

"What. The. Actual. Fuck, Kyle?" Dean threw the phone back at his assistant, who was shaking his head. "Who did this?" He was only barely controlling his voice. It wouldn't be long before he lost his temper entirely. "I need answers. Now."

"I'm working on it, Dean. I'm on it." And he was. Next to him, Kyle had pulled his laptop out and was already furiously typing away while simultaneously dealing with someone on his phone. He'd get to the bottom of it.

But Dean wasn't about to wait around for those answers. He knew someone who'd have them. He gritted his teeth as he pushed the button on his phone that would dial Bruce's number.

Chapter Twenty-One

"YOU LOOK AMAZING, PHOEBE." Kristen smiled and handed her a glass of champagne. "That dress is...wow."

It was *wow* and it was also not at all what she'd normally wear, but Kate had thrown it in her suitcase months ago along with the green dress she'd worn out dancing. *Just in case.* And with all of her usual choices all of a sudden feeling a little too tame, and ordinary, the black, backless sheath dress that clung to every one of her curves was the perfect choice. She felt sexy and special. Just the way all those months ago when shooting had started, she thought she was *supposed* to feel as the female star, and didn't.

It had taken awhile, but she finally got it now. She felt like a star. Well, maybe that was still a stretch. It was one thing to celebrate the wrap of a movie and another thing entirely to be a movie star. Baby steps.

Phoebe held her flute of champagne to her assistant, who'd become more like a friend, and they clinked glasses.

"You clean up pretty well yourself." Kristen looked radiant in a blue and green knee-length dress. Her hair was loose from her trademarked ponytail, and her smile was positively contagious. "I'm sorry Kyle couldn't be here. Will you guys see each other soon?"

Her smile dipped a little, but it was back in place a second later. "I'll join him in LA in a few days. I know it's going to be hard, given our professions, but we'll make it work. I have a lot more flexibility since I'm freelance. He works exclusively with Dean."

Phoebe took a sip of her champagne and for a moment, as the bubbles burst in her mouth, she let herself dream about a moment where she might be a big enough celebrity to warrant her own personal assistant, and not just one assigned for the filming. She almost laughed because she couldn't imagine a situation that would *ever* warrant such extravagance. She was only just getting used to the idea of fame and starting to get comfortable with what it might mean for her when the movie was finally released. But in reality, she was still light-years away from any actual fame. She was still a nobody. And for the time being, she was totally okay with it.

"I thought you knew." From the moment he'd picked up the phone and heard the venom in Dean's voice, Bruce had been talking faster than he usually did, trying to calm Dean before he erupted.

As far as Dean was concerned, there was no chance of it *not* happening.

"How would I know, Bruce?" He spoke through gritted teeth. "How could I possibly know that my private business had been sold to the tabloids? And the bigger question is *who* did it?"

"Dean." There was an edge of laughter in his voice that was starting to piss Dean off. "Deano," he tried again. "What do you mean, *how could you know*? You're fucking Dean Harrison, that's how you know your personal business is everyone's business. It comes with the territory, so don't act so goddamned surprised. And you know we've all been waiting for you and Phoebe to hook up anyway. Everyone has."

"No." He shook his head and tried to take a deep breath. Next to him, Kyle was almost yelling into the phone to someone about getting the photos removed. Dean knew from experience it wasn't likely to happen. He also knew that whoever had taken those photos likely had made a lot of money. The idea of some asshole profiting off his personal life in such a personal way pissed him off. But Phoebe...

Dean's stomach turned.

Oh shit. Phoebe.

In his ear, Bruce was still talking. "Look, I thought you knew that the added publicity was the reason we nailed down the meeting, Dean. Everyone wants a publicity machine on their side. The more eyeballs you get on those magazines, the more clicks you generate on websites, it's all money in the bank for the studio. They don't want a nobody. They want Dean *fucking* Harrison, and now they're going to get him. You will be the next *Super*, Deano. Do you know how huge that is? It's freakin' categorically huge!"

"When did you know?" Dean took a breath and forced himself to keep his voice even. "About the pictures, I mean?"

There was a slight pause. "I found out when you did. Maybe a few minutes before you called."

It was a lie.

"Bruce, I—"

"Flight attendants, prepare for departure." The crackling voice over the intercom of the airplane interrupted.

No.

Without another word, Dean disconnected the call and reached up to jab the call button at the same moment he stood up. "I need to get off the plane."

"Sir." The flight attendant ran down the aisle toward him, her hand outstretched as if she were going to physically stop him.

Nothing would stop him.

"I need you to sit down, sir. We're getting ready for departure."

"No." Next to him, Kyle had already tucked his laptop into his bag and was also standing, ready to go with Dean. "We need to get off the plane," Kyle said. "It's an emergency." His voice was calm and in control, the exact opposite of Dean, who was having trouble breathing. He needed to get to Phoebe. He needed to talk to her before she saw the pictures. He needed her to understand that it wasn't him. He didn't do this. He would *never* do this.

He also knew exactly how it looked.

Shit.

"I'm afraid that isn't possible." The flight attendant had placed herself between them and their exit. "There's nothing I can do. We're already—"

"I don't think you understand, miss." Kyle maintained his calm disposition, but there was no denying the firmness in his request. "It's not optional. We *need* to get off the plane."

She'd had too much champagne. It was going straight to her head. But still, Phoebe sipped at the glass in her hand as she moved her body on the dance floor. It had been a fun night. She couldn't remember the last time she'd laughed so much, or danced so much. Well, with the exception of hanging out with Dean at the club. But that was different. Just the thought of Dean and the little getaway they were going to have together made her feel warm and fuzzy inside.

Or maybe it was the champagne. Either way, she felt great.

"I think I might need a glass of water," she said with a laugh to Kristen, who was dancing next to her.

"No problem. I'll—"

"You'll do no such thing!" Phoebe put a hand on Kristen's shoulder. "And that's not what I meant. You're not working." She grinned and put the half-full glass of champagne on a table behind her. "I'll be right back."

Phoebe weaved her way through the crowd toward the bar. Faces blurred together between people she recognized, along with behind-the-scenes crew she didn't remember ever seeing before. So many people.

They all seemed to know her, though. Most smiled, some said hi, and some even whistled as she walked by. That was strange.

She'd definitely had too much champagne.

Finally at the bar, she squeezed herself between two people and waved to get the attention of the bartender, who was run off his feet trying to keep up with the heavy drinkers. "Just a water please."

"Water?" It was Mason she'd pushed in next to at the bar. He'd turned and loomed over her with his muscular frame. "It's a party, Pheebs. You're not supposed to order *water*," he teased.

She'd always liked his playful attitude, so in contradiction to his muscleman look.

Phoebe giggled a little. *Yup. Definitely too much champagne.* "I think I've had my fair share of alcohol for one night. But you're right." She turned to face the bartender who'd appeared at their end of the bar. "How about some sparkling water?"

"Living on the edge, Pheebs." Mason laughed, but as soon as Phoebe was handed her glass, he toasted her. "It's been a pleasure working with you. You are a true star." His smile was warm as they clinked glasses.

"Thank you, Mason. That means a—"

"Phoebe Flynn!" Layla sidled up to them then, followed by Eric, who looked a little shell-shocked. He stood behind Layla, his handsome face twisted into a frown as he kept an eye on his friend. "You little minx." She smacked Phoebe's arm in what was no doubt supposed to look like a friendly gesture, but there was something in the other woman's eyes that Phoebe didn't trust.

"What are you talking about?"

"Keeping the Max Silver reputation alive and well. Our girl here is no fool. She clearly knows how to get ahead in this industry, and it's all about whose bed she's in." She glanced at Mason and Eric to bring them into the conversation, but neither man looked as if they had any idea what she was talking about.

Phoebe's stomach turned, but it wasn't the alcohol in her system. There was no way Layla could possibly know the truth. She was fishing. She was still trying to get her to admit to something so she'd get her juicy gossip. Phoebe wasn't going to fall for it. It didn't matter how much champagne she'd had. And she definitely wasn't going to let this bitter woman ruin her evening.

"I told you before, Layla. You're totally on the wrong track. I'm not—"

"Sleeping with Dean Harrison?"

Mason and Eric both shot looks between the two women.

"I'm not."

Layla ignored her objections. "You do know that Dean sleeps with *all* of his costars, right? You're not special." There was venom in her voice. "But then again, you already know that. And you know that all of those women—Emma, Ashlyn, Jess—they all became big stars, too. Right?"

"Layla, I don't think—"

"Of course you don't, Mason," she hissed at him. "You don't think at all. But you're not paid to think."

"Damn, Layla." Eric jumped in. "What the hell?"

"Oh, don't pretend that you didn't know, Eric. You knew about it, too. Because why else wouldn't Phoebe be interested in you? I mean, when she can have the real thing, and not just the *double*." She rolled her eyes and focused back on Phoebe, who was rapidly losing her patience with this jaded, angry woman she'd once been naive enough to call a friend. "And if you can have the real thing *and* be a big star, why wouldn't you?"

"Enough, Layla." Phoebe worked to take back control of the situation. They were starting to attract a bit of a crowd. People who were no doubt all hungry to catch a little gossip to end their experience on set with. "There's nothing going on and I don't appreciate—"

"I didn't even believe it myself until I saw it with my own two eyes." From behind her back, Layla produced a tablet and shoved it in Phoebe's face.

No.

All the blood drained from her face and her entire body went numb as she took in the full-color image of her naked body intertwined with Dean's as they laid in what had been a *very* intimate moment on the island.

No.

"Phoebe?" It was Eric. He put a hand on her shoulder. "Do you need to sit down?"

"She doesn't need to sit down!"

Layla's voice cut through her like a knife. Phoebe blinked hard and focused on the vile woman. "Where did you get this?"

As soon as the question was out of her mouth, she knew the answer. The helicopter. The pilot.

"It's all over the internet, Pheebs." Layla reached over and scrolled through the pictures.

Dean and Phoebe walking on the beach.

Playing volleyball.

Wrapped in each other's arms in the water.

On the daybed in the early morning light while they were...

Her stomach heaved, threatening. The room spun.

"Here." Mason guided her to a stool and she sat, but only because her legs were going to give out if she didn't. Not because she had any desire to stay in the room with Layla, with the pictures, and with...*oh God.*

Everyone would have seen those pictures. Everyone would know she was with Dean. They would think she was just like the others. That she used him.

"You know what I heard?" Her big reveal complete, Layla's voice was suddenly cheerful and laced with joy. "Dean's manager was pushing him to lock her down."

Phoebe vaguely registered that Layla was discussing her as if she wasn't even there.

"The publicity of the stars dating is huge." Layla was still talking. "In fact, I heard that these pictures might have even been *intentionally* staged and leaked."

That snapped Phoebe to attention. "What?"

Layla grinned.

"You don't know what you're talking about, Layla." Eric wrapped his arm around Phoebe. "Come on, let's get you out of here."

"No." Phoebe shook him off and stood. "Tell me what you mean, Layla. *Intentionally staged? Leaked?* What do you mean?"

"What do you think I mean?"

No. No. No.

"I mean, it was either you..." She paused for effect. "Or Dean. I mean, you both had something to gain. Didn't you?"

Phoebe's stomach churned.

She knew she hadn't leaked anything, so that would mean that...*no.*

There was no way that Dean would do that to her. No way he'd violate her privacy. She'd been so concerned with not being like the others. She didn't want to date a player. Someone who was just out for the publicity. Who would use her.

She looked between Eric and Mason before her eyes once again landed on Layla. She'd been so naive. She'd thought these people were her friends. She'd thought that Dean...*no.* She couldn't think about Dean.

The sound of the busy bar faded away, and all she could hear were people murmuring and gossiping as news of the pictures got out. She lifted her head and looked around to see people looking at their phones, and pointing in her direction.

Her stomach heaved and she lurched up off the stool.

"I have to get out of here."

He'd damn near got arrested trying to get off the airplane. He was ready to bash down the door and risk a night or two in a Panamanian jail, although it wouldn't have gotten him any closer to Phoebe. But at least he would have been in the same country. If the plane took off, he'd be thousands of miles away in the United States. The distance was too much. Especially when he needed to get to her *immediately.*

Fortunately, Kyle was the voice of reason, and remained calm enough to talk him off the ledge, convince him to sit his ass down and let him deal with the flight attendants, and ultimately, the captain, who finally agreed to take the airplane back to the gate so they could get off and have their baggage removed. Certainly there would be some angry passengers, but Kyle would make some sort of arrangement to get them all VIP passes to his next movie or something that would probably come off as trite and entitled.

He probably should have cared more.

He didn't.

All he cared about was getting to Phoebe.

Preferably before she saw the pictures. But what were the odds?

The only glimmer of hope Dean had at all was that she was at the wrap party and hopefully everyone was too drunk and having too much fun to look at their phones.

When Kyle was done arranging another helicopter to take them back to Shelter Bay Marina, he made a quick phone call to Kristen, who, as it turned out, was Kyle's girlfriend. Dean felt the smallest flicker of guilt that he didn't even realize his assistant, and likely his only friend, was seeing anyone, let alone Phoebe's assistant. But he couldn't spare any mental energy on that particular detail at the moment. He'd worry about being a self-absorbed asshole later.

While Dean was busy sending texts that all went unanswered to Phoebe, Kyle was on the phone with Kristen.

"Well?" Dean asked as soon as he hung up. The helicopter had just arrived and they were waiting for the all-clear before heading out to the tarmac. "What did she say?"

He saw it in Kyle's face before he spoke. "They've seen the pictures."

"Who?" It was a dumb question, and they both knew it. "Who's seen them?"

"Everyone."

"Shit." Dean stared out at the dark night. "She won't answer her phone."

"We'll be there soon."

"Not soon enough."

Chapter Twenty-Two

PHOEBE THOUGHT her stomach might completely turn inside out. She was only vaguely aware of someone being nearby as she knelt by the shrubs and emptied the contents of her stomach.

He couldn't have done what Layla said he did. Not Dean. It wasn't like him. *Or was it? No.* It killed her that she even questioned it. That she questioned the man she was so sure she was falling in love with. The man who only a few hours ago had kissed her good-bye with the promise of a private holiday in a few days. He wouldn't have said that if he'd been using her, would he?

She didn't *think* he would do that. But then again...he was a really good actor and—

Again, she bent and retched into the shrubbery.

"Here." A napkin appeared in her periphery. She took it. Wiped at her face and rocked back on her heels. The fuzziness of the champagne was long gone, replaced by the distinct sharp edge of reality. "Are you feeling better now?"

Phoebe turned and for the first time realized it was Eric

standing next to her, who'd handed her the napkin. Eric who'd come after her to see if she was okay.

She nodded, even though she wasn't remotely feeling better.

He reached down and offered her a hand, which she took, and was hauled easily to her feet. Eric wrapped an arm around her shoulders and guided her to a nearby table and chairs. It was far enough away from the Dockside that hopefully they wouldn't be seen. The idea that everyone was looking at her and thinking—whatever it was that they were thinking—she didn't have the energy for it. Either they thought she was an opportunistic slut, just trying to advance her career by jumping into bed with Dean Harrison, or that he'd played her for a fool to gain the publicity that would seal the deal on the *Supers* movie.

She didn't know which was worse.

Phoebe sat, numb, in the chair next to Eric.

"Drink this." He handed her a bottle of water, the cap removed, and she took a tentative sip, not sure how her stomach would react to anything, even water.

"You know Layla's just jealous."

Phoebe shook her head.

"She is."

"Maybe so." Finally, she turned to look at Eric. "But it doesn't change the facts. There are pictures."

He nodded but didn't say anything else, because what was there to say?

Instead, they sat in silence for a few more minutes before Phoebe stood up. "I can't stay here," she said. "I can't be here even one more second. I have to go."

"Don't let this ruin your night, Pheebs. You've earned this. You need to go back—"

"I don't *need* to do anything of the sort." She shook her head so violently that she thought she might be sick again.

"What I need to do is get out of here. I need to go home and forget any of this ever happened. Any of it." She smoothed her hair back and swallowed hard. "This was a mistake." Suddenly unstable on her high heels, she teetered in the direction of the condos.

One more night. That's all she needed to get through, and then she would be home with Kate and her nieces, and she could forget this had all ever happened. She'd been a fool to think she could be a movie star. She'd been so naive to think that she could outsmart the media machine.

I won't be like those others.

I would never date my costar.

She'd been so stupid. But in a way, she wasn't like those women who came before her at all. She was worse. Because she'd been stupid enough to think even for a second that she was better than them.

She wanted to scream.

Phoebe's heel caught in the gravel of the path and she lurched to the side. She almost crashed to the ground, but Eric was there to catch her.

"Careful, Pheebs."

"I'm fine, Eric. Really." He had his arm around her shoulder again, only this time instead of leading her to the table, he was helping her down the path.

"I'll get you home, Phoebe. You shouldn't be alone."

"I'm fine, Eric." The idea of being with anyone at that moment was not appealing, let alone someone who looked way too similar to Dean. Just being near him was giving her the creeps. She tried to shake him off. "Thank you, but I can get there on my own."

He squeezed her closer. "Really, it's no big deal. I just really don't think you should be alone."

That's *exactly* what she needed. What she didn't need was

someone trying to think for her. She stopped walking abruptly. "Eric. I'm fine."

"Phoebe, I—"

"She said she was fine."

Phoebe froze.

Without taking his arm off her, Eric turned around to face Dean. "I really don't think you're the person to say that, man. You need to—"

"Let her go." Dean's voice was tight and controlled, as if he would rip Eric's arm off if he didn't remove it from her shoulders.

But she didn't need anyone to take care of her. Least of all Dean Harrison.

With a new strength she didn't know she was capable of, she spun around to face him and instantly, her breath caught in her throat the way it always did when she saw him.

Dammit. How was it fair that after everything he'd done, her body still reacted that way to the sight of him?

She took a deep breath and let it out slowly before saying everything she would ever need to say to Dean Harrison again. "Fuck you."

Her words hit him like a knife to the gut. But Dean wasn't to be deterred. "Phoebe, you—"

"You heard the lady." Eric stepped forward and Dean's temper flared.

If he'd been pissed at hearing about the leaking of the photos, he was straight up livid to see his friggin' stunt double standing next to *his*...Phoebe.

"Stand down, Eric."

He took another step toward Phoebe, ready to do whatever it took to get her away from Eric, to talk to him, and most importantly, hear what he had to say about the photos. Which wasn't much. Kyle hadn't been able to figure out where they had come from, who'd taken them, or who'd commissioned them.

He'd hung up on Bruce before he could hear his explanation, not that it would be a good one. Or even one that he would believe. But the idea that he might have something to do with the photos getting out to the media wasn't completely farfetched. It was a niggling feeling, like a burr that had been lodged in his sock.

But he'd deal with Bruce later.

The first and most important thing stood right in front of him. "Phoebe." He reached out. "Talk to me. I need you to know that—"

"Why would she talk to you?" Eric all but laughed in his face while he squeezed his arm around Phoebe.

There was no doubt in Dean's mind that Eric could kick his ass without even trying, but it wouldn't stop him from throwing the first punch. No way. In fact, it would probably feel really bloody good to do it. He clenched his fists at his sides and breathed through his nose. "This has nothing to do with you, Eric. I'm not going to tell you again. Stand. Down."

Sensing his need for a fight, Eric dropped his arm from Phoebe's shoulder and stepped forward. "I don't think that's going to happen, Harrison. You might think you're some sort of big shot around here and you can do whatever you want and treat people however you want for your own benefit, but that's not how I work."

"What the hell are you talking about?"

"I'm talking about the way you used Phoebe."

Behind Eric, Dean saw Phoebe shudder. His entire body yearned to go to her. To explain. To hold her and tell her how he felt. But he wasn't a complete idiot. He could see her pulling away from him right before his eyes. Panic started to well up inside.

"I didn't use—"

"Shut up, man." Eric stepped closer to him again while Phoebe only seemed to get farther away. "No one here is buying your innocent act. Very convenient, that you got just the right media attention at such a crucial moment, don't you think?"

He wasn't wrong. Not about the attention. It *did* look bad. It looked *very* bad. But it wasn't him. He'd never do that. And that's what Phoebe needed to know.

Dean looked past Eric, to the only person who really mattered. "You have to believe me," he pleaded. "Phoebe, I—"

"Think you're—"

"Shut up, Eric!"

"Fuck off, Eric!"

Both Dean and Phoebe spoke at the same time, but Dean let her finish her thought. "I can handle this," she continued. "I don't need you to defend me or fight some sort of battle for me or anything else. Just…go inside." He stared at her with his mouth open. "Go," she said again. "Please."

Dean bit his tongue to keep from adding something that wouldn't serve any purpose except to piss the other man off. Now wasn't the time.

He waited while Eric looked between the both of them and finally nodded. "If you need anything, I'll be—"

"I won't."

Eric nodded sharply, and then, suitably dismissed, he turned and walked inside, leaving them alone.

Finally.

She should have walked away. She should have taken her chance when she had it and let Eric deal with Dean. Or Dean deal with Eric. Whatever.

The moment she was alone with Dean, she regretted it. She at once wanted to go to him, and let him hold her and tell her it would be all right while simultaneously punching him in the face. The conflict within her raged and put her off-balance.

"Phoebe." He took a step toward her, but she held up a hand to ward him off.

"I need you to stay over there." She shook her head, changing her mind. "No. I need you to go. Why are you even here?"

"I had to come."

"No. You didn't."

"I did, Phoebe."

His face twisted. He looked tormented. He looked hurt. But he was a good actor. He was the best. Phoebe felt her walls go up around her.

"I needed to see you and talk to you and—"

"Make sure I knew that you'd betrayed me to land the *Supers* movie?"

"No." He ran his hands through his hair until it was standing up. "That's not what happened."

She bristled and pulled her shoulders back. "Isn't it?" She knew she sounded like a bitch. She didn't care. "Are you really going to stand there in front of me and tell me that the publicity from this *leak*," she used air quotes, "wasn't a huge publicity boost for you?"

He opened his mouth to speak, but she cut him off. "Because word on the street is that your manager's been pushing you for some juicy details about us."

Dean's face registered shock, but not denial.

"Do you deny it?" she pushed. "Did your manager want you to hook up with me for publicity?"

Once again, he opened his mouth to speak.

"Don't lie to me," she warned. "Not now."

He took a deep breath, and that's when she knew. It was true. What Layla said was true. Her heart cracked a little, but she wouldn't let him see her fall apart. Not now.

"Yes," Dean said slowly. Even though she was expecting it, the admission cut deeper than she could have expected. "Bruce has been pushing me to give him some gossip. He wanted me to date you and—"

"You obliged." She scoffed and squeezed her eyes shut. She couldn't look at him. She couldn't look at the man she thought she'd been falling in love with and see it in his eyes that he was anything but the man she thought he was. But how could she have been so wrong? The things he'd said to her? The way he'd helped her sister? That couldn't have been all an act, could it? The betrayal caused a physical ache that ripped at her.

It was too much.

"Phoebe. It wasn't like that."

Her eyes popped open, angry now. "It wasn't? Really?" She spat out the words. "You just admitted it to me, Dean. It was *exactly* like that. You needed the publicity to get the movie, didn't you?"

Again, he hesitated but eventually nodded.

She took a deep breath, needing the oxygen to give her the strength she wasn't sure she could muster on her own.

"Fuck you, Dean."

She needed to get away. She needed to get as far away from him and the movie, and this life that she was stupid enough to believe she might be able to have. Phoebe kicked off her shoes, and without bothering to stop and pick them up, started to head back to her condo. It's not as though she was going to need stilettos in Montana.

"Phoebe!"

He yelled after her, but she didn't stop walking.

"Phoebe!"

She could hear his steps on the gravel behind her, coming after her. But she refused to stop. She refused to let him see how hurt she was. What he'd done to her.

No. She couldn't let him know how he'd broken her.

Hadn't everyone told her what a talented actress she was? Maybe two could play at that game. He'd played her for a fool. He'd used her in the worst possible way. He'd earned her trust; she'd let him in; she'd dropped her defenses and been intimate with him. *So* intimate. And he'd exploited it. But she wouldn't give him the satisfaction of seeing her pain.

She squeezed her eyes shut, let out a long, slow breath, and spun around to face him in character. He was much closer than she'd expected and his nearness nearly unsettled her. Nearly. She straightened her shoulders, and with a voice as cold as Dean's bed was going to be without her in it, she spoke. "But really, I guess I should thank you, too, right?"

His face twisted in confusion.

"Now that the world knows that I was with Dean Harrison, my star should start to rise, too." She let out a little laugh and locked eyes with him. "I guess we both got what we wanted."

Phoebe turned and walked away before she could see his reaction. It didn't matter. Nothing mattered but getting the hell out of there.

This time, he didn't follow her.

Chapter Twenty-Three

WATCHING the sunrise reflecting off the mountains was one of Phoebe's favorite things in the whole world. Wrapped in a fleecy blanket against the bite in the air that early spring in the mountains held, and a hot cup of coffee in her hand, Phoebe was at peace.

Mostly.

She'd been home in Montana at Kate's house for the last two months, and although the pain of Dean's betrayal had faded, it had definitely not disappeared. Panama felt a lifetime away. Her time on the set was a distant memory. One she couldn't decide was a good or a bad memory.

There were days she missed the challenge of acting. The excitement of the set. The camaraderie of the cast and crew— mostly. And then she remembered what it was really like. The deception. The lies. The backstabbing. True, it wasn't everyone. But it had been the most important person.

Dean.

And that's when she remembered why she'd left it behind and come home. It was simple. Easy.

Phoebe wrapped the blanket a little tighter around her

shoulders. The days were getting longer now that spring was almost officially here. Which also meant she wasn't going to be able to hide forever. She was going to have to get a job and do something with her life.

"Auntie!"

Phoebe turned to see her youngest niece, Ally, standing at the back door, hollering at her. Instantly, she smiled. The girls had been a lifeline for her when she returned from Panama. There was nothing like the love of a child to bring her back to earth and remind her what really mattered.

"What's up, kiddo?"

"Mom wants to know if you want pancakes."

"Of course. Blueberry?"

Ally laughed. "Chocolate chip, silly."

"That sounds good, too." She grinned. "I'll be right there."

Ally nodded and then, as if she'd just remembered something else, she hollered, "Oh, and Mom says she's going to throw your phone into the yard if you don't answer it." With that, she disappeared inside and the door slammed behind her.

Phone?

Her phone hadn't done much ringing at all since the first week or two that she'd been home. Kristen had tried calling. Wes had both texted and called. Lorilee had left a number of messages and even Louis had tried to reach out. She'd ignored all of them. And eventually her phone had gone silent.

Not that she cared. The only one she wanted to hear from, she equally *didn't* want to hear from. Which worked out, considering he was the one person who hadn't reached out at all.

She'd come to appreciate the silence of her phone over the last few weeks.

"Phoebe!" Kate yelled from inside the house.

Apparently, her sister had also come to appreciate the silence of her phone.

When she got inside, Kate all but threw her still ringing phone at her. "Don't you have voicemail?"

"I do. But..." She looked at the caller. Lorilee. It was the fourth time she'd called. "Apparently she doesn't want to leave a voicemail." Phoebe moved to silence her phone and toss it back on the counter, but something stopped her. She stared at the screen.

"Just answer it already." At the stove, Kate flipped a pancake.

Phoebe stood and watched her big sister for a moment and marveled at how quickly she'd recovered from the surgery that had taken the lump from her breast. They'd been able to dismiss the nanny that Dean had hired as soon as Phoebe got home. Mostly because Kate had bounced back so quickly. She still had a course of chemo and follow-up to go, but her sister was a fighter. She'd beat it. She didn't hide from it. She faced it head on.

"Answer it," Kate said again, shaking Phoebe from her thoughts. "You can't hide forever. Just deal."

She was right, and it pissed her off. With a groan, Phoebe grabbed the phone and hit the button that took the call.

Dean's oar cut through the water in the bay that was almost as still as glass. Besides a sea lion or two, he was the only one out. Just the way he liked it.

He'd been hiding at the rental house in Washington since leaving Panama. At first, the idea of retreating to the house he'd rented to be alone with Phoebe felt wrong. The way she'd looked at him—the hurt and pain in her eyes—and knowing he'd put it there had almost broken him. But then, the way she'd shifted...she'd been cold, almost hurtful. Not the Phoebe he knew.

Or maybe he didn't know her at all.

Kyle thought that staying in the rental house that was supposed to have been their haven was Dean's way of punishing himself. And maybe he was right. At the very least, he wasn't wrong. But it was also Dean's way to be close to her. Or the Phoebe he'd known.

Because the Phoebe he'd been falling in love with wouldn't have looked at him the way she did. She wouldn't have said the things she'd said. No matter how hurt she was. And the longer Dean had to sit and think on it, the more he'd convinced himself that she'd used him, too. Maybe she had been all along. Maybe it was *her* who leaked the photos? He knew it wasn't him, so...

Maybe Kyle wasn't completely wrong.

Being alone, in a place that was supposed to be special, was a punishment. One he deserved.

He finished his morning kayak around the bay and returned to the launch, where he dragged his kayak up and out of the water, flipping it to keep the otters from getting inside. He walked up the path that led to his rental, a four-bedroom cabin tucked away in the forest with an oversized deck that looked out over the quiet bay. There were no close neighbors. No one who could spy on him, or see that he was alone and miserable. No one but the deer that roamed through the garden. Just the way he liked it.

He dropped his oar and lifejacket on the stairs of the deck, grabbed a beer out of a cooler, and flopped onto the large wicker chair, where he planned to spend the rest of the morning.

"A little early for that, don't you think?"

Dean spat his beer all over the deck as he shot up in his seat. He turned to see Kyle. His former assistant stood with two cups of take-out coffee in his hand as he leaned against the doorframe.

"How did you...where did you..."

"Here." Kyle handed him a coffee and took the bottle from his hand. "I think you could use this more than that." He took the seat across from Dean and waited and watched while he took a sip of the black coffee.

Kyle was right. Coffee was a better choice. Especially dark, thick, bitter coffee. Kyle was always right. Which was why right after the *Panama fiasco*, Dean had fired Bruce and promoted Kyle. He finally got the raise and the promotion he deserved, and Dean got a manager he could trust.

He still didn't know how the pictures had gotten out. Maybe Bruce had something to do with it. Maybe not. Maybe it was just an opportunistic helicopter pilot who'd taken advantage of the situation. Maybe—and this was his least favorite option—it had been Phoebe after all. Maybe she'd been playing him just the way the others had. Every time he let himself entertain that thought, even for a second, it made him physically ill. Still. He couldn't get her final words out of his mind.

Now that the world knows that I was with Dean Harrison, my star should start to rise, too.

I guess we both got what we wanted.

It had been months since he'd seen her, but when he closed his eyes, he could hear her voice perfectly and the cold little laugh as she'd walked away.

Which was why he didn't close his eyes. At least not without enough alcohol in his system to numb the effects of actually feeling anything.

The coffee was sour in his mouth. He grimaced and swallowed it anyway.

"Delicious, right?" Kyle sat across from him. "Washington has the best coffee. It's—"

"Foul." Dean sneered, but Kyle only laughed.

"Are you almost done with this self-pity act? Because I'm starting to grow weary of it."

"It's not self-pity."

Kyle crossed his leg and sat back in the chair, a smug smile on his lips that Dean suddenly had the urge to punch off his face. He swallowed hard and grumbled to himself. He was a lot of things. Especially at the moment. But violent was *not* one of them.

"What is it exactly?" Kyle wasn't going to let it go. "Is it more of a self-hatred? Or more of a hate the whole world kind of thing? Or maybe." He sat up and looked directly at Dean. "Maybe it's just an old-fashioned broken heart?"

"Fuck you."

"Right." Kyle sat back, satisfied with his diagnosis, which frankly wouldn't have taken a genius to have figured out. "You do know that I think you're being ridiculous, right?" He didn't give Dean a chance to respond before he continued. "No, I take that back. You're being an ass, Dean. A full-fledged, grade-A ass."

Dean shook his head in shock. No one had ever called him an ass. Especially not someone who was on his payroll.

Kyle put his hands on his knees and stood. "And I refuse to work for an ass."

Maybe it was the foggy head from the beer, or the whisky the night before, or the lack of sleep. Or all of the above. But it took Dean a moment to catch up to what Kyle was saying. "What?"

Kyle walked across the deck to the sliding door that led to the living room.

"What the hell, Kyle? You're quitting?"

Panic slid over him and settled in his gut. Kyle had worked for him for years. He knew Dean better than he knew himself some days. Kyle couldn't quit. If he left…*shit*.

Dean jumped to his feet and immediately swayed. He grabbed the back of the chair.

Kyle turned and shook his head in disgust. "Look at you. Dean, you're a mess."

He knew it was true. Still, he shook his head. "I'm kayaking every day. I get fresh air. I'm—"

"Full of shit."

He knew that was true, too.

Dean hung his head. "Don't quit on me, Kyle."

He didn't respond right away, and for a moment, Dean was sure he'd left.

But then, just when he was about to give up, Kyle groaned. "I'm not quitting, Dean. But I do have something to say."

"So you're really leaving?" Kate had come into Phoebe's room and was lying across her bed, picking up and examining the clothes she'd laid out to pack. She lifted a T-shirt with two fingers, made a face, and tossed it behind her. "For how long?"

Phoebe bent to pick up the shirt with a sigh and stuffed it in her bag before her sister could get it again. "A week, maybe. But I don't have to go. I can tell Lorilee that—"

"You're going." Kate sat up and shook her head. "For goodness' sake, *please* go." She laughed, but Phoebe frowned in response. "I'm fine, Phoebe. I don't see the doctor for two more weeks, but she cleared me to go back to work, remember? I don't need a babysitter. And between school and the daycare, the girls will be fine. Go. You need this."

"We could get the nanny back." Phoebe wasn't sure how exactly they'd get the nanny back as she wouldn't be paid her full amount for the movie until it was released, but she had some savings stashed away. They'd make it work if they needed to. Or find a cheaper one. Leave it to Dean Harrison to find the most expensive nanny in the state. But certainly there would be cheaper options. She'd find them.

"We don't need the nanny." Kate interrupted her thoughts. "Really. We'll be fine. And it'll be good for you to go, Phoebe. You need to get out of here."

Her sister's words stung and Phoebe didn't even try to hide the hurt. "I thought you liked having me home?"

"We do," Kate said quickly. "You know we love you and love having you here. But…"

"But?" Phoebe held a small stack of jeans.

Kate blew out a breath and shrugged. "You've been a bit of a downer lately."

"A downer?" She knew what her sister was saying was true, but it still stung. "I'm sorry, I didn't—"

"Can we talk about it?"

Phoebe turned to face her closet. She pretended to be searching for something to wear on the press junket that Lorilee was making her go on. A series of interviews and photo shoots to promote the movie, which was being fast-tracked and set for an early release. Apparently, the production company and all of the various stakeholders knew a good publicity opportunity when they saw it, and were more than ready to capitalize on it. She'd tried to get out of it, but it was in her contract, and Phoebe needed the money. She couldn't say no. Despite the fact that just thinking about seeing Dean in person again made her want to be physically and violently ill. She had no idea how she was going to survive sitting next to him and pretending they were friendly.

Lorilee had promised her a public relations expert would be there to help coach her through the difficult situations and questions. But Phoebe was pretty sure it was going to take a whole lot more than an expert to help her get through it.

"Phoebe?" Kate touched her shoulder lightly and asked again, "Can we talk about it? Are you ready yet?"

She took a deep breath and nodded, but then quickly shook her head. Kate had been so patient with her since she'd been back, especially because Phoebe knew she was hurt that Phoebe hadn't confided in her about Dean. And maybe she should have, but now…it was too late. The whole world knew. There were no secrets anymore.

"What's to talk about?" She turned around and pressed her lips together. "I'm just another Silver Starlet." She refrained from using some of the headlines the tabloids had selected, in particular, the most hurtful.

Silver Slut.

She'd become everything she hated. And all because she'd trusted that she was different. That *he* was different. She'd been an idiot.

"I think there's quite a lot to talk about, actually."

Phoebe felt a rush of love for her sister, who no doubt had been dying of curiosity for details of what had happened with Dean. She'd demonstrated incredible self-control by not asking. A fact Phoebe appreciated more than she could ever express because, after coming home, there was no way she could bear retelling all the details of what she'd thought at the time would be her great love story. It was too difficult.

"I wasn't using him," she said after a moment. She turned to face her sister. "I need you to know, Kate. I didn't plan it. No matter what the tabloids say, I'm not like those other actresses. Do you believe me?"

"Of course. That's not who you are." Kate took the dress Phoebe was holding from her hand and led her to the bed, where they sat side by side. "Tell me about him."

She knew what her sister was asking, and it was not about Dean the movie star. It was about Dean, the man she'd fallen for. Her lips twitched up in a smile and she allowed herself to think about him in that way for the first time in months.

Maybe she could talk about him. "He's funny. And kind. And he…"

Used me.

How nice was he really? He'd set her up and without any regard for her at all, he'd—

"Stay with me." Kate squeezed her arm. "Don't disappear into your head again."

Phoebe blinked and brought her sister back into focus.

"Tell me why you fell for him. Focus on the positive stuff. Because I know you, Pheebs. You're a smart woman. You make smart decisions, and you *know* people. You wouldn't have fallen for him if he wasn't a good person. You know that too."

She shook her head. "I thought I did."

"You *do*."

She wanted to believe her sister, but she couldn't get past the facts.

"I don't know what happened to make you doubt yourself, Phoebe, but you have to let it go."

She thought about that for a minute. *Let it go.* Kate was right. It had been two months. She should let it go. She needed to, because hanging onto it was killing her. But it wasn't just the betrayal. It was that she was so sure they were the real thing. It was that for the first time in her life, Phoebe was sure she'd found someone she could picture a future with. And then…it wasn't just the fact that she couldn't trust Dean—it was even worse: she couldn't trust herself.

"I was stupid," Phoebe said finally. "Same old story. Naive, trusting country girl seduced by a handsome, smooth talker. I'm not proud of it. I should have known better."

"Hey." Kate offered her a small smile. "It happens."

Phoebe snorted. "I guess you'd know, right?" She felt her sister's hand stiffen on her arm, and at once realized her mistake. "Oh, Kate. That's not what I meant." She turned and grabbed at Kate's hand as she stood from the bed. "Kate, I'm sorry. I didn't mean—"

"You did mean it." She turned around, her finger pointed at her face. "And yes. I've made mistakes. Sure, I've fallen for the wrong guy and yes, I've been taken advantage of. But at least I didn't run away."

Phoebe stood. "I didn't run away. I'm—"

"You've been hiding out here for months, feeling sorry for yourself, letting one little thing ruin this incredible opportunity."

"I'm not hiding, Kate." Phoebe worked hard to control her voice. "I came back to be with you."

"Bullshit!"

"I did! You needed—"

"No." Kate shook her head. "Do not use me as your excuse."

"It's not an excuse."

"Yes it is!" Kate cried. "You're hiding, Phoebe, and you know it. Stop being so scared of your life. Stop running away from everything good." She squeezed the bridge of her nose. "I'm not proud of all my decisions. But that's the difference between you and me. I'm not too scared to face the truth."

"I'm not, Kate. I'm just..." Phoebe couldn't find the words. But it didn't matter because Kate had long since turned and left her alone.

Chapter Twenty-Four

KYLE HAD MADE HIS POINT. And it was a good one.

He'd sat Dean down long enough, and with enough black coffee, to impress upon him the importance of getting his act together in order to fulfill his contractual obligations. When he was done with his press for the Max Silver movie, then, if he still felt like wallowing in the bullshit of his life, as far as Kyle was concerned, he was welcomed to do so.

But, Kyle added at the end of the conversation, once Dean agreed to pull it together long enough to take care of the press junket, despite the fact that he'd missed the meeting for the *Supers* movie, the producers were still interested in opening discussions with him about a role, and possibly a separate solo movie. Even through his foggy state of self-pity, Dean could recognize an amazing opportunity. Still, he didn't commit to anything.

One thing at a time.

He needed to work out the details for the series of interviews for the Max Silver movie. Interviews that would no doubt include very hard questions about Phoebe. Questions he wanted to stay as far away from as possible. Never mind the fact that there was a very good chance he'd be sitting next to Phoebe during those interviews.

"I told you," Kyle said, answering his questions for at least the tenth time that day. "We have a PR firm that will meet with you and Phoebe both together and separately to discuss the proper way to handle things. What to say, what not to say, that kind of thing."

Dean nodded. He'd met with plenty of PR agents in the past. Sure, they knew the best way to talk around a sensitive issue, but did they know the best way to actually handle the issue? Could they tell him how to make things better with Phoebe? How to fix it and make everything okay again? Could they coach him through what it would be like to see her again? To not pull her into his arms the second he laid eyes on her?

He sure as hell hoped so.

Two days later, in LA, he had his answer.

"Sorry, Mr. Harrison, I can't help you with that."

Kyle had assured Dean that Rebecca Dash, with Dash PR, was the best in the business. And maybe she would be able to help him spin things, but she certainly didn't seem to be very helpful as far as Phoebe was concerned.

"This will be your first event together," Rebecca continued. "And while I'm sure things might be a little *awkward* between the two of you, it is important that you remain professional. The best defense for this is to get ahead of it."

It was a little late for that, Dean thought, but he didn't bother to say anything. He only half listened while Rebecca went over the talking points, and gave him strategies to dodge any overly personal question about the two of them and what exactly the status of their relationship was.

There wasn't one. It was the truth, after all. But saying it out loud might cause him actual physical pain.

Kyle hadn't let him touch any form of alcohol for the last two days. Not even so much as a beer. He told him it was for his own good. But so far, having a clear head wasn't doing him any favors.

"I've already informed Ms. Flynn that you are here," Rebecca continued. "She will be—"

"She's here?" Dean sat up, suddenly paying attention. "Where is she?"

"She'll meet you on set. We've set up a room where the interviewers will rotate their time with you, and that way we can get most of the interviews and obligations done in one big day." Rebecca paused in her pacing and glanced at her clipboard before looking up at Dean with what could only be described as pity on her face. "She requested to have as little contact with you as possible."

Dean sat back in his chair, hard. It was probably for the best. He was way too conflicted about the woman. He'd been so sure he was falling in love with her. But then...the photos. *I guess we both got what we wanted.* She'd used him, too.

"I'd like to request the same thing." He spoke without really thinking, and judging by the look the PR woman gave him, that much was more than evident.

"Right," Rebecca said slowly. "So, I've been informed that neither of you would like to discuss the photographs, is that correct?"

Dean leapt out of his chair. "Of course it's correct. Why would I want to—"

Rebecca held out a hand to quiet him. "I'm just following up on my notes, Mr. Harrison. There's no need to get fired up. In fact." She tapped the pen to her lips. "I would strongly suggest that you do the exact opposite in the interviews, no matter what they bring up."

"They won't bring it up, will they?"

"We've asked them not to."

Dean had been in enough interview situations to know what that meant. "That doesn't mean anything," he grumbled.

"No. It doesn't. Which is why you need to remain calm." She consulted her clipboard. "So, as I mentioned, we've arranged to have all the reporters come to us, to make things as smooth as possible. One room, a few breaks, and you're done. Good?"

He shrugged.

"Great." Rebecca put her clipboard down by her side and for the first time since Dean had met her, smiled. It almost made her and her tightly pulled back ponytail look less severe. Almost. "It's time to get started. Follow me."

Phoebe had been prepped by the PR lady until she couldn't remember what her own thoughts were and what were things she'd been told to say. She went over the talking points in her head.

Exciting to film her first movie on set. True.

Panama is a beautiful country. True.

The cast and crew were amazing. Somewhat true.

She was thrilled about the early reviews. True. It was good if the movie wasn't a flop.

The new projects and opportunities coming in for her were exciting. Lie. Well, not completely. They *were* exciting. Lorilee had filled her in on all the offers. Some of which were *huge.* But she couldn't get excited about any of them. Not when she wasn't even sure she'd ever act again.

She'd been told that even though Dean was going to be sitting next to her, all the interviewers had been instructed not to ask about the leaked pictures or the state of their relationship. She was also told that there was a very good chance the interviewers would ignore that instruction.

Perfect.

"We're ready for you, Phoebe." Rebecca Dash popped her

head into her dressing room, waited for Phoebe's nod, and disappeared again.

Phoebe took a breath and looked at her reflection in the mirror. The makeup lady had done a good job. Her eyes sparkled and her skin glowed despite how she felt inside. Her stomach had been twisting and churning for the last few days in anticipation of seeing Dean, but there was no way around it, so she was just going to have to call on the very thing that had gotten her to this point: acting.

Just as she had done every day before going on set, Phoebe closed her eyes, took a few deep breaths and, when she opened them again, was in character. This time her character wasn't Misty Falls, but a colder, closed-off version of Phoebe Flynn.

She hoped she could pull it off.

The moment she stepped inside the room and saw—or more like felt—Dean's presence, all her confidence wavered. Her body reacted the way it did the first time she'd seen him in person. Every muscle clenched tight, her breath caught in her throat, and the floor tilted underneath her. When he looked in her direction, she thought she might pass out. His eyes looked straight into her soul, his lips curled up in the corners, just a little, and then the trace of a smile was gone. He nodded in greeting and turned away.

Oddly, Phoebe was thankful for his cold greeting. It made it all the easier to stay in character.

"Dean." She returned his nod and sat down in the chair next to him. She crossed her legs and tilted just slightly away from him, hopefully not enough for anyone to notice. Although, she was sure that Rebecca Dash would let her know if she was being overtly rude to him. The stiff PR woman had told her in no uncertain terms that she was absolutely not to come off rude or angry with Dean, as it would only fuel the rumors about the two of them. And although the press junket's main purpose was to promote the movie, if it was done right,

Rebecca assured her, it would also serve to stem or slow some of the gossip about how she'd used Dean for his fame.

It still made her sick to think that people thought that of her. It couldn't be further from the truth, and anyone who knew her knew she wasn't that type of person. That's all that mattered.

Still.

It mattered a little what the rest of the world thought. She couldn't help it.

Phoebe swallowed and smiled sweetly as the first interviewer sat down across from them.

Over an hour later, they'd completed three interviews, and nothing catastrophic had happened. Just as Rebecca promised, they'd stuck to the approved questions. Mostly. Only the young man from *Star* magazine had tried to sneak in a question that was over the line.

"Dean, can you tell me what it was like working with Phoebe?"

An approved question, Dean handled it smoothly.

He flashed his trademarked smile in her direction, and she, perfectly on cue, nodded and returned the smile. "It was an absolute delight," he said. The words sounded so fake coming out of his mouth, but no one else seemed to notice. "Phoebe is a true professional. We had a lot of fun on set and more than once we were able to hit a scene on the first take. It was really a great experience."

"And was it on set that you two first had a physical connection?"

Not an approved question.

Phoebe immediately stiffened, panic flooding through her while her perfect smile remained pasted on her face. She was about to look to Rebecca, who no doubt should be jumping in any second, but before she could, Dean reached his hand over and put it on her arm that was resting on the chair next to his.

His eyes met hers and with a slight nod to her, he turned back to the man who Phoebe now wanted to shove backward off his stool.

"As with any costar you work closely with," Dean began, "there was a connection between us, of course. We really had a lot of fun together on set as we got to know each other. For sure." It was a simple, non-answer, but Dean delivered it so smoothly, it didn't leave room for a follow-up.

Nor did Rebecca, who chose that moment to swoop in with her clipboard. "Okay, time is up. We need to keep on schedule." She turned toward them and added, "Take a few minutes to grab a snack and stretch your legs. Back in ten."

Phoebe didn't need to be told twice. She pulled her arm away from Dean's, that was still touching her, and bolted for her dressing room as quickly as was reasonably possible.

———

Dean was fuming and Rebecca knew it.

"You told me they—"

"They aren't supposed to," Rebecca cut him off. "But it's going to happen. You know that. It always happens. You handled it great. It wasn't even a thing."

He opened the door to his dressing room and spun around. "It *was* a thing. For Phoebe. I'm used to this shit. She's not. Make sure it doesn't happen again."

He disappeared inside and the door slammed behind him. Dean wasn't trying to be an asshole, but he needed time alone. Seeing Phoebe had been harder than he'd thought it would. More than anything, he wanted to pull her into his arms and kiss her deeply. His entire body yearned to have his lips on her, his hands on her curves and— He wasn't alone.

"What are you doing in here?" Dean barked at Kyle. He walked toward the mini fridge to grab a water. He'd promised

Kyle he wouldn't touch anything more during the press junket. He screwed off the cap and tipped it to his mouth, drinking deeply before turning around to face his manager.

Dean almost spat out his water when he saw Kristen, Phoebe's assistant from the set, standing with Kyle. "And…why do we have company?"

"Dean, this is—"

"Mr. Harrison. I'm sorry to—"

"One at a time." Dean was quickly losing patience. This was a hard enough day as it was. Having more people around to witness it wasn't helping. "I know who she is," he said to Kyle. "Nice to see you, Kristen." He spoke to the woman, who stood close to Kyle. "But I don't understand why you're here."

"She's with me." Kyle put an arm around her. "We haven't been in the same city for a while and—"

"You two?" Dean waved a finger between them both. "Right. I forgot. Congrats." He tried not to sound jaded, but even in his worked-up state, he knew he hadn't pulled it off. "But if you don't mind, you can take your reunion out of here."

"Mr. Harrison." Kristen stepped forward. "That's not the only reason I'm here." She looked to Kyle for guidance, and he nodded, so she took another step forward toward Dean. "I'm sure you know that when we were on set, I worked with Phoebe Flynn."

"Sure." He tipped the water bottle back again and finished it. Dean crushed the plastic in his hands and tossed it toward the recycle bin. "And?"

"And, I wanted to tell you something. For whatever it's worth."

She had his attention. He crossed his arms and stared at her.

"Well, it's just that…" she stammered, obviously nervous.

Kyle joined her and put a supportive arm around her. "It's

okay, Kristen. He's really not that scary." Kyle glared in Dean's direction. "He's just having a bad day."

An understatement. Still, he tried to relax his face a little.

"Okay." Kristen smiled a little. "Well, Kyle mentioned you were pretty upset with Ms. Flynn because of the pictures getting out."

Nope. He didn't want to hear it.

Sensing his objection, she spoke faster. "And I wanted you to know that there's no way Phoebe had anything to do with the pictures. I know."

That caught his attention. "You know, do you?" Dean could sense Kyle tensing next to his girlfriend. No doubt he was ready to take him down for being a complete and total dick to her. Dean couldn't blame him. He tried again to relax a little. "Sorry, Kristen. I just don't see how you can possibly know that she didn't do it." He felt like a first-class ass even saying the words out loud because he *knew* in his heart she hadn't done it. She couldn't have. And not just because she didn't have the means or the access to the helicopter pilot who Kyle was still trying to track down, but because it wasn't *her*. Phoebe *wouldn't* do it. He knew it in his heart. He knew it in his brain. Hell, he just *knew* it. But evidently it was going to take someone else telling him what he already knew to let himself believe it.

"Dean." Kyle stepped up. "Just listen."

"I'm listening." He leaned back against the wall and crossed his arms. "So how is it that you *know*?"

"Because I worked with her pretty closely." Kristen's face softened into a smile as she spoke. "And she is quite possibly the sweetest, most genuine woman I've ever worked with in Hollywood."

Dean could believe that. It's exactly how he felt about her, too.

"But it's more than that," Kristen continued. "She didn't tell anyone about the two of you. Not even her sister."

That caught Dean's attention. Phoebe was extremely close to her sister; certainly she would have told Kate. And Dean wouldn't have blamed her.

"She didn't tell me either," Kristen said. She glanced over at Kyle, and Dean shook his head.

"You told her."

Kyle nodded and shrugged a little.

"Should I be worried that you two were the ones who leaked the pictures?" The matching looks of shock and horror on their faces answered that question. If Kristen were even half as loyal as Kyle, he had nothing to worry about. "Whatever." Dean waved the idea away and gestured for Kristen to continue.

"Anyway, the reason I know she didn't say anything, to *anyone*, was because she was really upset that I even knew about the two of you. She told me how important it was to her to keep it quiet because of your...well, because of your reputation. Because she was so new to the industry, she was adamant about not getting messed up in all that stuff."

"Dean," Kyle said. "I've been trying to tell you and you *know* this logically, anyway. Phoebe couldn't have known about the helicopter, or Barbecue Island ahead of time. She didn't even know you were taking her there. And even if she did, she wouldn't have commissioned the pictures. Do you really think that?"

He didn't. He really didn't. But it was so much easier to protect his heart if he did.

Kristen spoke again. "Dean, Phoebe told me that she tried to fight her feelings for you because of all the tabloid bullshit. But she couldn't. Despite herself, and everything else, she had feelings for you."

"I'm falling for you, too, Dean."

Something inside him clicked and snapped into place.

"And I believe her," Kristen finished. "She would never have leaked any of that. It all devastated her."

He dropped his chin to his chest. Dean knew if he closed his eyes, he'd see the look on Phoebe's face the night of the wrap party. It was the same look that had haunted his dreams for the last few months. Because he knew the truth. He'd always known. Phoebe never would have betrayed their relationship that way.

"And, Dean?" Kyle chimed in. "If Phoebe really was an opportunistic woman, looking to use you to further her career, then why has she been in hiding since the film wrapped? Why hasn't she taken any roles? Or even entertained any? In fact, word is that she's done with acting for good."

"What?" Dean jerked his head up. "She's *done*? She's so bloody talented. Why would she quit?"

Kyle and Kristen exchanged looks, but didn't answer the question directly. They didn't have to.

Chapter Twenty-Five

LAST ONE. *Last one.*

Phoebe repeated the mini mantra over and over as she worked up the energy to sit down again in the interview chair. They only had one more interview to get through. And it was the big one. It was for *Celeb*, the online magazine and website that broke the story of Phoebe and Dean and published those terrible pictures.

She took a deep breath and squared her shoulders before opening the door to her dressing room and making her way down to the set.

Dean wasn't there yet. The interviewer, Rick Myers, a too-slick, too-trendy, and way too cocky for his own good, man sat across from her. His legs were crossed, a notebook on his lap, despite the video cameras that were set up around the room to record every move they were about to make.

Phoebe bristled. *This was a mistake.* He was already looking at her with beady black eyes. No matter what Rebecca said, he was going to break the ground rules and ask the questions he wasn't supposed to. She knew it. Phoebe glanced around, but Rebecca was nowhere to be found. Neither was Dean.

When she turned forward again, she realized her mistake. Rick was grinning at her as if he'd already won a battle she didn't know she was there to fight.

Fuck.

No amount of PR prep could equip her to face this moment. Rick Myers was going to rip her and whatever was left of her reputation to shreds.

Phoebe pasted on a smile, and without breaking eye contact with the man, she channeled the version of herself that was going to help her get through this interview and the rest of the day. She released a slow breath and when the exhale was complete, she was as ready as she was ever going to get.

There was a flurry of activity as Dean appeared, followed by Rebecca, Kyle, and Kristen. *Kristen?*

She shot her former assistant a quizzical look, and Kristen raised two fingers in a slight wave, accompanied by a warm smile.

"Are we all ready?" Rebecca looked a bit flustered, but she waited until Phoebe and Dean, who'd taken the seat next to her without even a glance in her direction, both nodded. "Great." She turned to Rick. "Stick to the approved questions and we have ten minutes. Go ahead."

The interview started much the same as all the others had, with the basic questions. Only, as they answered each question, there was an underlying tension running through all of them. Not only was Phoebe feeling it, but she could see it in the stiff way Dean held himself, and the annoyingly sly grin on Rick's face.

They answered all the usual questions and finally the interview was starting to wind down when Phoebe allowed herself to believe nothing bad would actually happen.

"So," Rick asked. "What's next for the two of you?" Phoebe froze, her breath in her throat, until he added, "What exciting projects are on the calendar?"

Oh. Work. Of course.

Phoebe released her breath and because he was looking at Dean, she let him answer first.

"Lots of exciting things in the pipeline." His answer was smooth and rehearsed. "Nothing I'm at liberty to announce quite yet," Dean continued. "But I'm sure *Celeb* will be the first to know." It was a dig, and they all knew it.

The same question was asked to Phoebe. Her answer didn't come as smoothly. "Well, Rick," she started. "Right now I'm weighing my options, but…" She paused and shook her head. "You know what?" She almost laughed. "I'm not weighing my options at all."

From off to the side, she could hear Rebecca gasp. They'd gone over the *correct* answer for this question, and Phoebe had gone off script. *Way* off script.

"What do you mean by that, Phoebe?" Rick was clearly enjoying the shift in conversation. He leaned forward in his seat and put his elbows on his knees, ready and eager to hear more. "You're not weighing any options? Does that mean you are—"

"Not going to be acting anymore, Rick."

"What the—"

"Why is—"

Rick and Dean spoke at once. Phoebe kept her gaze fixed forward, ignoring Dean and answering Rick's partial question.

"It was fun, Rick. But I don't think I'm cut out for it."

"The hell you aren't."

Out of the corner of her eye, Phoebe saw Dean sit up in his chair. He was turned toward her, but still she ignored him and kept talking to Rick.

"I really enjoy acting, Rick," she continued. "In fact, I can say that it's the first time I've done something that I've both been good at *and* enjoyed."

"And the early reviews coming in," Rick said. "They've all been very positive. Glowing, in fact." He glanced down at his notes. "They're calling you the next big thing. Hollywood's *it* girl." He looked up at her, confusion on his face. "So why is it you don't think you're cut out for acting?"

"Oh," Phoebe said as calmly as possible. "It's not the acting I'm not cut out for." Her smile was sweet. She could almost feel Rebecca panicking from where she sat. Dean was vibrating, but she didn't care. She needed to say what she needed to say. "I'm not cut out for all the backstabbing bullshit. The rumors, the lies, the deceit." She shook her head, feeling better than she'd felt in ages. "As much as I love acting, none of that bullshit is worth it. It's not the kind of life I want to live. And as I'm sure you know, Rick, my first experience with exactly how shitty this industry can be was a particularly devastating one." She reached up to pull the mic off her blouse. "And that is not the kind of life I want to live. So until or unless something changes, and I don't see that happening, I'm out."

With far more drama than she intended, Phoebe pulled her mic off, getting tangled in the cord as she did so, and got up from her seat.

"What the fuck, Phoebe?" Dean was up and out of his seat next to her. "This is your fault, Rick."

She was halfway out the room when she heard Dean say, "Phoebe! Don't go."

She turned to see Dean standing, his hand on his mic as well. His eyes were pinned to her. As were all the cameras in the room.

Reflexively, Phoebe looked to Kristen, but her former assistant only smiled and nodded her head as if this were the most normal interview ever.

"Please," Dean said. "Don't go. Not yet. There's something I need to say."

He wasn't sure that she would. But after a moment, Phoebe slowly walked back to her seat. He smiled in what he hoped was an encouraging way, but the careful mask she'd had in place all day stayed put.

"Thank you," he said as she took her seat and the tech people frantically ran over to hook up her microphone again.

Dean wasn't entirely sure what he was going to say, but he knew he had to say something. Hell, he should have said something months ago. It had gone on far too long. And even though he didn't know what the hell he was going to say, something was going to be better than nothing.

The moment they were sitting down again, Rebecca appeared in front of them, blocking Rick from their view. "What is going on here?" She looked between the two of them, searching for answers as to what had disrupted her perfectly crafted interviews.

Phoebe shrugged. "I only said what I felt. It needed to be said."

Rebecca looked to Dean.

"That's all I'm going to do, too," he said. "Just say what needs to be said." He looked to Phoebe. "Say what I feel."

One more time, Rebecca looked between them before throwing her arms up in exasperation. "Whatever."

As soon as she was clear, Rick pounced. He waved his hand to the cameras, and dove right in. "What was your reaction to Phoebe's announcement, Dean? Obviously, your relationship has made quite an impact on her and her career choices."

Next to him, Dean could see Phoebe tense. He'd asked her to come back when all she wanted to do was leave. Apparently for good. He couldn't let that happen.

"I don't think that's the real question here, Rick," Dean

said smoothly. "In fact, as a journalist, you should be ashamed of yourself for missing the point completely."

Rick barely reacted, not that Dean had expected much more. "And what's that?"

"The point is that one of the most talented actresses we've seen in decades is about to quit the industry after barely even scratching the surface of what she can do." He took a breath. "Why do you think that really is? And if you think it has anything to do with *me*, or a relationship of any kind, you're totally off base."

Before Rick could answer, Dean continued, "She's going to walk away because—and forgive me if I'm speaking out of turn here, Phoebe—" He waited until she gave him a small, curious nod, before he continued. "Because of you and every other tabloid publication out there who has to rely on made-up scandal and total bullshit to sell copies of their publication, or ad space on their site, because the talentless hacks who are writing and reporting for them can't come up with anything original and *factual*."

Finally, Rick reacted. He sat back on his stool; his face turned a satisfying shade of red, and his teeth clenched together, giving him a distinctive blockhead look. He opened his mouth to react, but Dean still wasn't done.

"I could tell you the truth of what happened between Phoebe and me on set."

Rick's eyes widened, and next to him Phoebe made a slight noise of protest.

"But I won't," Dean continued. "Because you aren't interested in the truth. Only the scandal that will sell, no matter what the cost. This time, that cost is this woman's well-being, and her entire career, that she's willing to walk away from, because of the shit you've dragged her through. And that's a goddammed travesty."

More than done with the weaselly reporter, Dean turned so he spoke directly to Phoebe. "You are, hands down, the most talented actor I've ever worked with. Don't quit. Not because of this." He waved his hand to encompass everyone else in the room besides them. "Not because of them." He lowered his voice and moved to take her hand, but at the last minute didn't. Dean needed her to hear him and what he needed to say without letting any of her feelings about him get in the way. He wouldn't blame her if she hated him. He hadn't been fair. Not even close. He looked down at her hand and back up into her eyes. "Not because of me, Phoebe. Don't quit what will be an amazing career, because of all of this."

She shook her head gently. "But I'll never know if my success was—"

"This seems like a good time to bring up the photos," Rick interjected in an attempt to regain control of the interview. "The photos have all but launched you into stardom, Phoebe. It seems that just as the others who came before you, you have definitely capitalized on Dean's fame."

Phoebe's lips pressed together, and she squeezed her eyes shut.

Dean had made it a policy over his career not to comment on such scandals. It had served him well not to fuel the media machine. But this was too much. He grabbed Phoebe's hand and squeezed. More to keep her from running than anything else, but also, not touching her was becoming far too hard. Maybe she did hate him, but he needed her to hear what he needed to say.

"Do you want to know about those pictures, Rick?"

The reporter looked like a cat who'd swallowed the canary as he nodded.

"The truth is, we don't know who took the photos and sold them, but what we do know without a doubt is that Phoebe had nothing to do with it. *Celeb* got it wrong, as did every other publication who reported or even insinuated that she had anything to do with it. Frankly, Rick, I'm surprised that you wouldn't have more professional integrity to check your sources. The facts are this…" He looked at Phoebe, who hadn't pulled away from his hand, and decided to go with the truth. After all, he had nothing left to lose. "Phoebe and I worked on set very closely together, and during that time got to know each other very well." He kept his eyes locked on Phoebe. The pain reflected back in her gaze gutted him, but he needed to keep going. "We developed feelings for each other and had a relationship. Because of the media scrutiny, we made the decision to keep things as private as possible. Neither Phoebe nor I had any intention of making our relationship public. At all."

"At least not until it served you. Isn't that right, Dean?"

Slowly, he looked away from Phoebe, who would no longer meet his gaze. "What are you trying to imply, Rick?"

"It's been reported that your former manager Bruce Warner used the publicity of your relationship with Phoebe to secure your role as Blast in the upcoming *Supers* movie. Is there any truth to that?"

It wasn't entirely untrue. But it wasn't the full story either. "Bruce Warner is no longer employed by me." Truth.

"But is it true that he used that publicity? And, in fact, encouraged you to have a relationship with Phoebe?"

"No final decisions about the *Supers* movie or the role of Blast have been decided," Dean said. Also true.

"You're not answering the question."

Dean looked at Phoebe, who was also waiting for his answer to the question, which was the only reason he answered it. "It is true that Bruce was an unscrupulous man who pushed me to capitalize on a relationship with Phoebe. However," he added quickly and firmly. "My feelings for Phoebe are real, and despite the pressure he placed on me, I never revealed the truth of our relationship to Bruce. Not once." He looked straight at her while he spoke. It was the truth, and he needed her to believe him. "Again, we don't definitively know who leaked the photos, or for what purpose. But I can say with one hundred percent accuracy that it wasn't Phoebe or myself."

Without looking, he felt Phoebe shift in her chair. He hoped like hell she was really hearing him.

"What about those who say you capitalized on your relationship with Phoebe to secure the *Supers* role?"

Dean stared straight into the camera as he answered the question. "To anyone who thinks that, let me say this. I in no way am interested in gaining a movie role of any kind because of rumors, scandal, or anything to do with my personal life. I have great respect for the *Supers* franchise, but if that is why they are considering me for the role, I withdraw my interest. The only roles I am interested in are ones I have earned with my talent and hard work, not for any other reason. Furthermore, if my former manager, or anyone else who was in my employ in any capacity, had anything to do with the scandal that affected Ms. Flynn, I would like to offer my sincerest apologies and assurances that they acted out of their own volition, and we will pursue legal action as far as the law allows." He turned to stare at Rick to be sure he got the message, too. "This applies for any future infringements on my privacy that affect my life or the lives of anyone I care about."

Phoebe needed a minute to absorb what had just happened.

No, she needed more than a minute.

The second Rebecca shut down the interview officially, Phoebe was up and out of her seat. She only barely registered the fact that Dean had been holding her hand. Hell, she only barely registered anything that had just happened or had been said.

The techs moved quickly to get her mic off her and she was gone, into her dressing room. She leaned back against the shut door and took her first deep breath. But only one before there was a knock on the door.

She ignored it and moved away.

"Phoebe?" The knock came again. "Open the door. Please."

There was no reason not to. She opened the door. Dean's profile filled the doorframe. His presence sucked the oxygen out of the room, making it hard to breathe.

How did he still have that effect on her? After everything?

For a second, she contemplated, digging deep and going within herself to find the walls she needed to protect herself from this. From him. But she was tired. Tired of pretending that she didn't care and that everything that had happened between them didn't matter. Because it did. More than she could even put into words.

She stepped back to allow him entry, and Dean closed the door behind him. As soon as she turned to face him, this time with enough space between them that she could breathe, he spoke.

"Phoebe. I don't know what to—"

"Did you mean it?" Her entire body shook and she wrapped her arms around her waist in an effort to still it.

He looked at her in question.

"Did you mean what you said?" she asked again.

"All of it." He took a step toward her, but she shook her head.

She needed space if she was going to get through this without falling apart.

"Every word," he said. "I meant everything I said. Everything."

She swallowed hard. "You know I didn't sell the pictures."

"Oh my God." He brought his hands up to his head and

pulled on his hair, leaving it looking adorably disheveled. "I know, Phoebe. I know you could never do that. I always knew. I just…I was hurt." He dropped his head in defeat. "When I saw you that night outside the Dockside, you were with Eric and—"

"You know that wasn't—"

"I know." He held up a hand and nodded. "I do. I just… my emotions were all over the place. I was so worried about what you were going to think and then you were so angry and… dammit," he muttered to himself. "I was an idiot. I knew then, just as I know now, that you had nothing to do with it. I think when you said that thing about your star rising along with mine, and the look on your face, and…well, there's no excuse. There's not. I was trying to protect myself and I think to do that, I needed someone to blame."

"Just like I did." She whispered the words, but the moment she said them, she knew it was true. She'd let her emotions and other people's opinions color what she knew in her heart to be true. The Dean she'd met and gotten to know. The Dean she'd been *falling in love* with wouldn't have sold her out. Never. And she *knew* it. She'd been scared and at the first sign of anything that could potentially hurt her, she'd run. Hell, she was still scared. But this time…

"You know I wouldn't hurt you on purpose, Phoebe." He reached for her then, and she let him. He took her hand in his and tugged her gently toward him so they were closer. "Just knowing you were hurting…Phoebe, not seeing you, not being with you…" He shook his head and reached for her other hand. "I can't do this."

Her heart fell. Hopes she didn't even know she had were dashed. "What do you—"

"I can't stand here and pretend that these last few months haven't completely destroyed me." He ran his hands through his hair. "I'm a mess. Hell, I'm every single cliché that's ever been written." The corners of his eyes crinkled when he smiled. "Phoebe Flynn?" Dean squeezed her hands so she was looking directly at him. "I told you once not too long ago that I was falling for you."

She nodded, her breath caught in her throat.

"But that was a lie."

She blinked hard as he continued.

"It was a lie, Phoebe, because I'm not falling. I'm completely and totally in love with you."

Again, he'd taken her breath away. But this was different. *Very* different.

"You what?"

"I love you." He looked straight into her eyes. "I think I've loved you almost from the moment I met you. You're funny, and strong, and sweet, and kind, and sexy, and you have absolutely all of my heart, Phoebe Flynn." He dropped one of her hands to reach out and cup her cheek.

Instinctively, she closed her eyes and leaned into his touch.

"Everything that happened…if I could take it all back, I'd—"

She silenced him with the kiss she'd been wanting to give him from the first time she'd seen him again. Everything that had happened—the misunderstandings, the hurt, the time apart, all of it—dissolved in an instant as Phoebe's lips pressed to his.

Dean pulled her close as she parted her lips and welcomed him to take it deeper.

There were a thousand reasons she shouldn't be kissing him. That she should be packing her bag and getting as far away from LA, and Dean Harrison, as possible. But with her older sister's words replaying in her head—*Stop being so scared of your life. Stop running away from everything good*—there was only one reason that mattered…

She broke the kiss long enough to say what she needed to say. "I love you, too."

He could have kissed her all day.

Having Phoebe back in his arms felt like finally coming home. No matter what happened, no matter what the fallout was going to be from that interview—and there would be some —he didn't care. He had everything he ever wanted and would ever need as long as he had Phoebe. And she *loved* him.

His heart was full. He was—

"Dean!"

Sharp banging on the door distracted him from his task of kissing the woman he loved while ignoring everything else in life.

Startled, Phoebe jerked backward and shot him a dubious look as Kyle once again rapped on the door.

"Open up. Now."

Phoebe shrugged.

Dean knew he wasn't going to be able to get rid of his manager and friend just by ignoring him. Not after the stunt he'd just pulled. With a sigh, he opened the door and Kyle, followed by Kristen, barreled into the small dressing room.

"Kyle." Dean nodded. "Kristen."

"Hi, Dean," Kristen said with an apologetic shrug. She waved her fingers in Phoebe's direction with a small smile that disappeared as soon as Kyle started to speak again.

"What the hell, Dean? Do you want to tell me what all that was about?"

"I stand by everything I said." Dean crossed his arms over his chest. "I appreciate that you didn't make this mess, Kyle. Bruce did. But I didn't say anything I didn't mean." Dean looked to Phoebe and reached out a hand. He needed her close. "Everything that went down with the pictures was bull-shit. Rick *should* be ashamed of himself. This whole industry should be ashamed. I didn't do anything wrong, and I definitely didn't betray Phoebe's trust or her privacy. You know that."

"Yes, yes." Kyle waved his hand, obviously impatient. "I get all that. I agree. I'm talking about the *Supers* gig. We've been working incredibly hard to nail that down and you go on record saying you don't want it."

"I didn't say that."

"You might as well have."

"What I said was that if they want me based on publicity and harming the reputation of the woman I love, I'm not interested. And I stand by it." He squeezed Phoebe's hand. He'd been dead serious when he'd said that, and he stood by it. Maybe it was the biggest role of his career but he didn't want it at that expense.

"*Supers* is huge."

"It *is* huge," Phoebe said next to him. She tugged on his hand a little bit until he looked at her. "Dean, don't throw your career away because of me."

His mouth dropped open. "Me?" Dean ignored everyone else in the room and turned to put both hands on her shoul-ders. "Phoebe, I'd throw it all away. All of it. If it meant that *you* wouldn't. You are so talented." She ducked her head, but he used two fingers to pull her chin up to look at him. "You asked me if I meant what I said earlier." She nodded. "I meant all of it, especially the part about you not quitting acting. Phoebe, you can't quit. Not when you're just getting started. Do not let the assholes of this industry keep you from doing something you were clearly born to do."

She shook her head with a soft smile. "I refuse to be successful because of my relationship with you, Dean. I told you that when we first met, and I mean it even more now after everything. I won't—"

"Woman." He shook her a little and tried not to laugh. "You are crazy if you think that anyone will watch this movie and see you on screen and even remember my name. Babe, you are going to be wildly successful *despite* me, because you are insanely talented." He looked to Kyle and Kristen, who stood together. "Tell her."

"He's right." Kyle spoke first. "Dean Harrison may be the lead of this movie, but you are going to be the star, Phoebe. Hands down. Everyone has been saying so."

Kristen nodded, a huge smile splitting her face. "It's true. It's all anyone could talk about on set. Wes is pumped that he *discovered* you." She used air quotes. "And I'm sure it's one of the things that made Layla so crazy jealous of you. You're already a bigger star than she'll ever be."

"It's true."

"Layla did…" Phoebe's face screwed up in question. "Not that it matters anymore, but do you think she had anything to do with the photos getting out?"

Dean looked at Kyle, but he was already typing something into his phone.

"I'm on it. I think I'm getting close to finding Lee, the helicopter pilot, too. If she had anything to do with it, I'll get to the bottom of it, Phoebe. I promise."

She shook her head and slipped her arm around Dean's waist. "Maybe it doesn't matter. I mean…" She shrugged. "I swear I'm not fishing for compliments here, but do you really think I have what it takes in this industry?"

He couldn't help it; Dean laughed. "You have what it takes to *own* this industry."

She spun around so she was once again in his arms. She stood on her toes to kiss him before pulling away again. "Well,

I really hope that the *Supers* franchise still wants you for Blast then!"

Confused, he tilted his head. "Why's that?"

Her smile was coy and sexy. "Because it turns out they want me for the lead, Firestar." She winked. "You'd get to be my sidekick."

He threw his head back and let the laughter take over.

"Gladly, babe. Gladly."

Chapter Twenty-Six

THE PREMIERE for *Run From the Sun* came quickly and four months later, Phoebe found herself dressed in a silver sequin designer gown that hugged her body in ways she didn't even know were possible, and wearing incredibly high heels that made her legs look even longer. Her hair and makeup had been done by Louis and Susie, whom she'd specially requested, and they'd made her look every bit the glamorous movie star even though she still couldn't help but feel like an imposter.

"I can't even look at you." Kate shielded her eyes and turned away in a laugh. "Those diamond earrings are worth more than my house."

It was true. When Kristen, who'd since been hired as Phoebe's manager, had insisted on borrowing the diamonds from one of LA's big-name jewelers, she'd been hesitant. They wanted her to wear what equated to a ridiculous sum of money on her *ears*.

"Is it too much?" Phoebe clutched her ears, and immediately snatched her hands away lest she damage the jewelry.

But Kate just laughed. "You look stunning, sis. Really." She reached across the space and clutched Phoebe's hands. "You deserve this. I'm so proud of you."

Phoebe blinked hard to fend off the tears that for some reason had been threatening all day. If she cried, her makeup would run and Louis would never forgive her. "Don't be silly, Kate. It's you I'm proud of. Going back to school after all this time and—"

"No." Kate cut her off. "This is your day. And thank you so much for bringing me as your date and letting me share it with you."

Thankfully, Kate had forgiven Phoebe for saying all the thoughtless things she'd said, as sisters were wont to do. They'd hugged and cried and made up, as they'd done countless times before. Phoebe had heard Kate's message loud and clear. A fact she was eternally grateful for. Even if her big sister's delivery could have been a bit softer, it was what she'd needed to hear. "Are you kidding?" Phoebe said. "I wouldn't want to do this with anyone else."

The limousine came to a stop as Kate tilted her head and blinked dramatically. "Anyone? Are you sure?"

Phoebe laughed and swatted at her. "I am totally sure." She sat back and took a deep breath. "Here we go." The limo door opened and a gloved hand reached in to help her from the car.

The red carpet was every bit as overwhelming as Kristen and Lorilee had prepped her for. Lights flashed all around her and people in all directions called her name. Just as she practiced, she kept her smile on her face, and her sister by her side.

Phoebe answered countless questions about who she was wearing, who her date was, and of course, where Dean was. She answered them all with a smile and a wink—even the question about Dean, with a dismissive, "It's still early. I'm sure he'll be here."

She worked the runway and, to her surprise and delight, enjoyed every moment of it.

"You look stunning, Pheebs." Wes Reacher joined her for a few pictures and kissed her on the cheek. "I'm so glad you're here tonight. This movie is what it is because of you."

"Wes, you don't need to say that."

"It's true." He held up his hands. "Honestly. It was an absolute joy to work with you and I'm proud to say I was your first." He winked as she smacked his arm lightly. "Have fun tonight. You deserve it."

She was almost at the door. She'd done her rounds, stopped at all the cameras and microphones. She'd waved. She'd smiled. She'd been polite and friendly. She'd done everything anyone could have wanted or expected of her.

Except...

"Dean!"

"Dean Harrison!"

"Over here!"

"Dean!"

And then... "Phoebe? Did you know Dean would be here? And with a date?"

Phoebe held her pose and smiled through all of it. The cameras flashed; reporters yelled. It was all good because Phoebe had prepared herself for just this moment. She'd been thinking of it for days, wondering how she would react. Because Dean wasn't there with a date. He was there with *two* dates.

The cameras flashed. The reporters hollered and shouted.

Phoebe took a deep breath and turned around to face Dean and his two stunning dates.

She was breathtaking.

She wore a silver sequined dress that caressed her curves in a way that he wished he was doing at that exact moment. Her long, dark hair hung down low on her back. And Dean knew that the moment he saw her piercing eyes, he would be rendered speechless.

His dates, one on each arm, were beautiful. They'd spent hours in the hair and makeup chair. Their dresses were stunning, high-end designers. But as gorgeous as the young ladies on his arm were, they had nothing on Phoebe.

The flashes blinded him. The questions hammered his ears. But Dean could only focus on one thing.

One dazzling woman in silver. His Silver Starlet. The only one who had ever mattered.

And then she turned around.

Dean let his eyes travel up from her toes on the red carpet she deserved so badly, up her delicious sequined body, and finally to her beautiful face and the smile that made his heartbeat stutter.

He was rendered completely helpless as Phoebe crouched down in her gown, and held out her arms to her two young nieces. Dean's dates.

Ally and Olivia ran to their auntie and she didn't hesitate to hug them tight.

Over the heads of Phoebe and her nieces, Dean met Kate's smile. The look of pride on her face put a smile on his face that he didn't think would ever come off.

In fact, if the last few months were anything to go from, he didn't see that smile disappearing any time soon.

From the moment he declared his love to Phoebe in that dressing room after that fateful interview, everything had been ridiculously good.

Even the things that weren't good became okay with Phoebe by his side.

Dean watched as she embraced the little girls. Dean had grown close to them both over the last few months. After all, it was hard not to get to know someone well when you lived under the same roof. After the press junket, they'd left LA, and Phoebe insisted on taking Dean back to Montana to see Kate. As far as she was concerned, he *had* to meet her big sister. It was a mission he was happy to join her on. As was sleeping in Phoebe's childhood twin-sized bed. A bed he very quickly upgraded to a queen-sized a few weeks later when it became clear that they weren't going to be leaving Montana anytime soon. He loved the woman, but he also loved his sleep.

Dean had been more than happy to stay in Montana in Kate's small house. It was cozy and close, with a busy family and not enough bathrooms, but Dean couldn't get enough of it. Living in the little bungalow, pouring cereal and looking for missing socks as everyone rushed out the door to school and daycare, was everything Dean had always wanted. A family. It was the perfect chaos of a family that loved each other. He soaked up every moment of it.

Just as he was going to love every moment of watching Phoebe on the red carpet.

She kissed each of her nieces before standing tall, one of her hands in each of theirs. Ally and Olivia's appearance sparked a whole new set of questions for Phoebe, all of which she answered with grace. And then it was his turn.

Dean had ignored the shouts and hollers trying to get his attention. Still, he ignored them as he only had eyes for Phoebe.

As he approached, Dean stopped and kissed Kate on the cheek before crouching down and kissing each of the girls in turn. And then it was all Phoebe.

As planned, Kate gathered up the girls and took them just over to the side so Dean could wrap his arm around his woman and give her the kiss he'd been dying to give her since he saw her in that sexy silver number.

"Congratulations, baby." Dean pressed a slow, but red-carpet appropriate kiss on her lips. "This is your night."

Still with his arm around her, Dean took a step back and looked at the closest reporter. "Isn't she incredible?"

The journalist nodded and smiled awkwardly, but ultimately agreed. How could she not?

"Dean? Phoebe? Are you a couple? How long have you been dating? What's happening?"

The questions were fired from all directions. Dean just stood next to his woman and let her field each question in turn, which she did effortlessly. Dean watched with pride as Phoebe, shoulders back and smile in place, answered every question with ease.

She was excited to be there.

Yes. She was in a relationship with Dean.

Of course she was excited about upcoming projects.

"Dean?" Phoebe turned to him, and his eyes locked on hers. The only person he had eyes for. "What do you think?" Her question was extra sweet, and totally expected.

Dean stepped forward, so while Phoebe was still taking center stage, he was closer to her for the announcement. "I think we should let them know," he said. "Tell them what they can expect from us in the future."

"Us?"

"Dean!"

"Who's us?"

The questions went wild but Dean took them all in stride, stepped back and let Phoebe take the lead. This was her night, after all.

"Yes," Phoebe said smoothly. Her arm tightened around his waist, and he squeezed hers in return. "Dean and I are together," she said. "And, it's not about publicity or anything Hollywood." She laughed and looked at him.

"That's right." Dean jumped in. "Our love is anything but Hollywood." Phoebe shot him a look, but he could only laugh and squeeze her tight. Dean turned so he could look in her beautiful eyes before he said, "It's the most real thing I've ever felt."

Her smile melted him completely. But they didn't have time to have more than the smallest moment. They had a very important announcement to make.

"What's coming next for the two of you?"

It was the question they were waiting for. Phoebe turned to him. Dean winked and held his hand out toward her, giving Phoebe the chance to say what she needed to.

Her smile dazzled and Dean had to laugh. She'd come so far with the spotlight on her. Where she used to shrink away from it, Phoebe seemed to thrive now under the light. "Well," she grinned and looked around, "I'm really happy to announce that both Dean and I have accepted the roles of Blast and Firestar in the upcoming *Supers* movie."

Phoebe stepped back so she stood side by side with him, and Dean couldn't have been more proud or happy than he was in that moment.

They were together. They were happier than he could have ever imagined. And they were moving forward together, with their career. And more importantly, their lives.

Chapter Twenty-Seven

IT HAD BEEN JUST over a year since Phoebe had taken the role of Misty Falls and arrived in Panama to shoot a movie that would completely change her life, in all ways. Since the movie premiere, everything seemed to be on fast-forward. The critics loved it, they loved her, and they loved Phoebe and Dean together. Their announcement about co-starring in the next, massive *Supers* movie had blown up. People were excited to see them work together again, and so were they. Shooting began in less than a month. It would be another physically demanding, intense shooting schedule. Especially for Dean, who was going to be doing all of his own stunts. He'd been training hard, and he was ready for it, but it would be a busy six months while they shot the movie.

Which was why it was so important that they take this time to escape off the grid together. And what better place than Casa del Sol, the eco resort Phoebe had visited with some of the stunt doubles when she'd first arrived in Panama. They were still friendly with Mason, and even Eric, now that he understood that she was happily with Dean, and they would be nothing more than friends. Layla was a different story. Once they discovered for sure that she, and Lee, the helicopter pilot she'd seduced and promised riches to, was behind the photo scandal, they'd completely cut her out of their lives.

Dean, true to his word, wanted to send his lawyers after Layla, but Phoebe had stopped him. There was no point. Besides, it had become such a public scandal that Layla was virtually unhireable in the industry now, and last they'd heard she was back in her hometown in Iowa, working as a personal trainer. She'd made her choices, and she had to live with them. There was nothing more that Phoebe and Dean could do. Nor was Phoebe interested in revenge. She was more interested in moving on.

Which was exactly what she was doing.

Phoebe swung back and forth gently on the wooden swing that hung from the eaves of the thatched roofed hut she and Dean were calling home for the next week. She let her head fall backward as she pumped her legs gently, but just enough that the turquoise water appeared below her. Colorful fish darted through the water just below the surface. A gentle breeze washed over her as the sun started to set on their tropical retreat.

She closed her eyes, perfectly satisfied in the moment.

Two strong arms wrapped around her, stopping her mid-swing.

She opened her eyes and looked up, directly into the eyes of the man she loved a little more every day.

"Well, hello there."

He bent down to kiss her, sending heat directly through her. His kisses never failed to elicit that type of reaction from her. She loved it.

"Did you have a nice nap?"

He groaned against her lips before moving his kiss down to her neck. "I'm feeling very rested now. In fact…"

She giggled as his hands slipped up and under her bikini top to cup her breasts.

Dean held her effortlessly. The new workout regime he'd been on for the last few months to get him *Supers* ready had created next-level definition in his muscles, and a rippling wall of abs. But that wasn't the hardness that Phoebe currently felt pressed up against her back as he kissed her.

"You were right," he said between kisses. "This place is absolutely magical."

The owners, Heather and Ash, who were now pregnant with their first child, had done some work since the last time Phoebe had been there. They'd built a few new huts up the hill in the rain forest that were perfect for those seeking ultimate privacy. There was the hut Phoebe and Dean occupied, positioned at the end of a long walkway out over the water. And a collection of smaller thatched huts along the shore, some of which were hostel style. The main building housed a kitchen, dining area, and living room-style seating area where all the guests could gather for the gourmet meals and drinks and games in the evenings.

It was a completely different type of holiday than Dean had ever been on, which was exactly why Phoebe wanted him to experience it. He was so used to hiding from people and the spotlight, but at Casa del Sol, among all the other guests, they could just be Phoebe and Dean. Which was exactly what they wanted to be.

Phoebe twisted her head around so she could kiss Dean properly, despite her precarious position on the swing. "I know we should be getting ready for dinner, but…"

"Dinner can wait." His kisses grew more urgent, his hands moving over her body when she slipped from his grasp.

The swing she was sitting on moved out over the water and away from Dean. Phoebe laughed. "The one that got away, huh?"

She swung back over the deck, but instead of Dean capturing her again the way she thought, he grinned mischievously. "Make no mistake, my love. I'll never let you get away again." He let her swing out over the water one more time before capturing her once more in a tight grip.

Phoebe held onto the ropes and leaned back into his chest. "Got me."

Dean ran a hand up her arm and unwound her fingers from the rope where she held tight. He held her hand in his for a moment, stroking each finger, which made her groan in pleasure and close her eyes.

Her eyes popped open a moment later when he slipped a ring on her finger. "Dean? What is—"

Still holding her on the swing, Dean bent down on one knee, and Phoebe's breath caught in her throat. "Phoebe," he started. "I love you more than I can possibly begin to explain. You have opened me up to a whole new world of possibilities and family I never could have imagined. Your love has completed a part of me that I didn't even know was missing. I can't imagine going another moment without making sure you never have to doubt that again. Will you do me the greatest honor of being my wife?"

A tear slipped down her cheek and she nodded, and then nodded again. "Yes," she finally said. "A million times over."

He kissed her then, sealing the moment.

"And, Dean? No matter what could ever happen, I will never doubt your love for me." She looked down at the huge diamond that sparkled on her finger and held her left hand to his chest, over his heart. "Ever."

He kissed her again, as Dean lost hold of the swing.

Phoebe moved far out over the water. She looked back over her shoulder and winked right before she slipped off the wooden seat and into the ocean with a splash.

When she surfaced, Dean was in the water with her, just as she knew he would be. He wrapped his arm around her, pulled her close, and kissed her.

"Now I've got you right where I want you."

His hands moved quickly, tugging her bikini top from her body. He tossed it to the deck and let his hands travel down her sides. She moaned when his fingers slipped between her legs and plunged into the heat there. Dean tugged at the string keeping her bottoms together and that scrap of clothing also was tossed to the deck. Not to be undone, Phoebe unlaced his board shorts and tugged them down, wrapping one hand around his silky, hard length before twining her legs around his waist.

His fingers moved quickly inside her, bringing her closer and closer to release. Phoebe kissed him hard and pressed herself tight against him. Before she could explode, he removed his fingers, and used both hands to lift her hips a little, and bring her down on his length.

As the sun set over the ocean, with the water giving them perfect cover in case anyone happened to look out and see them, they came together in a burst.

Phoebe nestled her face into Dean's neck. "This place is the definition of paradise."

"No, babe." Dean lifted her head up, so she was looking at him when he said, "It's you. You are my paradise. Always."

I hope you enjoyed your trip to paradise and Dean and Phoebe's love story.
But what happens after they leave Paradise? Find out in an exclusive bonus scene HERE!

**If you're looking for more Happy Ever Afters, I have exactly what you need!
Read an excerpt of the first in my newest series, Choosing Happily Ever After right after this!**

Choosing Happily Ever After

Please enjoy this excerpt from Choosing Happily Ever After

SHE WAS GORGEOUS. All dressed in white, of course. The veil covered her face, but there was no doubt that beneath the gauzy film was the hint of a smile while she tried to bite back the tears that threatened to spill down her cheeks despite the bride's insistence earlier that she *"absolutely will not cry. I'm just not a crier."*

Hope Turner had seen it a million times before. And they almost always cried.

At least a little.

"Are you ready?" she asked the bride, who clutched her father's arm tightly. "Just like we practiced."

"Only this time it's for real."

Hope nodded. "It is."

She'd also seen this a million times. A bride and groom who laughed and joked their way through the rehearsal the night before and then completely came undone at the actual ceremony the moment they realized that it was, in fact, *real.*

"And you *are* ready," she added. "It's going to be great." The bride nodded and looked straight ahead. That was Hope's cue.

She whipped out her phone, which also served as a control station for basically everything, and tapped a button. A moment later, the traditional wedding march—the bride's choice, not hers—filled the outdoor ceremony space Hope had dubbed Riverbend, due to the fact that it was, in fact, in the bend of the river. She had her pick of perfect ceremony sites on Ever After Ranch, but this was her favorite.

Hope stepped back and let the bride's father lead her down the grassy aisle toward her groom, whom, she was absolutely certain, would also be dabbing his eyes through the entire ceremony.

The bride made it safely to the end of the aisle, hugged her father, and took her groom's hand as the ceremony began. There was a time when there was nothing Hope enjoyed more than listening to the couple recite their vows. After all, it didn't get any more romantic. But lately, there hadn't been time to enjoy the details of the beautiful weddings she put on. There was just too much to do.

Which was why, as soon as the officiant began speaking, Hope scurried away in the golf cart that she'd recently started using to get from place to place around the ranch, back up to the Barn, where the reception was to be held to double-check with the catering staff that everything was set up. Just as she'd instructed, champagne was poured and ready to go on trays by the entrance. The servers stood by with canapés to keep guests entertained while the newlywed couple went for a few photographs around the property.

Hope did a quick spin of the reception space, a refurbished barn that was her pride and joy and also the reason that her business was booming in the last few years. It was rustic elegance that spoke to the dreams of many engaged couples. It didn't hurt that it had the capacity for large gatherings, and a wedding coordinator who could handle anything that was thrown at her. She'd come a long way from the little girl who, along with her twin sister, used to beg her parents to help with the few weddings that they'd host on the lawns of their sprawling mountain property. Back then, it hadn't been a business. Not really. Just a little bit of *fun money*, her mom used to call it. Something to do when things were slow with the ranching business, or more usual, when there was a special request to hold an event on their property. The Turner ranch had always been gorgeous.

And Hope had seen the potential. Of course, not even her grandest dreams could have prepared her for how successful Ever After Ranch would be and just how busy she'd find herself in such a short time.

Satisfied that the reception was ready, Hope gave a few final instructions to the catering staff, who she already knew didn't need them, and raced back down to the ceremony space just as the officiant was declaring the happy couple husband and wife.

Perfect timing.

She quickly pressed another button on her phone and new music played over the speakers. The crowd cheered and the bride and groom danced down the aisle with their arms in the air, and ever so slightly red eyes, just as Hope predicted.

It wasn't until hours later, after the photographs, the speeches, and dinner, with the guests all happily dancing the night away on the hardwood floors of the barn, that Hope had a minute to hop in her cart and head back to the ceremony site to clean up any garbage that guests had left behind, pack up the speakers and sound system, and take care of anything else that couldn't be left out in the elements.

The stars and the moon lit up the night sky and in desperate need to sit down, Hope gave in and did just that. She tipped her head up and let herself take it all in.

When was the last time she'd stopped and just looked up?

She couldn't remember. But that's what it was like to build a business. Exhausting. Which would explain why she could barely keep her eyes open. She felt it deep in her bones. An overwhelming exhaustion. It was different than her usual tiredness. Of course, she was taking on more bookings than ever before. Maybe it was time to bring on an assistant.

Or her sister.

Hope almost laughed out loud at herself. There was no way. Nevertheless, it was worth a shot. Well, it was worth *another shot.* Still chuckling, she pulled out her cell phone and pressed the button for her twin sister.

"It's late on a Saturday," Faith answered. "Shouldn't you be busy perpetuating the myth of happy ever after and charging tens of thousands of dollars for it while you're at it?"

Hope shook her head and rolled her eyes. "Hi to you, too, sis." Where Hope was a die-hard romantic, which had led to the idea of her business in the first place, her twin sister, although identical in appearance, couldn't be more opposite in her feelings about love and marriage. "So I was thinking…"

Might as well get right to the point.

"No."

"You don't even know what I'm going to ask." She groaned and moved the phone to her other ear. "At least wait until I—"

"You're going to ask me to come home to Glacier Falls and run the ranch with you," her sister said matter-of-factly. "Just like you always do when I answer the phone at eleven p.m. on a Saturday night. And just like it always is, the answer is no. I hate that shit, Hope. You know that."

She did.

"But you love me."

"I do."

"So do it for me. To help me out." She knew it was pointless, but she tried anyway. "Besides, it will be fun. We can be the wedding sisters again, like when we were kids."

It was one of Hope's favorite memories, when their mother would dress them up in frilly dresses and give them baskets of flower petals to throw on the newly married couples. Guests had loved the identical blonde-haired, little girls. Hope had loved it too. Faith, not so much. But even so, there had been a handful of times when Hope had managed to convince her sister from time to time to dress up and reenact their own weddings, taking turns with who got to be the bride and who had to play the groom.

"If you're trying to convince me, that's the wrong way to do it." Faith laughed and then added, "Seriously though, if you need help, Hope, hire someone. Because as much as I love you, I'll be staying in the city. Sorry." She actually did sound a little sorry this time. "Put an ad on the town's Facebook page or something. You'll get someone."

"Yeah, maybe. But hey, you can't blame a girl for trying. Let's talk tomorrow, okay?" Hope smiled into the phone. Distance and lifestyle may separate them, but they were still close. "Love you."

"Love you too, Hope," Faith said. "And Hope? Get some sleep. You sound exhausted."

She hung up the phone and tucked it away before going to gather up the rest of the things that couldn't wait until morning. Hope fell heavy into her golf cart and checked the time. There was still at least two hours before she could announce last call. And then she got to start the process of cleaning up.

Hope closed her eyes, but only for a moment. She couldn't risk falling asleep. Maybe Faith was right; maybe she really should hire someone. She was exhausted already and the wedding season was only just beginning. Before she could talk herself out of it, Hope opened the Facebook app on her phone and typed up a quick help wanted ad.

After all, it couldn't hurt.

"I'm not saying it's not good to have you back…"

"It's just strange," Levi Langdon finished for his cousin, Logan. "I get it. It is strange." Levi lifted the bottle to his lips and let the cold beer slide down his throat. As strange as it was to be back in his hometown after almost ten years, it also felt good. Really good. Like putting on an old sweater. Or in this case, an old pair of work boots to help Logan out on his family ranch. The ranch he'd grown up on and couldn't wait to leave.

"But I'm not complaining." Logan grinned. "I've missed you and it was good to be out there today. When was the last time we rode the fence line like that together?"

Levi chuckled and shook his head because they both knew the answer. He'd been twenty years old, Logan a year ahead of him, and they'd both been caught drinking Logan's dad's beers. Both were of legal drinking age in Canada, not that it mattered to Uncle Harold. They were *his* beers. An already hard man got even harder when someone took his beers. Especially his dead sister's kid. For whatever reason, Uncle Harold had a special place in his heart for Levi. And it wasn't a good one.

Their punishment had been to ride the fence line and repair some downed wire in the middle of the night. Of course, Levi's punishment had also included a punch in the face that only narrowly missed breaking his nose, but he'd sported the shiner for weeks. It was the last time they'd rode the fence together, because it had also been the last time Levi had spent the night under his uncle's roof.

He'd had enough. Besides, he was already living on borrowed time on the Langdon ranch. A fact Uncle Harold had no trouble reminding him of on a regular basis. He should have left years ago but he'd been trying to save up enough money to get an apartment in the city. Or at least enough to set him up. But leaving early couldn't hurt. Hell, it would probably hurt a whole lot less.

At least that's what he'd thought at the time.

Levi blinked hard and shook his head. Coming back to Glacier Falls was hard enough. He didn't need to relive every goddamn heartbreaking moment.

"Right." Logan lifted his own beer, obviously remembering that night as well. "Hey, about all of that." He wiped his mouth on the back of his sleeve. "I'm really sorry that my dad treated you like that back then. I don't—"

"Want you to worry about it," Levi answered for him. "It wasn't your fault and you can't own the actions of your parents. Hell, we'd both be in trouble if that were the case." He hadn't known his dad, but all accounts were that he was a deadbeat asshole who'd left his mom knocked up and alone. Levi didn't even know what his last name was, having been given his mother's family name. And it didn't matter; he'd never cared to know who the man was.

Levi had nothing but love for his mother, what he could remember of her anyway. She'd died when he was only ten and he'd gone to live with her brother's family in Glacier Falls. It had been a mixed blessing. Logan had been a cousin, best friend, and brother all rolled into one. Katie had been like a little sister to him, and Auntie Deb had done her best to love and protect young Levi from the unexplainable anger of her husband that only got worse the older he got.

Leaving them had been just as hard as it had been easy leaving Uncle Harold. But now Uncle Harold was gone, having died three months earlier from a heart attack. And Levi was back.

"Still," Logan said. "I'm sorry he was such a dick to you.

He never could explain it, and I know you don't want to hear it, or you wouldn't believe it anyway, but he really wasn't like that with Katie and me."

"That I do believe." He took another long pull from his beer. "It doesn't matter now," he said again, meaning it. "I'm looking forward to catching up with you all. I've missed all of you."

"Just us?"

If he hadn't been on the other side of the shop, Levi likely would have punched his cousin or at least given him a shove. He hadn't even been back for a full twenty-four hours. There was no need to stir the pot. Logan knew damn well that his family wasn't the only thing he'd missed about Glacier Falls. Far from it.

"How is Hope?"

Hope Turner, the love of Levi's young life. Or at least he'd thought she was at the time. With her long blonde hair and innocent blue eyes, he'd been completely wrapped around her little finger. He would have done anything for that girl.

Except stay in town.

As much as he loved her, he knew in his heart that if he stayed, Uncle Harold would slowly beat down his spirit—and his body—and in a small town, there was nowhere else to go. Leaving her had been the hardest thing he'd ever done and as much as he wanted to, he couldn't ask her to go with him, because he knew her heart was in Glacier Falls. She loved her small town, and more than that, the ranch she grew up on. She was never leaving. He knew it just like he also knew if he asked her, it would break her heart to have to choose. So he'd let her go.

To his credit, Logan didn't make a smart-ass comment the way Levi was so sure he would. Instead, he slowly put his beer down on the workbench he sat on and crossed his arms. "Ten years, and you've never once asked about her."

Levi nodded. It was true.

"That must mean you're finally over her."

He laughed but didn't answer right away. There would be a part of him that was never completely over Hope Turner. But he'd been a kid the last time he'd seen her. A lot changed in ten years. "It's been a long time."

"That didn't answer my question." Logan raised an eyebrow at him before hopping down off the bench and moving across the shop to the beer fridge. They hadn't even been in the house yet, a fact Levi felt a little guilty for. But it was late and he hadn't told anyone he was coming. He'd surprised Logan by joining him in the field earlier, but it was getting late now. He'd just have to surprise Aunt Deb and Katie in the morning. He accepted another beer from his cousin but paused before opening it when Logan said, "Hope's killing it with her business. Turned her family ranch into a wedding venue, of all things."

Levi laughed and shook his head but he wasn't surprised. Ever since they were kids, Hope talked about the few weddings they held out on their property. She'd always been a hopeless romantic. "I'm glad it's working out," he said. "But I'm not surprised. She always knew exactly what she wanted."

Again, Logan raised his eyebrow, but didn't say anything. "She must be doing even better than last year." He handed Levi his cell phone. "She just posted on Facebook that she's looking to hire some help."

Levi took the phone without trying to look too eager. He was pretty sure he failed, but he couldn't help it. Talking about Hope had his pulse racing. He'd managed to avoid her on social media all these years, largely because he wasn't on any social media, but it didn't mean he hadn't thought about how easy it would be to see what she was up to. Was she married? Did she have kids? Was she happy? All things he could know if he'd joined the Facebook phenomenon. Which was precisely why he didn't. But that didn't stop him from grabbing his cousin's phone and looking at the familiar, yet different, beautiful face on the tiny screen.

Hope Turner.

She looked the same, but also so different. She definitely wasn't the innocent girl he'd left. Although she still had the sweet look of complete trust in her eyes, there was also something else in her expression. Something deeper.

Levi forced himself to look away from her profile picture and scroll down on the screen to the post Logan was referring to.

Help wanted: General handyman, jack of all trades. Must love love.

He couldn't help but laugh. She was still a hopeless romantic. Some things never changed.

What if there were a few more things that hadn't changed?

Levi looked up at Logan, who clearly saw the expression on his cousin's face. "Looking for a job, are you, cuz?"

Read the rest of Choosing Happily Ever After and find out what happens when Levi responds to that help wanted ad. Can you ever really get a second chance when so much time has passed?

About the Author

Elena Aitken is a USA Today Bestselling Author of more than forty romance and women's fiction novels. The mother of 'grown up' twins, Elena now lives with her very own mountain man in the heart of the very mountains she writes about. She can often be found with her toes in the lake and a glass of wine in her hand, dreaming up her next book and working on her own happily ever after.

To learn more about Elena:
www.elenaaitken.com
elena@elenaaitken.com

www.ingramcontent.com/pod-product-compliance
Lightning Source LLC
Chambersburg PA
CBHW031025260626
47153CB00017B/2127